Anne Thackeray Ritchie

Toilers and Spinsters, and other Essays

Anne Thackeray Ritchie

Toilers and Spinsters, and other Essays

ISBN/EAN: 9783744746014

Printed in Europe, USA, Canada, Australia, Japan

Cover: Foto ©Andreas Hilbeck / pixelio.de

More available books at **www.hansebooks.com**

THE WORKS

OF

MISS THACKERAY

VOLUME VII.

TOILERS AND SPINSTERS

AND OTHER ESSAYS

LONDON
SMITH, ELDER, & CO., 15 WATERLOO PLACE
1890

TOILERS AND SPINSTERS

AND OTHER ESSAYS

BY

MISS THACKERAY

LONDON

SMITH, ELDER, & CO., 15 WATERLOO PLACE

1890

TO

CHARLOTTE AUGUSTA RITCHIE

IN PARIS

THE FRIEND AND HELPER

OF

MANY TOILERS AND MANY SPINSTERS

NOTE TO THE READER.

Many of these Essays were written long ago ; and, although I have tried to correct the past by present reports, some of the statements may be no longer applicable after fifteen years.

A. T. T.

1876.

CONTENTS.

TOILERS AND SPINSTERS.

Je garde la fidélité à tout le monde, j'essaye d'être toujours véritable, sincère, et fidèle à tous les hommes, et j'ai une tendresse de cœur pour ceux à qui Dieu m'a uni plus étroitement, et soit que je sois seul ou à la vue de tous les hommes, j'ai en toutes mes actions la vue de Dieu, qui les doit juger et à qui je les ai toutes consacrées.—PASCAL.

IF one is to believe some people, there are a certain number of unmarried ladies whose wail has of late been constantly dinning in the ears of the public, and who, with every comfort and necessary of life provided, are supposed to be pining away in lonely gloom and helplessness. There are a score of books written for their benefit with which they doubtless wile away their monotonous hours. Old Maids, spinsters, the solitary, heartbroken women of England, have quite a literature of their own, which demands a degree of public sympathy for this particular class which would be insulting almost in individual cases, except, indeed, that there are not individual cases, and very few, who, while desiring such com-

B

miseration for others, would not quite decline to present themselves as its deserving objects.

To come forward, for instance, and say, ' Oh, alas, alas! what a sad, dull, solitary, useless, unhappy, un-occupied life is mine! I can only see a tombstone at the end of my path, and willows and cypresses on either side, and flowers, all dead and faded, crumbling beneath my feet ; and my only companions are memories, and hair ornaments, and ghosts, prosy, stupid old ghosts, who go on saying the same things over and over and over again, and twaddling about all the years that are gone away for ever.' This is no exaggeration. This is what the ' thoughtful ' spinster is supposed to say in her reflective moments. There are Sunsets of spinster life, Moans of old maids, Words to the wasted, Lives for the lonely, without number, all sympathising with these griefs, such as they are, urging the despondent to hide their sufferings away in their own hearts, to show no sign, to gulp their bitter draught, to cheer, tend, console others in their need, although unspeakably gloomy themselves. One book, I remember, after describing a life passed in abstract study, in nursing sick people, in visiting unhappy ones, in re-lieving the needy, exclaims (or something very like it) :—
' But, ah! what at best is such a life as this, whose chief pleasures and consolations are to be found in the cares and

the sorrows of others? Married life, indeed, has its troubles;' these single but impartial critics generally go on to state; ' but then there is companionship, sympathy, protection '— one knows the sentence by heart. ' Not so is it with those whose lonely course we should be glad to think that we had cheered by the few foregoing remarks, whose sad destiny has been pointed out by a not unfeeling hand. Who knows but that there may be compensation in a lot of which the blank monotony is at least untroubled by the anxieties, and fears, and hopes of the married ?'

These are not the exact words, but it is very much the substance, of many of the volumes, as anybody who chooses may see. Where there really seems to be so much kindness and gentle-heartedness, one is the more impatient of a certain melancholy, desponding spirit, which seems to prevail.

But what have the ladies, thus acknowledging their need, been about all these years? Who has forced them to live alone? Is there nobody to come forward and give them a lift? What possible reason can there be to prevent unmarried, any more than married, people from being happy (or unhappy), according to their circumstances— from enjoying other pleasures more lively than the griefs and sufferings of their neighhours? Are unmarried people shut out from all theatres, concerts, picture-galleries, parks, and gardens? May not they walk out on every day of the week? Are they locked up all the summer time, and only let out when an east wind is blowing? Are they forced to live in one particular quarter of the town? Does Mudie refuse their subscriptions? Are they prevented from taking in 'The Times,' from going out to dinner, from match-making, visiting, gossiping, drinking tea, talking, and playing the piano? If a lady has had three husbands, could she do more? May not spinsters, as well as bachelors, give their opinions on every subject, no matter how ignorant they may be; travel about anywhere, in any costume, however convenient; climb up craters, publish their experiences, tame horses, wear pork-pie hats, write articles in the 'Saturday Review'? They have gone out to battle in top-boots, danced on the tight-rope, taken up the Italian cause, and harangued the multitudes. They have gone to prison for distributing tracts; they have ascended Mont Blanc, and come down again. They have been doctors, lawyers, clergywomen, squires—as men have been milliners, dressmakers, ballet-dancers, ladies' hair-dressers. They have worn waistcoats, shirt-collars, white neckcloths, wide-awakes. They have tried a hundred wild schemes, pranks, fancies; they have made themselves ridiculous, respected, particular, foolish, agreeable; and small blame

to them if they have played their part honestly, cheerfully, and sincerely. I know of no especial ordinance of
nature to prevent men, or women either, from being ridiculous at times; and we should hate people a great deal
more than we do, if we might not laugh at them now and
then. To go back to our spinsters, they have crossed the
seas in shoals, been brave as men when their courage came
to be tried; they have farmed land, kept accounts, opened
shops, inherited fortunes, played a part in the world,
been presented at Court. What is it that is to render
life to them only one long regret? Cannot a single
woman know tenderest love, faithful affection, sincerest
friendship? And if Miss A. considers herself less fortunate
than Mrs. B., who has an adoring husband always at home,
and 10,000*l.* a year, she certainly does not envy poor
Mrs. C., who has to fly to Sir Cresswell Cresswell to get rid
of a 'life companion' who beats her with his umbrella,
spends her money, and knocks her down instead of 'lifting
her up.'

With all this it is dismally true that single women
many, and many of them, have a real trouble to complain
of; and one which is common also to married people,
that is, want of adequate means; and when the barest
necessaries are provided, life can only be to many a long
privation; from books, from amusement, from friendly

intercourse, from the pleasure of giving, and from that
social equality which is almost impossible without a
certain amount of money; but then surely it is the want
of money, and not of husbands, which brings such things
to this pass. Husbands, the statistics tell us, it is
impossible to provide; money, however, is more easily
obtained.

For mere sentimental griefs for persons whose comforts
are assured, and whose chief trouble is that they do not
like the life they lead, that they have aspirations and
want sympathy, I think fewer books of consolation might
suffice. The great 'Times' newspaper alone, as it turns
its flapping page, contains many an answer to our questions; and it might supply more than one need for each
separate want, and change how many vague things, dull
dreams, hopeless prayers, into facts and human feelings,
into boys and girls, into work, into pains and sympathy,
into old shoes, and patches, and rags, and darns, into
ignorance and dawning knowledge and gratitude. The
whole clamour is so much mixed up together that it is
very difficult to separate even facts and feelings from one
another. It is not the sorrow of others which makes the
happiness of those who are able to find out some means
for lessening that sorrow, but the relief of their relief
which can only be truly earned and felt by those who

have worked for it. And the best work and the most grateful surely. No one can witness the first-fruits of such good labour without coming away, for a little time at least, more Christian and gentle-hearted.

But it can only be by long patience and trouble that such things can be achieved. For to sympathise, I suppose people must know sorrow in equal measure; to help they must take pains; to give they must deny themselves; to know how to help others best they must learn themselves.

And the knowledge of good and of evil, as it is taught to us by our lives, is a hard lesson indeed; learnt through failure, through trouble, through shame and humiliation, forgotten, perhaps neglected, broken off, taken up again and again.

> With pauses oft a many and silence strange,
> And silent oft it seems when silent it is not;
> Revivals, too, of unexpected change . . . .

This lesson taught with such great pains has been sent to all mankind—not excepting old maids, as some people would almost have it: such persons as would make life one long sentimental penance, during which single women should be constantly occupied, dissecting, inspecting, regretting, examining themselves, living among useless little pricks and self-inflicted smarts, and wasting wilfully, and turning away from the busy business of life, and still more from that gracious gift of existence, and that bounty of happiness and content, and gratitude, which all the clouds of heaven rain down upon us.

When one sees what some good women can do with great hearts and small means, how bravely they can work for others and for themselves, how many good chances there are for those who have patience to seek and courage to hold, how much there is to be done—and I do not mean in works of charity only, but in industry, and application, and determination—how every woman in raising herself may carry along a score of others with her—when one sees all this, one is ashamed and angry to think of the melancholy, moping spirit within us which, out of sheer dulness and indolence, would tempt some of us to waste so many hours of daylight in gloomy sentiment and inertness.

Statistics are very much the fashion now-a-days, and we cannot take up a newspaper or a pamphlet without seeing in round numbers that so many people will do so and so in the course of the year; so many commit murder, so many be taken up for drunkenness, so many subscribe to the ' London Journal,' so many die, so many marry, so many quarrel after, so many remain single to the end of their lives, of whom so many will be old maids in the course of time. This last number is such an alarming one, that I am afraid to write it down; but it is natural to suppose that out of these latter thousands a certain number must be in want of some place where they can have lunch and tea more quietly, and cheaply, and comfortably served than at a pastrycook's shop. Fifteen years ago good tea and bread and butter for sixpence, and dinner off a joint, with potatoes, for ninepence, were to be had at a little reading-room in Langham Place, which things must, I should think, have been a boon to a good many who were perhaps out and about all day, earning their sixpences and ninepences. The ladies might not only partake of all these, and other delicacies, and join in intellectual conversation, but go upstairs and read the 'Times,' and the 'Englishwoman's Journal,' and the 'Cornhill Magazine,' &c. &c., and write their letters on neatly stamped paper when the meal was over.

The governesses and hard-working ladies, however, did not seem to frequent this liberal-minded little refreshment-room as much as might have been expected; changes were made, the Englishwoman's reading-room was closed after a useful and original life of some ten years' duration; and the Berners Street Club[1] was then started with the same object.

[1] 1873.

It is a well-furnished home-like place, with arm-chairs, food, literature. I went there one evening in the dusk and found some ladies comfortably established at one of the tables in the dining-room with something smoking before them and a waitress in attendance, while upstairs a reader was sitting in the drawing-room absorbed in a novel and an armchair. The housekeeper let me see the tariff of the charges. There is a dinner at one o'clock, to which some students from the Royal Academy often come; later in the day people order what they want from the *carte.* Notwithstanding the rise of coals and meat, the prices are not less moderate than they were at the former club fifteen years ago :—

	s.	d.
A cup of tea	0	2
A plate of hot meat	0	6
Potatoes	0	1
Cold meat	0	4
Pudding	0	2
Bread and butter.	0	1
Claret	1	4
Tarragona port	3	0

were among a few of the items.

It is a nice old house with a Georgian face, an old-fashioned staircase; the dining-room is downstairs, and the reading-room is above, with a request for silence and missing volumes to be returned, on the door. In the drawing-room any amount of conversation is tolerated, and visitors, ladies and gentlemen too, are admitted.

The drawing-room table seemed to me, as far as I could judge, to be as liberal and well supplied as the dining-room. Half-a-dozen morning papers, for breakfast, hot from the printing-press; no lack of solid reading, besides lighter stores upon the shelves neatly served in calf, and monthly *entrées* of magazines and quarterlies. These refreshments may be partaken of all the days of the week, from eight in the morning till half-past ten at night. The annual subscription is a pound, and the entrance-fee five shillings.

Perhaps some people may think some great moral experiment is involved in the existence of this little place, but it is a pity to mix up social science with cups of tea; and this establishment has no more sinister intention than that of providing a little rest, food, and intelligent relaxation for any who may wish to avail themselves of it. It cannot of course attempt to compete with any of the clubs in Pall Mall, economy is studied perforce; perhaps at some future time, when women's work is better paid, and education is a liberal profession for women as well as for men, economy may give way and more spacious comfort be secured.[1]

---

[1] On the ground floor of the Ladies' Club in Berners Street, there is the office for the franchise of women.

An uninterested person, not long ago, coming in and receiving a courteous reply to a few passing questions, could not help feeling ashamed of a

Somebody says somewhere, that it is better a thousand times to earn a penny than to save one. I have just been learning how, in a few cases, this penny may be earned by women.

There are—to give the first instance which comes to me—Schools of Art all over the kingdom, where young men and young women are taught the same things by the same masters. It is a fact that the women generally take higher places than the men in the examinations; and when they leave, a person in authority has assured me that he did not know of one single instance where they had failed to make their way. They can earn generally

certain conscious and accepted ignorance, as there contrasted with the courage and liberality which has prompted certain ladies to attempt to urge the rights of the lazy and uninterested people who have not even cared to take trouble to think out a serious subject. These ladies feel that justice (if justice it is) has nothing to do with that acknowledged apathy of ' half the women of England' who do not care for votes, and whose supineness is scarcely a good reason for *not* giving the Franchise to those persons who happen to care for it.

The ideal woman as one imagines her is no social failure. She is calm, beautiful, dignified and gentle, not necessarily accomplished, but she must be intelligent. a good administrator, wise and tender by instinct; for my own taste, she should have perhaps a gift for music, and a natural feeling for art and suitability in her home—and beyond this home she should have an interest large enough to care for other people and other things, nor should that which affects the world and her own country-people's welfare be indifferent to her. If she is able to rule her household, to bring up her sons and daughters in love and in truth, and to advise her husband with sense and composure, she may perhaps be trusted in time with the very doubtful privilege of a 5,000th voice in the election of a member for the borough.

from one hundred to two hundred a year. This is by teaching privately or in government schools, and by designing for manufacturers. One girl that I have heard of was engaged at two hundred a year to invent patterns for table-cloths all day long for some great Manchester firm. I think the melancholy books themselves nearly all most sensibly urge upon parents their duty either to make some provision for their daughters or to help them early in life to help themselves. For troubles come—sad times come—and it is hard to look out for a livelihood with eyes blinded by tears.

It is now about sixteen years since a society was started, called the 'SOCIETY FOR PROMOTING THE EMPLOYMENT OF WOMEN,' of which the object is so good that I should think there must be few who will not sympathise with it.

'Miss Boucherett and a few ladies,' says the report, 'feeling deeply the helpless and necessitous condition of the great number of women obliged to resort to non-domestic industry as a means of subsistence, consulted together as to the best way in which they might bring position and influence to their aid. . . . They resolved on the formation of a new society, which would have for its object the opening of new employments to women, and their more extensive admission into those branches of employment already open to them.' The report goes on to describe briefly enough some of the difficulties which at once occurred to them. Among others, where they should begin their experiment. 'For highly-educated women we could for a time do nothing; women of no education could do nothing for us. That is to say, we could open no new channels for the labour of the former, and our experiments would have failed, owing to the inefficiency of the latter. But we felt convinced that in whatever direction we made an opening the pressure upon all ranks of working women would be lessened.'[1]

It has not been idle during the past fifteen years.

This society has continued in apprenticing girls to hair-dressing, printing, law-copying, dial-painting, sun-glass engraving. It is making enquiries in other directions, but it finds many obstacles in its way. Apprenticeship is expensive, very few of the girls who come to them can give the time to learn a new trade. They almost all want immediate work and payment, and something to do which needs no learning nor apprenticeship. Can one wonder how it is that women earn so little and starve so much? I once saw a dismal list belonging to the secre-

[1] This quotation was made many years ago; in November 1873, calling at the office I saw the unemployed women of to-day still sitting on a bench awaiting their fate, and heard the murmurs of a committee still at work within.

tary of the society, which tells of certain troubles in a very brief and business-like way.   Here is—

'Miss A., aged 30, daughter of a West Indian merchant, reduced to poverty by his failure: highly educated, but not trained to anything.   Just out of hospital. Wants situation as nursemaid, without salary.

'Miss B., aged 30.   Father speculated, and ruined the family, which is now dependent on her.   He is now old, and she has a sister dying.

'Miss C., aged 50.   Willing to do *anything.*

'Miss D., aged 30.   Obliged by adverse circumstances to seek employment: unsuited for teaching.

'Mrs. E., widow, with four daughters, aged from 14 to 23.   Not trained to anything, imperfectly educated, lost large property by a lawsuit.

'Mrs. F., husband in America, appears to have deserted her.   Wants immediate employment.

'Mrs. G., aged 55; husband, a clergyman's son, ill and helpless.   Would do anything.   Go out as charwoman.   Orderly and methodical in her habits.   Applied at St. Mary's Hospital, refused as being too old.

'Miss H., aged 30, clergyman's daughter, governess seven years.   Dislikes teaching, is suffering in consequence of overwork.'

One has no training, no resources ; another poor

thing says she is neither well educated nor clever at anything; she had a little money of her own, but lent it to her brother, and lost it.

' Miss I., energetic, willing to do anything.

' J., middle-aged woman, not trained to anything in particular; tried to live by needlework, and failed.'

Here we are only at J, and there are yet alphabets and alphabets of poor souls all ready to tell the same story, more or less, whom this friendly society is endeavouring to help.

At that time the society had already opened two little establishments that were making their way in the world with every chance of prosperity and success. One was the law-copying office in Portugal Street, and the other the printing press in Great Coram Street, which, as I was told, was better known, and where twice as many hands were employed.[1]

To this printing-house in Great Coram Street we went, my friend A. and I; A. telling me, as we drove along, of all the thought, and pains, and money the house had cost. The money it is already giving back; the kind thought and trouble will be paid in a different coin.

One of the best hands in the office, A. said, is a poor printer's daughter from Ireland, who learnt the business there at her father's press. After his death, she fell into great poverty and trouble, and could find no work nor way of living, when one day she happened to pick up an old torn newspaper, in which she read some little account of the *Victoria Press*. She set off immediately, begged her way all the way to London, and arrived one day covered with grime and rags, to ask Miss Faithfull to take her in. There was another printress whom I saw diligently at work, a little deaf and dumb girl, who had been trained in the office. I scarcely know if I may say so here, but I know that the printers in this office are trained to better things still than printing.

The workwomen are paid by the piece at the same rate as men are paid. The money is well-earned money, for the work is hard; but not so hard—and, I think, some of these very women could tell us so—as working button-holes fourteen hours a day at five farthings an hour, selling life, and spirit, and flesh, and blood, in order not to die. Here are eighteen and twenty shillings to be made a week between nine and six o'clock, except, of course, when some sudden press of business obliges them to work on late into the night.

On the ground-floor there is an office, a press-room, a store-room; down below, a dining-room, where the women cook their dinners if they like, and rest for an hour in the middle of the day. On the first floor are work-rooms. The front one is filled up with wooden desks, like pews, running from the windows, and each holding three or four young women. At right-angles with the pews run long tables, loaded with iron frames and black sheets of type, which are being manipulated by two or three men in dirty-white paper caps. There are also men to print off, and do all the heavy work, which no woman's strength would be equal to.

It is a very busy, silent colony; a table of rules is hanging up on the wall, and I see NO TALKING ALLOWED printed up in fiery letters. All the tongues are silent, but the hands go waving, crossing, recrossing. What enchantresses, I wonder, weaving mystic signs in the air, ever worked to such good purpose! Backwards, forwards, up and down, there goes a word for a thousand people to read; hi, presto! and the GUINEA BASSINET is announced in letters of iron.

Besides all the enchantresses, there is a little printer's devil, who haunts the place, and seems to have a very pleasant time there, and to be made a great deal of by all the womankind. He has a pair of very rosy cheeks, he wears a very smart little cap, with 'Victoria Press' embroidered upon it, and he goes and waits in the halls, and sends up for the ladies' manuscript, just like any other printer's devil one has ever heard of.

'The Society for the Employment of Women apprenticed five girls to me,' says Miss Faithfull, describing their start, 'at premiums of 10*l.* each. Others were apprenticed by relations and friends, and we soon found ourselves in the thick of the struggle. . . . . When you remember that there was not one skilled compositor in the office, you will readily understand the nature of the difficulties we had to encounter. Work came in immediately from the earliest day. In April we commenced our first book.'

Everybody, I think, must wish this gallant little venture good speed, and all the success it deserves. Here is one more extract about the way in which the printers themselves look at it :—

'The introduction of women into the trade has been contemplated by many printers. Intelligent workmen do not view this movement with distrust. They feel very strongly that woman's cause is man's, and they anxiously look for some opening for the employment of those otherwise solely dependent upon them.' And I feel bound to add that I have seen exactly a contrary statement in another little pamphlet, written by another member of the society.[1]

[1] This account was written in the year 1860.

The other place to which we went was a law stationer's in Portugal Street, Lincoln's Inn, where are a series of offices and shops in which lawyers' clerks, I believe, go and buy all those red tapes, blue bags, foolscap papers, plain or over-written, in stiff, upright, legible handwriting—which seem to play such an important part in the legislature of the country. Blue paper, white paper, of a dozen tints, ruled, unruled, abbreviations, erasures, ordered, permitted, forbidden— all these things are decreed by certain laws, which are as much the laws of the land as 3 Vict. or 18 Geo. III., which one reads about in the newspapers. All this was good-naturedly explained to us by the manager of this copying office, into which we were invited to enter by an elaborate hand hanging up on the wall, and pointing with a pen, which was ornamented by many beautiful flourishes. I was rather disappointed to find the place perfectly light and clean, without any of the conventional dust and spiders' webs about. The manager sitting in a comfortable little room, the clerks busy at their desks in another—very busy, scarcely looking up as we go in and working away sedulously with steel pens. I am told that the very first thing they learn, when they come in, is to stick their pens behind their ears.

There were about ten of them, I think. The manager

told us that they were paid, like the printers, by the piece, and could earn from fifteen to twenty-four shillings a week ; receiving three-halfpence a folio, or twopence a folio, according to the difficulty of the work. They go on from ten till about six. This business, however, cannot be counted on with any certainty ; sometimes there is a press of work which must be done, and then the poor clerks sit up nearly all night, scratching with wearied pens, and arrive in the morning with blear eyes, and pale faces, and fit for very little. Then, again, there is comparatively nothing going on ; and they sit waiting in the office, working and embroidering, to pass the time. The idea of clerks embroidering in their office, and of young women with pens behind their ears, bending over title-deeds and parchments, seemed rather an incongruous one ; but young women must live somehow, and earn their daily bread ; and a great many of these had tried and failed very often before they drifted into Miss Rye's little office.

It was opened some ten months ago, she told us, by tne Society, and was transferred to her in November, and already begins to pay its own expenses. It was very uphill work at first. The copyists were new to their work ; the solicitors chary of reading it. Many of their clerks, too, seemed averse to the poor ladies. Others, however, were very kind; and one, in particular, came to see Miss Rye of his own accord, to tell her of some mistakes which had been made, and gave her many useful hints at the same time. Without such help, she said, they never could have got on at all. Now the drudgery is overcome, the little office is flourishing; the steel pens find plenty of work to do.

One of the copyists is a widow, and supports two children; another is a Quaker lady, who writes the most beautiful hand imaginable. Applicants come every day to be taken in, and Miss Rye says that if they seem at all promising she is only too glad to engage them; but many and many of them lose courage, cry off at the last moment, find the occupation too severe, the distance too great, would like to come sometimes of an afternoon, and so go off to begin their search anew after that slender livelihood that seems so hard to win—so hard in some cases, that it is death as well as life that poor creatures are earning, as they toil on day by day, almost contented, almost cheerful.

Ladies—those unlucky individuals whose feelings have been trained up to that sensitive pitch which seems the result of education and cultivation, and which makes the performance of the common offices of life a pain and a penalty to them—might perhaps at a pinch find a livelihood in either of these offices, or add enough to their store to enable them at least to live up to their cultivated feelings. At any rate, it must be less annoying and degrading to be occupied with work, however humble, than to contemplate narrower and narrower stintings and economies every day—economies which are incompatible with the very existence of cultivation and refinement. Scarcely any work that is honest and productive can be degrading. If a lady could earn 60*l.* a year as a cook, it seems to me more dignified to cook than to starve on a pittance of 30*l.* or 20*l.*, as so many must do.

Work may be wearily sought indeed, but it is to be found. By roadsides, in arid places, springing up among the thorns and stones. Patient eyes can see it, honest hands may gather; good measure, now and then pressed down and overflowing. Only poor women's hands are bruised by the stones sometimes, and torn by the thorns.

I seem to have been wandering all about London, and to have drifted away ever so far from the spinsters in whose company I began my paper. But is it so? I think it is they who have been chiefly at work, and taking us along with them all this time; I think it is mostly to their warm sympathy and honest endeavours that these places owe their existence—these, only a few among a hundred which are springing up in every direction:—

springing up, helpful, forbearing, kindly of deed, of word, gentle of ministration, in the midst of a roaring, troublous city. Somehow grief, and shame, and pain, seem to bring down at times consolation, pity, love, as a sort of consequence.

1873. The writer has left these last few pages as they were written at the time, fifteen years ago or more, not because of the description they contain of things which have passed away, but for the sake of things that cannot pass away—a remembrance of the hands that marked this portion of the writer's life. One hand—that which ruled and blessed at home—wrote a title to the rambling little paper. The guiding companion whom I have called A. is no longer among us, but the light of her sweet wisdom still burns as from a shrine, and falls upon many a dark and tortuous way, and its radiance still cheers and encourages many a lagging pilgrim. Adelaide Anne Procter is a household name to many and many of us, and her voice is not silent.[1]

---

[1] A book beside me opens at her lines on ' Incompleteness : '—

Learn the mystery of progression duly,
   Do not call each glorious change Decay ;
But know we only hold our treasures truly
   When it seems as if they passed away.

Nor dare to blame God's gifts for incompleteness ;
   In that want their beauty lies ; they roll
Towards some infinite depth of love and sweetness,
   Bearing onwards man's reluctant soul.

The writer can recall the scene in the little copying office in Lincoln's Inn, and still see the noble, worn face, the slender form leading the way, and the bright-haired lady who came smiling into the room with a welcome to her visitor. Maria Rye has also in these long fifteen years won for herself a place in the ranks of those who have not grudged to give their life's toil and generous hearts to others.

Homes, husbands, sons, and daughters, such sacred ties are sweet, but they are not the only ones nor the only sacred things in life, and some examples seem indeed to show us that love may be strong enough and wide enough to take the world itself for a home, and the deserted for children, and the sick and the sorrowful for a family. Married or unmarried, such lives are not alone.

Before concluding this little article, written from its double point of view and from the two ends of fifteen years, I cannot help adding a few words about some of the changes which have taken place in women's work since it was first published.

As regards this special Society for the Employment of Women, Miss King, the present secretary, tells me that among the experiments (some abandoned perforce, others continued) hair-dressing has perhaps been most thoroughly successful and well established. The following extract about *Dispensers* is also very interesting and hopeful :—

'The demand for female dispensers is still small, but the efficiency displayed by those already engaged in this occupation will almost, as a matter of course, ensure an increase, and during the year two applications have been made for female dispensers, which the committee was unable to meet, having no one qualified to undertake the duties.   The opinion of a doctor who has large experience in dispensers, both male and female, is interesting.   He writes of a lady who was employed in a dispensary which he superintended: "She was one of the most efficient dispensers I have had under my direction, and I have had several, both male and female.   My experience has led me to prefer an intelligent female to a male dispenser.   I find they are more careful, neater, more courteous to the patients, and that although still a novelty, they are in no way taken exception to."'

Miss King also tells me that there is a class at the Society's office for book-keeping and arithmetic, which seems to answer admirably, and I again extract from the report showing the practical use of such instruction :—

'Women who have obtained certificates seldom have to wait long for employment, and the reports received by the Society of the manner in which they discharge their duties are in almost all cases satisfactory. Captain Costyn, secretary of the Westminster Palace Hotel, wrote in April last as follows to the secretary: " For some time two young women educated in the institution have been employed in the office of this company, and, I am glad to say, before long a third will be established here. The conduct of the two has been so creditable, and the aptitude they have displayed for business so great, that I am induced to communicate with you and to ask whether it would be agreeable to you to receive particulars of any vacancy which may occur in the head office, though I trust the day may be distant when I lose the services of either. I may mention that in a fortnight all the clerks will be females." '

The report goes on to say that 'persons who have once had book-keepers from the Society constantly return for others when those they have obtained through the Society form engagements, or they require additional hands; and book-keepers who have once made a good start seldom find it necessary to put their names again on the register, which is, perhaps, the best guarantee that could be given of their success.'

Book-keepers in the house earn from 15*l.* to 50*l.* a year; out of the house from 10*s.* to 25*s.* weekly; for law writing the average for the year is only from 8*s.* to 15*s.* a week.

Miss King has collected an interesting table of the

proportional wages of women; of these the highest are for trained artists and painters on china,[1] who can earn from 3*l.* to 5*l.* weekly, and who seem to be the only well-paid workers on the list. There are curious trades and details in the list. 18*s.* a week for sticking pins into paper is a liberal and unexpected item. Among the best paid workers are the colour stampers, who can earn from 20*s.* to 25*s.* The wages seem to rise immediately when the occupation ceases to be mechanical, and intelligence comes into play.

These women, well or ill paid, have learnt their art, can use their tools, and are fortunate in having wherewithal to gain their honest daily bread, and to be able to look the future in the face. 'But what is one to do,' says the secretary, 'for persons of 40 or 50 who come to one wanting employment for the first time, who have never learnt anything nor done anything in their life before? Though I write their names down on the registry, it is of little use; and yet it is a case of daily occurrence: nor does it much matter if it is that of a man or a woman.' Let us hope, according to the present rate of progress, that in another forty years every woman will have learnt a trade.[2] As regards teachers, Miss King told

---

[1] They should be grateful to Sir Henry Cole for this.

[2] I must not omit to mention an excellent institution called the Ladies' Sanitary Association, also having an office at 22 Berners Street.

me that people now constantly ask for certificated teachers for their schools and their children, and it necessarily follows that such teachers stand in a far better position than they did before these certificates were given.

There is certainly a different feeling about education now from that which formerly existed. The London Association of Schoolmistresses, established for the purpose of meeting and talking over matters concerned with education, indicates a new spirit and interest in the work. The Cambridge scheme for local examination has been of real and practical benefit, and there is also the system for education by correspondence. One friend, whom I will not name, has given leisure, energy, and resource to the work, and has sown his seed broadcast in the endeavour to raise the aim and widen the span of the ordinary school-girl mind. It is not so much at the onset of life, in the early spring-time, that the result of such teaching will tell; but a little later, when the time for the harvest comes round, and the fields are ripening, then the sheaves may be reaped and sorted, and the work of the labourer and the effort of the soil repaid.

In education, that mighty field, as you sow the seed, that strange incongruous seed of human intelligence cast forth hour by hour in books and words, in the secret meditations and works of the dead as well as the deeds of the living, so it grows again, new, revivified, gathering life from every breath of air and ray of light. But, nevertheless, it happens not unfrequently that while some good soil is utilised and worked and turned to good and useful ends, other soil not less good and fruitful is neglected or ill-treated and scantily supplied, diluted with platitude, planted with parsley and cucumbers and with asparagus, when under more favourable circumstances it might have grown wheat or wholesome crops in bountiful measure.

What Arnold did for schoolboys and schoolmasters, inventing freedom for them and a rescue from the tyranny of commonplace and opposition, and bringing in the life of truth and commonsense to overwhelm schoolroom fetishes and opposition, some people have been trying to do for home-girls, schoolgirls, and their teachers, for whom surely some such revolution has long been needed. Of late years a very distinct impression has grown up (by the efforts of the people I am alluding to) that even schoolgirls and governesses are human beings, with certain powers of mind which are worthy of consideration, and for whom the best cultivation, as well as the worst, might be provided with advantage.

The College for Ladies has proposed to itself some such aim of good teaching and intelligent apprehension.

There is also a home at Cambridge for the use of ladies who wish to attend the professors' lectures. When the home began, with Miss Clough as its principal, it only consisted of eight or nine pupils; there are now more than twenty, and the numbers are steadily increasing. The little home has moved from Regent Street, where it was first opened, to an old house in a green garden not far from the river, where the very elms and gables seem to combine in a tranquil concentration. The girls meet together, they are taught by people who do it from interest in the teaching itself; they come into contact with cultivated minds, perhaps for the first time in their lives.

'We teach the girls first for the examination which the university has instituted specially for women,' writes a friend; 'then if they like to stay on, we teach them further, just what we teach the young men. About half of them are preparing to be teachers; the rest come for pure love of learning. We do not want to have only the professional ones, though we are specially anxious to aid these. . . .

'I am glad that you hear people speak favourably of the results of our examination. What we want to do is just what you describe—to aid in the great stimulus that is everywhere being given to girls' education. .This is good for all, while for the few to whom the acquisition of knowledge can be the pleasure or even the business of life, we want to provide guidance and encouragement, and a little material evidence if possible. . . .'

' I have taught some of the girls. It was an instructive change from teaching men. Most of them insist on understanding what they learn, and won't take words for thoughts. Even the stupider ones that I have met with in my teaching do not write the absolute rubbish which stupid men write. I mention this because most people would expect the opposite.'

What is it, then, that we would wish for, for ourselves and for the younger selves who are growing up around us ? Eyes to see, ears to hear, sincerity and the power of being taught and of receiving the truth ; and thus, as I hear A. F. saying, by being taken out of ourselves, and farthest removed from this narrow domain into the world all about us, do we most learn to be ourselves and to fulfil the intention of our being. All nature comes to our help. all arts, all sciences. What is there that does not contribute to the divine reiteration ? The problem of education is merged into that of life itself, when people begin to sort themselves out and to fall into their places, and then for the women who do not marry comes a further question to solve ; and some write books, and some write articles, and some put on long black cloaks, and some wear smart chignons, and the business of living goes on. For the motherly woman, those who have homely hearts, there are real joys and fulfilments undreamt of perhaps in earlier life, when no compromise with perfect happiness seemed to be possible.

The rest of the human race is not so totally devoid of all affection and natural feeling that it does not respond to the love and fidelity of an unmarried friend or relation. There are children to spare and to tuck up in their little beds, young people to bring their sunshine and interest into autumn; there are friendships lifelong and unchanging, which are among a single woman's special privileges; as years go by she finds more and more how truly she may count upon them. Nor are her men friends less constant and reliable than the women with whom she has passed her life. Some amount of sentiment clings to these old men and women friendships: and some sentiment, perhaps, belongs to every true feeling; it is the tint that gives life to the landscape.

As for work, whichever way we turn are the things that we have left undone. 'Come, pluck us! come, pluck us!' cry the fruits as they hang from the branches. There are a thousand plans, schemes, enterprises, fitted to their different minds. Some go into sisterhoods and put their lives into the hands of others, who may or may not be wiser than themselves; others wander into the wide realms of art and worship at æsthetic altars; others are nurses, administrators. We need not despair of seeing women officially appointed as guardians of the poor. Regarding the much debated question of religious and secular organisation, I cannot refrain from quoting a passage from a book,[1] that speaks straightly and wisely in solution of a problem that has occurred to many hundreds of women before this :—

'Secular associations do not undertake to discipline the souls of their members, nor to afford them any special opportunity of expressing their devotion to God as the common Father, but they can no more hinder the expression of such feelings than they can hinder the growth of the soul. On the contrary, they give all the scope that naturally belongs to charitable action, for the expression of such feelings in deed as well as in word. They neither seek for nor value pain and humiliation as a means of proving devotion; on the contrary, they avoid all that might injure health, or distract attention, or encourage spiritual vanity as interruptions to the one main object— the good of the poor. Those who wish to see charitable organisations organised upon a purely secular basis wish

---

[1] *The Service of the Poor*, by C. E. Stephen.

it not only because they believe singleness of aim to be the first condition of perfect success; not only because the poor will probably be most effectually served by those who do it from pure love of them, without thought of their own spiritual interests; not only because secular association breaks none of the domestic interests and social ties which they believe to be divinely appointed, and full both of blessing and power for all good ends; but also because they think that to provide an organisation for the systematic cultivation and exhibition of love and devotion, is to depart from Christian simplicity, and must tend in the long run to injure true humility, sincerity, and even the love and devotion themselves which are thus artificially stimulated.'

' L'homme n'est ni ange ni bête,' says Pascal; 'et le malheur veut que qui veut faire l'ange fait la bête.'

But the angels and the beasts, far apart though they may be, come together both toiling in the field of life, each doing their part in the work: the beasts cultivate the ground, the angels reap and store the good grain. The bread of life itself cannot come to fruition without labour, and the sacrament of brotherly love, union, and faithful promise must be kneaded with toil.

Farewell rewards and fairies,
Good housewifes now may say,
For now foule slutts in dairies
Doe fare as well as they;
And tho' they sweepe their hearths no less
Than maydes were wont to do,
Yet who of late for cleanliness
Finds sixpence in her shoe?

I.

WE have all heard of a benevolent race of little pixies who live underground in subterranean passages and galleries. While people are asleep in their beds these friendly little creatures will come up from their homes in the depths of the earth and dust, and sort and put our houses in order, and repair the damages and waste of the day, light the fires, fill the cans, milk the cows. There is no end to their good offices. They reject all thanks, and are apt to disappear and give warning upon small provocation. Sir Walter Scott has written their history, and as one reads one might sometimes almost fancy that an allegory is being told of some little servant-maid of modern times—I do not mean the comfortable, respectable upper house and parlour-maid of villa and crescent-life, but of the little struggling maid-of-all-work dwelling under our feet or in the narrow passages and defiles of our great city. Do they when their work is finished sometimes emerge from their subterranean haunts, sit by flowing streams, float along upon lily leaves, or sport in moonlit fields, dancing in circles? I am afraid no such pleasant recreation is reserved for our poor little household drudges.

Most people who have ever rung bells, found their hot water ready set for their use, their breakfast waiting their convenience, will be interested in a Report recently laid before the House of Commons—the Blue Book which concerns these little maids.

It is written in the simplest way. Its rhetoric is made up of a few dates and numbers. Its phrases represent so much work done rather than words strung together. It has romance enough in its pages, and pathos and tragedy. They are classed *a*, *b*, and *c* for convenience. This remorseless record of life as it exists for a certain number of people is tabulated for easy reference: so are the sorrows and indifferences of which it treats in a few quiet words. The history of these 650 girls will be found in an appendix, says one sentence.   No wonder that reviewers hesitate to pronounce upon such a literature.

'In January, 1873, you told me,' says Mrs. Senior, ' that you wished to have a woman's view as to the effect on girls of the System of Education at Pauper Schools. You asked me if I would undertake to visit the workhouse schools and report to you the conclusions at which I arrived. . . . .

'I have given my attention almost exclusively to questions affecting the physical, moral, and domestic training at the schools.   I have not attempted to judge of the scholastic work, as I required all the time allowed me for looking into the matters on which I knew that you more especially desired the judgment of a woman.   I divided the enquiry into two parts:

'1. As to the present working of the system in schools.

'2. As to the after career of girls who have been placed out in the world.'

This first part means many months of ceaseless investigation into metropolitan schools, country schools, orphanages, reformatories, &c.; the boarding-out system, as carried out in Cumberland and the North, &c.

The second division represents no less labour of a different kind.

' My next endeavour was to ascertain the history of the girls who had been placed in service from the schools during the last two years. I obtained the names and addresses, more or less exact, of about 650 girls who had been placed out in service in the years 1871–2 in all parts of London and its suburbs, and the history of each girl, as derived from the books or otherwise, was sought to be verified by personal investigation. The very great number of visits to be made, and enquiries to be set on foot, involved in this first investigation, could not within the time allowed be undertaken by myself personally, but the work was effectually carried out by the help of several indefatigable friends.

' I enquired myself personally into the cases of fifty of these girls,' says Mrs. Senior, who has not been content with merely writing a report. She has lived it, heard it speak, gone straight to the human beings concerned in her Tables. Her own personal investigations are contained in Appendix G ; in Appendix F are the histories investigated by her assistants.

'In order to ascertain the school history of each child,' she continues, ' I have usually found it necessary to consult, besides admission and discharge books, five enormous alphabetical registers, numerous volumes of relief lists, creed registers, service register, and chaplain's visiting books.'

This is but a small part of the labour to be undertaken in writing a report of which every detail almost is a living figure in the great and terrible sum which is set before us all to work out as best we can, not only in Blue Books and pamphlets. Anybody may supply a running commentary upon the text, by looking about and using that useful power of common sense with which we are more or less gifted. The facts and data are not past things and distant conclusions—they are now, and round about us. The children are there, the schools are there, the maid-servants are in the kitchens, the report is published, and anyone may read it who chooses.

II.

We should be indeed ungrateful to the work of those wise and far-seeing people who first turned their attention to the crying evils which existed in workhouse schools, and who first insisted upon separate schools for the children, if we did not begin by acknowledging that whatever is done now, and whatever further improvement may be found possible, theirs was the first and decisive step in the abolition of a great abuse. The workhouses are necessarily refuges for every species of failure in life, in conduct, in mind, in body. Such depressing and contaminating influence is the very last to which young children should ever be subjected. States of mind are as catching, especially at an early age, as some states of body. To see people who have neglected their opportunities, deserted their duties, succumbed to every sort of temptation, provided for by the state in a sort of semi-Hades of apathetic discontent, must certainly have no good effect upon the younger generation, already inheriting, perhaps, many of the proclivities that have brought this dismal fate upon their seniors.

The children, seeing their father a willing prisoner in fustian, their mother plodding doggedly along the ward in her blue-striped livery, come to look upon this unsatisfying place as a future to look to. Apathy seems to them a natural condition, low talk and common ways will be familiar sounds, they insensibly imbibe the fetid influence of the condition to which all these people have been brought; by misfortune was it?—or by wrong-doing?—who shall say, or whose the wrong-doing that has doomed these poor souls.

'The atmosphere of a workhouse that contains adult paupers is tainted with vice,' says Mr. Tufnell, in his Report on the training of pauper children. 'No one who regards the future happiness of the children would ever wish them to be educated within its precincts.'

A matron of thirty years' experience to whom I once spoke, shook her head and said that she found it practically impossible to prevent ill effects from the contact of children and adults in the workhouse under her care.

Miss Cobbe says, speaking of the state of workhouses so lately as 1861—'Whatever may be our judgment of the treatment of the male able-bodied paupers, very decidedly condemnatory must be our conclusion as regards the management of female adults, for whom it may be said that a residence in the workhouse is commonly moral ruin. The last rags and shreds of modesty which the poor creature may have brought in from the outer world, are ruthlessly torn away by the hideous gossip over the labour of oakum picking, or in the idle lounging about the women's yard.' And in a note we read—'In one metropolitan union it was found on enquiry, that of eighty girls who had left the workhouse and gone to service, not one had continued in a respectable condition of life.'[1]

The commissioners appointed to enquire into the system felt that nothing but evil could come to the children if things were allowed to continue in the state in which they found them. They worked with uninter-

[1] This statement applies to twelve years ago.

mitting energy and decision, and it was at their suggestion that separate and district schools were first instituted; separate schools being schools attached to one
workhouse only, and built at a distance from the house;
district schools being peopled by the children from three
or four different workhouses, all brought together for
greater convenience in teaching and organising.

Great sums of money have been spent. Fine buildings
have been erected. Hundreds and hundreds of little
paupers are now being struck off, taught, drilled, and
educated by good teachers, with careful superintendents,
in large houses, costing large sums of money. There can
be no comparison between the present and the past, and
there is not one of these children that does not owe
gratitude to those who first laboured to deliver them from
the house of bondage to which they seemed condemned.
But it does not follow that because money has been spent,
no further improvement is possible; and because some
people have been wise and devoted, that no further good
is to be done.

It seems as if every fact and theory of life had to be
rediscovered by each of us practitioners of life in turn.
We read about things, see them happen, listen to advice,
give it more or less intelligently; but we each have to find
out for ourselves what relations such things bear to our-

selves—what is human in all this printers' ink, which of the figures come to life in our own case, instead of being units or statistics—which among our fellow-creatures are actually living persons for us; duties and claims, wants, necessities, possibilities.

The writer happened to come across a living statistic on the side of good and hopeful things, a bright-faced little creature in a Sunday bonnet, who gave her some account of her experience in her first place. She had been brought up in a separate school and had gone out about thirteen.

'Oh, I've been a servant for years!' said the little thing, who was ready enough to tell us all about herself. 'I learnt ironing off the lady; I didn't know nothing about it. I didn't know nothing about anything. I didn't know where to buy the wood for the fire,' exploding with laughter at the idea. 'I run along the street and asked the first person I sor where the wood-shop was. I was frightened—oh, I was. They wasn't particular kind in my first place. I had plenty to eat—it wasn't anything of that. They jest give me an egg, and they says, " There, get your dinner," but not anything more. I had to do all the work. I'd no one to go to: oh! I cried the first night. I used to cry so,' exploding again with laughter. 'I had always slep in a ward full of other girls, and there I was all alone, and this was a great big house—oh, so big! and they told me to go down stairs, in a room by the kitchen all alone, with a long black passage. I might have screamed, but nobody would have heard. An archytec the gen'lman was. I got to break everything, I was so frightened; things tumbled down I shook so, and they sent me back to Mrs. ——, at the schools. They said I was no good, as I broke everything; and so I did—oh, I was frightened! . . . . Then I got a place in a family where there was nine children. I was about fourteen then. I earned two shillings a week. I used to get up and light the fire, bath them and dress them, and git their breakfasts, and the lady sometimes would go up to London on business, and then I had the baby too, and it couldn't be left, and had to be fed. I'd take them all out for a walk on the common. There was one a cripple. She couldn't walk about. She was about nine year old. I used to carry her on my back. Then there was dinner, and to wash up after; and then by that time it would be tea-time agin. And then I had to put the nine children to bed and bath them, and clean up the rooms and the fires at night; there was no time in the morning. And then there would be the gen'lman's supper to get. Oh! that was a hard place. I wasn't in bed till twelve, and I'd be up by six. I stopped there nine months. I hadn't no one to help me. Oh, yes, I had; the baker, he told me of another place. I've been there three year. I'm cook, and they are very kind; but I tell the girls there's none 'on 'em had such work as me. I'm very fond of reading; but I 'aint no time for read- ing.' . . . .

She was a neat, bright, clever, stumpy little thing, with a sweet sort of merry voice.

'You would think Susy a giant if you could see some of them; you have no notion what little creatures they all are,' said Mrs. ——, when I made some remarks about the child's size—and almost immediately came another visitor, smaller, shorter, paler than the first. This little maid had come to talk over the chances of a friend, to whom she seemed much attached.

'There is one thing about her,' said this mite, with some dignity; 'she don't come up to my shoulder. It's aginst her getting a good place.'

This little woman had been single-handed in a school where there were 50 pupils to let in twice a-day, as well as two sets of lodgers to attend to. The owners of the house were very kind, but too busy themselves to help, and the poor pixie had struggled until her health had broken down. Her feet were swelled ; she could no longer hold out when Mrs. —— found her. It is a terrific battle if one comes to think of it. One little soldier single-handed against a house and its wants, and the dust and the smuts, and the food and the inmates, and the bells, and the beds, and the fire and water to be served up in cans and stoves and plates. Atlas could carry the world on his shoulder, but what was his task compared to poor little Betty's?

III.

The writer has a friend among District Schools, who has more than once admitted her into the wards under his direction. At the time when he and his wife were appointed to their present position, the schools were in a bad and unsatisfactory state; notwithstanding all advantage of situation and arrangement, and liberal support, the health of the school-children was not what it should have been! Regularity, economy, uniformity—all these things seem desirable enough; but there is a point where we must all acknowledge that such things are intended for men's use, and not for their constraint alone, and my friends have made it their business to find out where that point exists.

Mrs. Senior suggests, among other things, some sort of home life in the schools: wards broken up, if possible into divisions, which might rectify their weary uniformity —some system of home government; the nurse, perhaps, acting as mother, and the elder girls attending to the little ones and babies. 'The children want *mothering*,' says the Blue Book, in the natural tones of a woman's voice.

About some necessities there can be but one opinion— air, water, room, change, well-cooked food, ease, backs to the forms—all these things our Blue Book recommends, not in official language, but in a voice that speaks far more truly the real feeling which is now abroad. Judging from signs we see daily (perhaps even more among the rulers than among the ruled), the great age of red tape seems coming to a close. The good goddess Hygeia must be smiling as she sees her temples rising, her votaries assembling, singing her praises in public and in private, and worshipping her with many ablutions and ceremonies of mighty import!

My friends, Mr. and Mrs. ——, who have partially tried one of Mrs. Senior's plans in the establishment under their direction, say that their experiment has had a most excellent result. They began of their own accord by creating a nursery, without any idea of the good effects which were to follow, but they very soon found that the girls allowed to attend to the children delighted in the work, softened to the little ones, and the children themselves got on better than when they were lost in the great body of the house. The nursery is detached from the main building, and when we walked in, it was broad daylight—eight o'clock—June bed-time. The little paupers were going to bed in the great bright wards. All the windows were open; the children were taking off their blue stockings and heavy little boots. We met one three-year-old pattering adventurously down a passage, and carrying its shift in its hand. There were about a dozen little creatures in one room, where an elder girl was undressing them. They could take off their thick boots for themselves; one ambitious Jenny was tugging at a string with a serious flushed face; a friend about her own size was looking on with deep interest. We said 'Good-night' to Jenny, who was too much absorbed to respond, but the little friend stuffed her hand into mine. It was a pretty sight in the next room to come upon all the babies toddling round their tub and plashing the water with their hands. They were plump, comfortable little bodies, waiting their turn to be scrubbed, and they certainly did credit to kind Mrs. ——'s efforts for their comfort.

I don't think they spoke, these small nymphs in blue stockings and unbleached calico; they looked up at us with sweet, innocent faces; one said 'Coo-bye;' one laughed and showed us her bed behind the door; another, a little baby boy, toddled forward half naked from the group—he was the youngest, and accustomed to be noticed; and so the kindly waters of the tub—that tepid evening stream that floats so many babes, that sparkles to so many little plashing hands—came flowing with its kind, refreshing depths into the workhouse nursery. The setting sun was shining through the tall open windows, and soft June breaths were blowing in.

For many years all these windows had been carefully filled in, the master told us; but now at last they have removed the ground glass, and let in the sight of the green, and the sunset and the summer-time. In the schoolroom especially the difference was very noticeable.

It was a Sunday evening, and while I was talking to Mrs. —— I had heard a distant sort of hymn in the air. The girls were singing as we came into the great schoolroom, about fifty girls were sitting upon the benches, and a music-master was at a harmonium playing and beating time.

They sang very sweetly, with very shrill and touching voices, one little class apart chaunted the hymn, and the others joined in. It was something about soldiers of the cross, with a sort of chorus.

As I stood by the superintendent he pointed to the

window, through which we could see a dazzle of June and green and distant hills, and a great field, across which a long procession of these young soldiers went winding and rewinding in the sweet basking evening. One thought of the battle before them—all the hard work, the troubles, and friendlessness of their poor little lives. They were not abashed, and chaunted on with all the might of their young throats, an unconscious prayer for safety, for help, for courage, and defence. While the hymn lasts they are safe enough. Then one day it breaks off for each of them. ' At sixteen,' says the Board, they are free, and the little soldiers struggle off to meet the world. They can cater for themselves; come, go, loiter as they will; they have had experience enough, advice enough; or, for a change, there is the workhouse, where they will find a new teaching, and a new code of morality.

———

IV.

Perhaps to the general reader it may not be the details, or the classifications, or the results of the enquiries contained in this Blue Book, that will seem most interesting, but the feeling which is unconsciously shown by its very

E 2

statistics—the unaffected goodness of heart and womanly mothership for all that is young, childish, foolish, and suffering. No one can deny facts and the inevitable fatality of causes, of which the effects are, in this instance, the little stunted beings that crowd our schools and educational establishments. But such Reports as these do at least suggest a sort of law leading both to good and to evil —a fatality of good as well as of wrong doing—and make one believe that the genuine interest which some people are feeling, and which has already shown itself in such satisfactory and practical details, may reach many a poor child, by signs more and more comfortable, and tangible, and cheerful.

Where a book ends and the reader begins is as hard to determine as any other of those objective and subjective problems which are sometimes set. Here, as we read, the paragraphs turn into every day; into the writer, into the children, into one's own conscience, into other people's— into work, trouble, necessity, into the influences by which people affect one another. Books teach us to think; then comes action to interpret thinking into signs and ceremonies; then come human beings who enact the signs, who are our consciences, revealed, perhaps, our thoughts, responsive, who are in themselves hope fulfilled, who combine in some strange way all the moods, questions, facts, that we see tangibly spread out before us.   It is almost as if one could look round at times and see the whole secret history of conscience mapped out in actual things, and doings; some of them stupid, jealous, shamefully incomplete; others gentle, and generous, and effective.

Two facts Mrs. Senior wishes us to bear in mind, if we try to draw some conclusion from that view of life which her report presents to us.   One is, that the schools have to deal with bad material.   The poor little heroines of this epic are stunted, stupid, unreceptive for the most part, though some people may well ask, Why should they be clever?   How can they grow tall?   and What is it that they have to receive?   They come to the schools because there is no home in the world outside for them, because their parents have come to grief, or to trouble of some sort.   They have to go out into the world again with their unsatisfactory little bodies and minds, because the schools can keep them no longer, at an age when other more fortunate children are shielded and loved and cared for, to struggle for themselves with difficulties, mistresses, incapacities, and dangers of every description.   So much for the second division of Mrs. Senior's report.   As regards that which applies to the changes she would wish to see in the schools, she says these apply to the system itself, and not to the working of it.   She says, ' I believe that, as a class, there are few people so painstaking, kind-hearted, and indefatigable, as the present lot of officials connected with pauper and district schools.'   It is, perhaps, because of this that, for some years past, some of these officials and managers have been dissatisfied with the results of their hard and constant work—of all this money and trouble given. ·In district schools, as elsewhere, experience had to be paid for; and when such vast numbers are collected together, every trifling experiment must necessarily count a thousand-fold, and be multiplied again and again.   The evil is gigantic, and almost impossible to grapple with.

V.

At present, one great difficulty consists in the classification of the children to be provided for.   There are the orphans, whose only home is the parish and the school; the deserted children, whose parents may reappear to claim them, as well as those whose parents are incapacitated temporarily or otherwise; and there are, thirdly, the casuals, who are sometimes taken in and out by their parents as often as *eight times* in a year, and for whom, under existing circumstances, any legislation must be very indefinite.

The real body of the school consists of the children who have no other home to turn to, and no personal ties to lean upon, and whose welfare, as Mrs. Senior says, should, in any doubtful question, be made the main consideration.

Some masters say that, were the classes divided, and the good influence of the permanent scholars removed from the casuals, these poor little creatures would become so demoralised that they would not have a chance for improvement.   Speaking in a general way, Mrs. Senior says that in large schools the officers hold that more good than harm is done by mixing the children; while the officers in smaller schools (who have perhaps better means of judging of individual cases) hold the contrary.

She goes on to say—'The difficulties of managing the pauper schools, even under the present system, are so great that one can heartily sympathise with the dread expressed by some officers of a change which, it appears to them, would add to their difficulties. We are none the less bound, however, to look simply at the question whether the presence of the casual children does or does not cause any moral deterioration to the permanent children, whose interests are chiefly at stake.'

Here is a picture of the state of things that might occur, with every careful endeavour for right doing. 'To

the eye of the visitor the outward order of the schools is in
most respects perfect, and it seems generally agreed that
the presence of a mass of children already drilled into
order has the best effect on new comers. We cannot,
however, judge by external order of the real effect of the
presence of the casuals. Whatever evil they may have
learnt during their vagrant life, they know that it is for
their interest to submit to discipline while at school, to
conceal what could bring them into discredit with their
superiors, and to avoid conduct and language that would
entail punishment. Whatever discipline may exist in the
school, the children in the playground and dormitories are
under little supervision.'

'In one school I saw a child of six years old whose
language was so horrible that the matron was obliged to
send her, as soon as lessons were over, to one of the dormitories in order to get her away from the other children.
She was probably too young to know that it was to her
interest to hold her tongue in the presence of officers. In
a few years she would be more cunning, and keep her bad
language for the playground and dormitories. Another
matron told me of a family of sisters who used to go in
and out and return each time more and more versed in sin.
From another I heard, among many examples, of a family
of children who were constantly on the tramp, sleeping

like animals in sheds, wandering about the country; children who were at first good and tractable, but who returned each time with more and more knowledge of evil.'

'Among many officers I found one who spoke even more strongly than the rest, and whose opinion I consider of great value. She fully recognised the large amount of mischief which can be done in a school even by one child, and felt that the *least* important duty of a mistress is the supervision of children during school hours.'

Many of the changes Mrs. Senior recommends are simple, feasible, and will apply to our own children in our own homes as well as to those in this strange cosmopolitan refuge which the necessity of the times has imposed upon our citizens.

If our children have round shoulders, shorn heads, weak eyes—if a certain number of them seem dull, stupid, and incapable of the common duties of life—if their nurses and teachers complain of their bad temper, untruthfulness, apathy, we must feel that for these special children, much as we have done already, we have not yet done enough.

Suppose they are ill, with long and chronic ailments, if we leave them for hours and hours unoccupied in a bare room learning a habit of idleness and dullness only too easy to acquire, and sometimes impossible to forget, we must feel that in one sense only we are doing our duty. You cannot inculcate moral qualities by word of command; intelligence, self-reliance, trust, sympathy—these things can't be dealt out in copy-books or written upon a slate.

Teachers and managers of schools have themselves raised the standard of that which is expected; and as the standard is raised, there will be less and less machinery, and more and more of natural feeling introduced, if it pleases Heaven to give us all more wisdom and knowledge of the laws which govern life and human beings,—from members of the Cabinet down to little pauper children.

A wise and experienced person writes:—

'We teach them indeed to read and write, and read and sing hymns. All that part of their education is probably quite as good as what is given in the day-schools of the ordinary poor. Also we teach them that part of religion which may be conveyed in the form of question and answer. But it is only the sum of all that makes human nature, more emphatically woman's nature, beautiful, useful, or happy. Her moral being is left wholly unculti-vated. She possesses nothing of her own, not even her clothes or the hair on her head. How is she to go out inspired with respect for the rights of property, and accus-tomed to control the natural impulses of childish covetous-ness? Worse than all, the human affections of the girl are all checked, and with them, almost inevitably, those religious ones which naturally rise through the earthly parents' love to the Father in Heaven. The workhouse girl is the child of an institution. She is driven about with the rest of the flock, from dormitory to schoolroom, and from schoolroom to workhouse yard, not harshly or unkindly, but always as one of a herd, whether well or ill cared for. She is nobody's Mary or Kate, to be individually thought of'

VI.

Having gone carefully into the details of the management of these school, Mrs. Senior, as I have said, proceeded to follow up the results of this management; and her figures, as compared to those in the note of Miss Cobbe's article, are less discouraging than they might seem at a first glance.

'Following out the scheme already stated, we took some trouble to trace out the careers of the girls brought up in the great amalgamated schools and in the separate schools, and, with the help of some experienced persons, to compare them together and divide them into classes. The result was as follows:—

	Girls brought up in District Schools.	Girls brought up in Separate Schools.
Good	28	51
Fair	64	82
Unsatisfactory	106	78
Bad	47	35
	245	246

Some idea may be formed of the difficulty and trouble which these few numbers have given to those who compiled them, and who have tried to add up this sum in human nature, by a glance at the Appendix, where will be found a history of each one of these cases traced out from records in school books, to the endless streets, suburban roads, lines of brick and rail, and humanity along which these little entries drift to their fate. The girls themselves have been produced from their back kitchens, and the mistresses encountered in their parlours. Out of complaints and cross-complaints, and good sense and moderate judgment, the daily story becomes a figure again counting in its place.

It is not long ago since I heard someone (with a right than which there is none greater) speaking of the force of contained power and of simple statement as compared to that of vehemence and picturesqueness of language. Here, in the Appendix of Mrs. Senior's Report, are histories, of which I have selected two or three at random. They are not very eventful, and their force most assuredly consists in this power of facts, tending towards the same results; uneventful units, whose histories count in the great sum just as surely as those of the others for whom they rub and scrub and toil.

I might multiply examples, but they are but repetitions of one another and all in the same way seem to point more or less to two necessities—that of some greater individuality of training when in the schools, and of more complete system of supervision when the school has become daily life.

Here is poor C. D., whose career, as it is traced from book to book, seems typical enough. She is clever, with 'high' notions, and goes to service; and then she loses her places again and again, reappears in one book and another, 'admission, dismissal, readmission.' Here she is under the heading of 'distress from service,' sent to a home; then follow six admissions, six discharges; lastly, she goes to Highgate Infirmary, and there comes the last entry of all, 'Died June 22, 1871, of phthisis, aged eighteen.'

There are naughty girls, and a certain number of good ones, in the lists published by Mrs. Senior.

G. goes from place to place, has fainting fits, hates going to her aunt between places, as relations don't like being at expense. First place—-too hard, not in bed till past twelve sometimes.   J. M. S., one eye, half witted, no friends, twenty years of age.   J. T., deserted child, no friends, whitlow, round shoulder.

As specimens of the class which may well be termed unsatisfactory, come—

No. 1. Pilferer, untruthful, idle, incorrigibly dirty.

No. 2. Very dishonest, dirty. Mistress, a kind person, keeps her because she cannot give her a character.

No. 4. Being refused leave to go out, howls till a crowd is collected.

No. 5. Improving, but throws herself on the ground when people attempt to teach her.

No. 12. Clean, destructive, curiously apathetic.

No. 20. Very bad temper, unkind to children, dishonest, untruthful, dirty. Two mistresses give an equally bad account.

Finally come the girls who have absconded with or without valuables, who are known to be leading immoral lives.

By 15 Vict. capt. ii. sec. 3 & 4, the guardians are required, so long as the servant is under sixteen, and resides within five miles of the workhouse, to visit the person at least twice in every year, and report in writing if the person is subjected to cruel treatment in any respect.

At some of the schools the chaplains keep up with the

girls in their places after the official hour has struck for them. But when one remembers the average length of a man's life, and the number of girls that pass through the schools, it will be seen how impossible a task this must be for any single person to accomplish thoroughly.

'We have found,' says the Report, 'many really admirable mistresses, homely women, taking a maternal interest in the girls; sparing no pains to teach and inspect personally the work of the house, and who understood that the little servant needed some pleasure and relaxation. Without any parade we have often heard from a mistress of a shilling given now and then to the girl to be spent in her own pleasure, of little presents to her subscribed for by the children.' But at the same time the statistics show how many there are among them who disappear entirely, and in the case of workhouse girls we know too well what this disappearance means.

A friend of Mrs. Senior, writing to her, says :—

'The answers given to me by the mistresses of girls sent to service from the metropolitan pauper schools were so uniform in character that I think the system of training must be in a great measure answerable for characteristics so general and so strongly marked. I have made enquiries as to 40 girls.

'The girls were all without exception well taught in

reading and writing; in arithmetic, as far as I could ascertain, they were fairly competent.

'All without exception were well taught in needlework, as regards the mere execution of stitches; and *all with one exception were unable to arrange or do any sort of needlework without constant supervision.*[1]

'All without exception are well taught in the elements ot religious knowledge.

'All without exception are curiously apathetic in temperament, described to me as not caring for anything, taking no interest, not enjoying, seeming like old people. All with one exception were stunted in growth and physical development, even where the health was good.

'If we compare the girls in pauper schools with girls kept at home by family necessity, or sent to service at fourteen or fifteen, I think we shall find the following differences :—The house girls have infinitely more life and energy, and it is much easier to teach them their work. They are often very troublesome to learn at first, but at least half of them are fairly good tempered; those with defective tempers are seldom invincibly stubborn or outrageous, and there is no difference between their physical development and that of all other classes.'

---

[1] This seems an excellent illustration of the defect of too much system in education.

A matron of a workhouse said to me the other day—' I knew a nice, good girl who was dismissed then and there by her mistress for what do you think, ma'am? for falling asleep in the day-time. I say it is not natural for a girl of sixteen to go fast asleep in the day-time, unless she is tired out and can't keep up any longer.'

' People turn them off and let them go, without a thought,' she continued. ' I myself met a poor child wandering about in the street, not knowing where to turn. I took her home, and she is now my servant; but there is no knowing where she might be if I hadn't chanced to meet her.'

Three girls, who were just going out to service from a district school, came into the superintendent's parlour the other day while I happened to be there; they were girls of sixteen, but they looked scarcely thirteen in their crops and pinafores. One of them appeared utterly stupid, and seemed to stare at my questions instead of answering them. The second was silent but intelligent, with wondering blue eyes and a very sweet expression. The third girl talked a good deal, but only by rote; she had been out already, but had been sent back by her mistress, she said. When I asked her what she had done in her place, she wandered off into some housemaid's catechism.

F

'What did you think about the first morning when you awoke?' said Mrs. ——.

'I couldn't think where I was,' said the girl; 'it was so small all round, with paper on the walls.'

'And what happened next?' said Mrs. ——.

Here the little housemaid started off rapidly. 'Rise at 'alf-past five, throw open the window, light the kitching fire, then do the parlour, carefully turning down the 'earth rug for fear it should be spiled, then sweep and dust the sitting-room, scattering tea-leaves,' &c.

Perhaps the little thing's practice had not been equal to her precept; happily for herself she was still of an age to be received into the school and into her pinafore again. If she breaks down a second time, she will only have the workhouse for a refuge.

I have been told in one district school that the most troublesome and unmanageable girls are those who have, by the desire of the guardians, passed through a workhouse, and remained there for some time before being despatched to the school.

* * *

VII.

Women are, perhaps, naturally more suspicious and nervously impressionable than men, and for this very reason are better able to observe those details which so greatly concern little children and young girls. Surely it is a wise and far-seeing legislature that allows for this difference; that attempts to suit the intelligence at its command to the work to be accomplished.

Here we find a woman doing woman's work, patiently following . out detail after detail, minutely inspecting wards, and clothes, and apparatus of every kind, reporting conscientiously, and bringing forward her long year's work. It is for other minds to generalise and legislate again upon this work, which seems to have been honestly carried out, and unweariedly pursued to its end.

Miss Cobbe describes an experiment that was tried by some ladies at Bristol not long ago. They acquainted themselves with the addresses of the girls going into service, called on each mistress, expressed their interest in the little servant, and asked permission for her to attend a Sunday afternoon class. Invariably it has been found that the mistresses take in good part such visits, made with proper courtesy.

Mrs. Senior would further add to this a system of Government supervision. The scheme, which is simple enough, consists of a certain number of paid agents to visit the young servants in their places; a certain number of ladies to befriend them; a certain number of post-cards ready addressed for the girls to post upon leaving their situations; one central office, or registry, where their names might be entered into books; and lastly, a certain number of small homes for them to go to in the intervals of service, where they may find help and advice. It is nothing new; but after all it is not anything new that any of us want; only the old blessing of asking and receiving, of friends and helpful succour answering to the call of our forlorn voices.

And what prayer, in words, in works, in goodwill, was ever prayed that was not answered in one way or another? We look life in the face, and hear of the laws that seem to rule its progress; we watch years go by, read Reports, see people in every sort of trouble, failure, and flurry, trying to regulate and order the disorder. Some are praying to God, others praying to men. As we watch the rout go by, as we travel along it ourselves, we cannot but be struck by the importance of every day, as well as by its profanity, by the meaning of its trivialities, amenities, and co-operations, all dominated by a law of which we dimly recognise the rule—a law to which we may open our hearts if we will, as it reaches us in this our common every day, our sacred every day. And by this supreme law each one of us in turn is touched. You are responsible to it, you wretched orphans flung upon evil shores; you are responsible, wise matrons, safe in port, anchored and sheltered from storm; you children, awakening in rows in the wards of the great refuges; you rulers and overseers, looking out afar; you critics and penny-a-liners and young men, maidens and old maids, according to your light and your power of life.

And besides this solemn law of the duty, varying in degree for each of us, there is also a gift, divine though we call it human, a multiplying, renovating charity, of pity and goodwill. It does not fail though the multitude is so great, and though the bread and the fishes that have been given by the Master to dispense among the hungry crowd seem so inadequate to their wants.

ARACHNE IN SLOANE STREET.

THE readers of the ' Spectator ' will remember the journal of the candid Clorinda, who at one in the afternoon calls for her handkerchief and works half a violet leaf. At the end of the week Clorinda moralizes as follows ;—

' Upon looking back to this my journal,' she says, ' I am at a loss to know whether I pass my time well or ill, and indeed never thought of considering how I did it before I perused your speculation upon that subject. I scarce find a single action in these five days that I can thoroughly approve of, excepting the working upon the violet leaf, which I am resolved to finish the first day I am at leisure.'

Clorinda has evidently some respect for her needle. In her day the golden age of embroidery was not quite over. I have no doubt that the violets of her time, though stiffly drawn, were harmoniously shaded. The faded wreaths may still be to be seen, perhaps in some museum or repository of ancient goods, shaming the forward steam-propelled ornamentation of later generations by their modest graces. It would be indeed strange if hand-work did not surpass machinery in that same quality which makes a drawing superior to a photograph, a letter to a printed circular. Hitherto it has given us many yards of indifferent and formal produce in the place perhaps of as many inches of really good and worthy ornament; but now, says the Report, it has become probable that furniture will be decorated by the hands of women quite, or nearly, as cheaply as by machinery. 'Hand-work is not only more beautiful, but it is thoroughly durable (the Exhibition of Ancient Needlework at South Kensington proved this), and each example has an individual interest and value.' The Report then goes on to point out 'the peculiar advantage of this employment for gentlewomen who find themselves obliged to earn a living. The work is fascinating in itself, and brings out the best powers of the worker, while its endless variety and intellectual interest obviate all the weariness of monotony.'

I cannot help contrasting this quotation and that from Clorinda's journal with a description I met with by chance a few days ago in George Sand's novel of Mauprat. It is of Edmée, the heroine, and her wool-work :—

'Elle était penchée sur sa tapisserie, et de temps en temps elle levait les yeux sur son père pour interroger les moindres mouvements de son sommeil. Mais que de patience et de résignation dans tout son être! Edmée n'aimait pas les travaux d'aiguille; elle avait l'esprit trop sérieux pour attacher de l'importance à l'effet d'une nuance à côté d'une nuance, et à la régularité d'un point pressé contre un autre point; mais depuis que son père, en proie aux infirmités de la vieillesse, ne quittait presque plus son fauteuil, elle ne quittait plus son père un seul instant; et ne pouvant toujours lire et vivre par l'esprit, elle avait senti la nécessité d'adopter ces occupations féminines. Dans une de ces luttes obscures qui s'accomplissent souvent sous nos yeux sans que nous en soupçonnions le mérite, elle avait fait plus que de dompter son caractère, elle avait changé jusqu'à la circulation de son sang.'

As one reads the page one can imagine the pattern that Edmée is tracing as she numbs away the time of her lover's absence; and her stitches mark the length of the slow-passing hours in line upon line of dull, unmeaning ornament, and dismal monotonies. No wonder that George Sand, great and impatient mistress of vivid colouring, of mystical workmanship; a weaver of unexpected and harmonious patterns, the unwinder of complicated threads of fate and life, speaks with scornful disparagement of the mechanical labour of Edmée's hands; but not so would she write of intelligent work with some interest and meaning in its intention. Clorinda, with unconscious art, might have given Edmée a hint as to her pattern. I am sure she would have liked to peep (with bright eyes enhanced by that fascinating patch which took so long to place) behind a certain red curtain that a friendly hand held up one bright' spring morning not long ago; I dare say Edmée herself might have exclaimed, seeing a pleasant and unexpected sight; Clorinda would certainly have noted it all down in her journal on her return to her home, and to the attentions of Mr. Froth.

Behind the red curtain is a long and lofty room, into which the sun comes streaming, and where some twenty ladies are at work at tables and embroidery-frames, among shining heaps and folds of satin, veils of silver paper, packets of silk, bright tinted patterns. The heads are bent; the stitches are falling; there is a certain sense of serenity and application which strikes you as you come in—of colour and sunshine upon it. For one thing, a work-room of ladies is not a usual sight, and one is naturally impressed by some feeling of quiet refinement, in the place of that stolid dulness and indifference which so often weighs upon one's spirits, and one's conscience too, as one looks into some of those work-places, for which one feels in some measure responsible.

Perhaps there may have been a time when such sights as this in Sloane Street were more usual than they are now. One has read of the châtelaines sitting, surrounded by maidens, in the castle-hall, and working many a scroll and patient conceit of tapestry against their lord's return. One has seen the result of Queen Matilda's perseverance, as she turned her days and years into long histories (what a strange chance it is, by which people turn the vaguest of things, secret impatiences, weariness, want of money or interest, into tangible, hard shape, into stitches, into black lines upon paper, into coming and going, into other people's affairs, visiting cards, as the case may be !)

Here most certainly was a useful impulse of bene-volence and cultivated instinct come to life; a new possibility among all the impossible things which are in the world.

No one noticed us as we came in. The stitches went on falling into their places. I could have imagined some such scene in the days when a Raphael himself might have come walking in with a design for tapestry, or when a Botticelli did not disdain to trace a pattern for the petticoat of a goddess. The two châtelaines, whose special interest lies among these workers, were standing in the midst directing. The work-mistress was going her rounds, the secretary was bringing her report, the workers were silently progressing. As Lady A——— went by, some of them looked up to smile at a familiar face. Patterns were flowing in a prim and measured cadence upon moon-lit and sun-lit stuffs. Here is a honeysuckle border starting from its suave satin ground, crisp and stately and harmonious.

When the lady for whom these honeysuckles were made went to Court in her raiment of fine needlework, no wonder that the people looking on admired as she passed. Most of them said it was rare old brocade—an heirloom in the great family to which she belongs; but our ladies have shown that they can do as well as the workers who lived in the golden age of art. Some of the appliqué work is so well restored, that it is impossible to tell the difference between that of our ladies and their century-ago ancestresses. I saw a noble crimson flood of damask embroidered with a stately pattern which Titian himself might have liked to paint; and then again came great sun-flowers turning their faces to the sun, upon brown and upon velvet. One beautiful screen was shown us of pearl-green satin, blooming into a garden for a royal princess. Pink delicate hollyhocks rearing their full and stately heads, birds suddenly flying into a silken existence, corn heads, lilies uprearing on their stems. Surely the fairy princesses must have come hither for their magic court robes, sunlight and moonlight stuffs and starry mantles. It remains to be seen whether the School will be able to stamp the mark of its work upon this Manchester age. That the work is charming is beyond a doubt, as also that it rises to the dignity of art, being kindled with that *something* beyond mere mechanism which should belong to all manual labour, of whatever kind it may be. The ladies are in some measure artists ; their stitches are set with a certain intelligence and cultivation which tells even in a pattern traced upon a sampler. 'The colour of that bird's wings kept me awake last night,' I heard the work-mistress saying. No wonder that the bird plumes in harmonious tints upon its satin. As I think of the place, numberless pleasant, handsome things occur to me. There was a peacock dazzling upon a sunset blaze of gold, there were gentle little daisies flowering upon a melodious green ground.

The Report says that the School was started, first of all to revive a beautiful and practically lost art ; secondly, to provide private and suitable employment for gentlewomen wishing to earn a living.

The story of the rise of the School I heard from a lady connected with the place. The original foundress, she told me, had always been interested in the art, and had herself designed and worked some embroidery for her own house. One day an upholsterer, who was at work for her, happened to say, 'If this kind of thing were for sale, I could always command a price for as much of it as I could get.' These words struck the lady, who began to think of the possibility of using her gift to some useful end, as she remembered some girls to whom she had given her patterns and instruction at different times. Some of these were young ladies to whom à suitable employment would be of all boons the most welcome. She spoke to them on the subject, and established a little class in her own drawing-room. Then she went to a friend, another kind châtelaine, who listened to her scheme for a while, and then suddenly held out her hand and said, 'Let us be partners,' and so the thing was done. The proposed scheme was to open a workroom, where ornamental work should be produced with some intention and harmony of colour and charm of design, and at the same time to employ those ladies whose cultivated instincts would be valuable in such an occupation.

The little enterprise was started, but struggled with many difficulties. The first manager, Mrs. Dolby, whose experience and special gifts had seemed to be the mainspring of the whole enterprise, fell ill and died at a time when one of the two ladies so much interested in the success of the venture was herself ill and confined to her bed. The staff of workers was organised, but everything else had to be found out day by day. Mrs. Dolby's loss was irreparable; nobody else had any knowledge of the practical working of such a scheme. ' Fortunately at this crisis Princess Christian, who had become interested in the scheme, came forward, and " her unfailing encouragement and unselfish personal exertions" in a measure helped to carry the undertaking through at a time when it was in the greatest danger of collapse.'

I cannot help further quoting an interesting passage from the Report:—

Up to that time the School had profited by Mrs. Dolby's large experience and exceptional knowledge of the highest branches of needlework, and her rare powers of tuition. But since her death, as no really efficient substitute could be found, it has been forced painfully to work out every detail, and to solve each problem as it arose by the slow and expensive process of many failures, crowned at last by success—a success, perhaps, the more complete because earned by experience. This, however, was not the only obstacle. There was the difficulty—a very real one—of training in regular, careful, and accurate habits of work, ladies accustomed to easy leisure rather than professional work; the difficulty of admitting all without distinction of creed (which, without great and patient care, might have led to painful discord); the difficulty of organising a staff among the ladies themselves, ignorant of business, and with only a few months' experience of art-work, while there was none to lead them but an amateur with only an amateur's experience, and a complete stranger to commercial affairs. Then there were the further difficulties of valuing and classing work; of having materials specially made and dyed (sometimes dyed at the School) to reproduce the rich harmony of ancient colour; of forming a code of regulations; in short, of initiating nothing less than a thorough business system for which there was no precedent. Many of these hindrances being much increased by the humble size of the School's original quarters (a small room over a bonnet shop), it was decided by H.R.H. the President and Council last May that the first thing to do was to find a suitable house. The house was found (31 Sloane Street), fortunately well adapted for the purpose, and the School was settled there in July, 1873.

From this time the history of the School may be said properly to begin. Though only known to a circle of private friends, orders have been sent in to a large extent —in many cases of such a value as to require large sums to be expended in executing them ; and one of the most satisfactory proofs of the confidence which has been so quickly earned is the quantity of ancient needlework of the utmost value and rarity which has been confided to the School to be transferred, repaired, added to, or copied, &c.

Forty-three ladies are now (Oct. 1873) on the regular books, and their numbers are being added to from time to time. Each lady pays an entrance fee of 5*l.*, and she must reside in London, and practically devote her life to the work, as in any other profession.

Work is not paid for by time, but by the piece, so that the most skilful and rapid worker earns the largest sums.

Some of the ladies live in the house, and a dinner is provided for them at a certain hour. Where it is possible, they take the work away. The secretary, Miss Turner, told me that in some cases she was able to look after younger girls, or absentees from sickness. There is a natural and kindly *esprit de corps* which I need not dwell upon, but which seemed to me not the least of the advantages to be gained by such co-operation.

It is no use—so Miss Turner told us—for persons to come who have not already worked with some natural aptitude—'with fingers instead of thumbs,' as she said, laughing ; and it is no use for ladies not living in London to apply; many of those we saw were married and living in homes of their own; one or two were young girls. There had been but few cases of incompetence and incompatibility; for by long experience, Miss Turner, who is deeply interested in her work, can now tell who is likely to do well in the School, and she only admits those of whom she has good hope.

I think we must all allow the real gratitude which we must feel to those who try to discern, behind the dull contrivance and commonplace of daily toil and life, the secret of an artistic fitness and beauty which certainly exists in most things and most places, but which so many cares and preoccupations combine to choke and to hide away. Those who have means and leisure beyond the actual calls of a daily and laborious existence are doing practical and useful work when they try to make things more full of interest and beauty for others.

We all have our household gods, whether or not we recognise the fact; and we all pay them homage in a fashion of our own—gods of association, of harmony, of fancy, of long-expected realisation. These supernatural visitors hide unsuspected in many a shabby place and corner. Some are visible only to certain people and at certain times; others, again, disclose their secret to any who have the gift to recognise their divinity; and I, for my part, honestly believe that nothing exists which may not be made more worthy by their touch, and none of us that may not benefit by recognising their existence in our daily life. What god from Parnassus has laid his hand upon those shabby garret walls—upon the torn curtain hanging from the pole—the broken jar standing in the sunshine, with its sprouting balsaam plant? The curtain is weather-seamed and stained by wet; the jar is cracked, the wall is smoked; but the blue serenity of the sky outside shows beyond the balsaam pot and the ragged curtain; some mysterious harmony in those shabby russet tones is melting to tranquillity upon the gray; the faded blue of the drapery is falling into shadow, the bright culminating flash of the flower flames a life into it all. Art seems to be a sort of soul to life that reaches us and uplifts with a strange yet gentle might of inspiration. I could imagine that a real and mighty work of art might even share in that same life which belongs to natural things—brightening and changing from day to day; fading and dimming sometimes, and then again behold it re-created for us, and standing as in a shrine, supreme and triumphant and revealed.

So, not long ago, was she of Milo revealed. Suddenly, and for one instant, she seemed to thrill with a divine and mighty life ; not life such as ours, struggling for something—it knows not what—or clinging to definite things, passionately apprehending for one moment and forgetting the next. This was something beyond—absolute, dominant and self-sufficing—that seemed to thrill with the sound of some faint Olympian music, stirring, not to effort, but to an existence more complete and more supreme.

And it is no small thing to learn from others—to see the golden radiance of the gods where it falls, upon the head of a goddess or the mere fringe of a garment; nor shall we live our own lives the less completely for such warmth and revivification.[1]

[1] Arachne has lately changed her quarters, and is now winding her silken threads in the South Kensington Museum.

HEROINES AND THEIR GRANDMOTHERS.[1]

Fantasio. Qui sait? Un calembour console de bien des chagrins, et jouer avec les mots est un moyen comme un autre de jouer avec les pensées, les actions et les êtres. Tout est calembour ici-bas, et il est ainsi difficile de comprendre le regard d'un enfant de quatre ans, que le galimatias de trois drames modernes.

Elsbeth. Tu me fais l'effet de regarder le monde à travers un prisme tant soit peu changeant.

Fantasio. Chacun a ses lunettes, mais personne ne sait au juste de quelle couleur en sont les verres. Qui est ce qui pourra me dire au juste si je suis heureux ou malheureux, bon ou mauvais, triste ou gai, bête ou spirituel?

Why do we now-a-days write such melancholy novels? Are authoresses more miserable than they used to be a hundred years ago? Miss Austen's heroines came tripping into the room, bright-eyed, rosy-cheeked, arch, and good-humoured. Evelina and Cecilia would have thoroughly enjoyed their visits to the opera, and their expeditions to the masquerades, if it had not been for their vulgar relations. Valancourt's Emily was a little upset, to be sure, when she found herself all alone in the ghostly and

---

[1] *Too Much Alone. City and Suburb. George Geith.*—Mrs. Riddell.

mouldy castle in the south of France; but she, too, was naturally a lively girl, and on the whole showed a great deal of courage and presence of mind. Miss Edgeworth's heroines were pleasant and easily pleased; and to these may be added a blooming rose-garden of wild Irish girls, and of good-humoured and cheerful young ladies, who consented to make the devoted young hero happy at the end of the third volume, without any very intricate self-examinations; and who certainly were much more appreciated by the heroes of those days, than our modern heroines with all their workings and deep feelings and unrequited affections are now, by the noblemen and gentlemen to whom they happen to be attached.

If one could imagine the ladies of whom we have been speaking coming to life again, and witnessing all the vagaries and agonising experiences and deadly calm and irrepressible emotion of their granddaughters, the heroines of the present day, what a bewildering scene it would be! Evelina and Cecilia ought to faint with horror! Madame Duval's most shocking expressions were never so alarming as the remarks they might now hear on all sides. Elizabeth Bennett would certainly burst out laughing, Emma might lose her temper, and Fanny Price would turn scarlet and stop her little ears.

Perhaps Emily of Udolpho, more accustomed than the others to the horrors of sensation, and having once faced those long and terrible passages, might be able to hold her own against such a great-granddaughter as Aurora Floyd or Lady Audley. But how would she deal with the soul-workings and heart-troubles of a modern heroine? Emily would probably prefer any amount of tortuous mysteries, winding staircases and passages, or groans and groans, and yards and yards of faded curtains, to the task of mastering these intricacies of feeling and reality and sentiment.

Are the former heroines women as they were, or as they were supposed to be in those days? Are the women of whom women write now, women as they are, or women as they are supposed to be? Does our modern taste demand a certain sensation feeling, sensation sentiment, only because it is actually experienced?

This is a question to be answered on some other occasion; but, in the meantime, it would seem as if all the good humours and good spirits of former generations had certainly deserted our own heart-broken ladies. Instead of cheerful endurance, the very worst is made of every passing discomfort. Their laughter is forced, even their happiness is only calm content, for they cannot so readily recover from the two first volumes. They no longer smile and trip through country-dances hand-in-hand with their adorers, but waltz with heavy hearts and dizzy brains, while the hero who scorns them looks on. Open the second volume, you will see that, instead of sitting in the drawing-room or plucking roses in the bower, or looking pretty and pleasant, they are lying on their beds with agonising headaches, walking desperately along the streets they know not whither, or staring out of window in blank despair. It would be curious to ascertain in how great a degree language measures feeling. People, with the help of the penny-post and the telegraph, and the endless means of communication and of coming and going, are certainly able to care for a greater number of persons than they could have done a hundred years ago; perhaps they are also able to care more, and to be more devotedly attached, to those whom they already love; they certainly say more about it, and, perhaps, with its greater abundance and opportunity, expression may have depreciated in value. And this may possibly account for some of the difference between the reserved and measured language of a Jane Bennett or an Anne Elliot, and the tempestuous ccn-fidences of their successors.

Much that is written now is written with a certain exaggeration and an earnestness which was undreamt of in the placid days when, according to Miss Austen, a few assembly balls and morning visits, a due amount of vexation reasonably surmounted, or at most 'smiles reined in, and spirits dancing in private rapture,' a journey to Bath, an attempt at private theatricals or a thick packet of explanations hurriedly signed with the hero's initials, were the events, the emotions, the aspirations of a lifetime.

They had their accomplishments, these gigot-sleeved ladies: witness Emma's very mild performances in the way of portrait taking; but as for tracking murderers, agonies of mystery, and disappointed affections, flinging themselves at gentlemen's heads, marrying two husbands at once, flashing with irrepressible emotion, or only betraying the deadly conflict going on within by a slight quiver of the pale lip—such ideas never entered their pretty little heads. They fainted a good deal, we must confess, and wrote long and tedious letters to aged clergymen residing in the country. They exclaimed 'La!' when anything surprised them, and were, we believe, dreadfully afraid of cows, notwithstanding their country connection. But they were certainly a more amiable race than their successors.

It is a fact that people do not unusually feel the same affection for phenomenons, however curious, that they do for perfectly commonplace human creatures. And yet at the same time we confess that it does seem somewhat ungrateful to complain of these living and adventurous heroines to whom, with all their vagaries, one has owed such long and happy hours of amusement and entertainment and comfort, and who have gone through so much for our edification.

Analysis of emotion instead of analysis of character, the history of feeling instead of the history of events, seems to be the method of the majority of penwomen. The novels that we have in hand to review now are examples of this mode of treatment; and the truth is, that, except in the case of the highest art and most consummate skill, there is no comparison between the interest excited by facts and general characteristics, as compared with the interest of feeling and emotion told with only the same amount of perception and ability.

Few people, for instance, could read the story of the poor lady who lived too much alone without being touched by the simple earnestness with which her sorrows are written down, although in the bare details of her life there might not be much worth recording. But this is the history of poor Mrs. Storn's feelings more than that of her life—of feelings very sad and earnest and passionate, full of struggle for right, with truth to help and untruth to bewilder her; with power and depth and reality in her struggles, which end at last in a sad sort of twilight that seems to haunt one as one shuts up the book. In 'George Geith,' of which we will speak more presently, there is the same sadness and minor key ringing all through the composition. Indeed, all this author's tunes are very melancholy—so melancholy that it would seem almost like a defect if they were not at the same time very sweet as well as very sad. Too Much Alone is a young woman who marries a very silent, upright, and industrious chemical experimentalist. He has well-cut features, honourable feelings, a genius for discovering cheap ways of producing acids and chemicals, as well as ideas about cyanosium, which, combined with his perfect trust in and utter neglect of his wife, very nearly brings about the destruction of all their domestic happiness. She is a pale, sentimental young woman, with raven-black hair, clever, and longing for sympathy—a *femme incomprise*, it must be confessed, but certainly much more charming and pleasant and pathetic than such people usually are. Days go by, lonely alike for her, without occupation or friendship or interest; she cannot consort with the dull and vulgar people about her; she has her little son, but he is not a companion. Her husband is absorbed in this work. She has no one to talk to, nothing to do or think of. She lives all alone in the great noisy

life-full city, sad and pining, and wistful and weary.
Here is a little sketch of her :—

'Lina was sitting, thinking about the fact that she
had been married many months more than three years,
and that on the especial Sunday morning in question she
was just of age. It was still early; for Mr. Storn, according to the fashion of most London folks, borrowed hours
from both ends of the day, and his wife was sitting there
until it should be time for her to get ready and to go to
church alone. Her chair was placed by the open window;
and though the city was London, and the locality either
the ward of Eastcheap or that of Allhallows, Barking (I
am not sure which), fragrant odours came wafted to her
senses through the casement; for in this, as in all other
things save one, Maurice had considered her nurture and
her tastes, and covered the roof of the counting-house
with flowers. But for the distant roll of the carriages,
she might just as well have been miles away from
London. . . . She was dressed in a pink morning dress,
with her dark hair plainly braided upon her pale fair
cheek, and she had a staid sober look upon her face, that
somehow made her appear handsomer than in the days of
old before she married. . . .'

This very Sunday Lina meets a dangerous fascinating
man of the world, who is a friendly, well-meaning creature
withal, and who can understand and sympathise with her

sadness and solitude only too well for her peace of mind, and for his own; again and again she appeals to her husband: 'I will find pleasure in the driest employment if you will only let me be with you, and not leave me alone.' She only asks for justice, for confidence—not the confidence of utter desertion and trust and neglect, but the daily confidence and communion, which is a necessity to some women, the permission to share in the common interests and efforts of her husband's life; to be allowed to sympathise, and to live, and to understand, instead of being left to pine away lonely, unhappy, half asleep, and utterly weary and disappointed. Unfortunately Mr. Storn thinks it is all childish nonsense, and repulses her in the most affectionate manner; poor unhappy Lina behaves as well as ever she can, and devotes herself to her little boy, only her hair grows blacker, and her face turns paler and paler, day by day; she is very good and struggles to be contented, and will not allow herself to think too much of Herbert Clyne; and so things go on in the old way for a long, long time; and we turn page after page, feeling that each one may bring some terrible catastrophe. At last a crisis comes—troubles thicken— Maurice Storn is always away when he is most wanted; little Geordie, the son, gets hold of some of his father's chemicals, which have cost Lina already so much happiness and confidence, and the poor little boy poisons himself with something sweet out of a little bottle. All the description which follows is very powerfully and pathetically told—Maurice Storn's silence and misery, Lina's desperation and sudden change of feeling. After all her long struggles and efforts she suddenly breaks down, all her courage leaves her, and her desperate longings for right and clinging to truth.

'She said in her soul, "I have lost the power either to bear or to resist. I have tried to face my misfortune, and I feel I am incapable of doing it . . . why should I struggle or fear any more? I know the worst that life can bring me; I have buried my heart and my hopes with my boy. Why should I strive or struggle any more?" And Lina had got to such a pass that she forgot to answer to herself, Because it is right—Right and wrong, she had lost sight of them both.'

Poor Mrs. Storn is unconscious that already people are beginning to talk of her, first one and then another. Nobody seems very bad. Everybody is going wrong. Maurice abstracted over his work, Lina in a frenzy of wretchedness; home-fires are extinct, outside the cold winds blow, and the snow lies half melted on the ground. The man of the world is waiting in the cold, very miserable too—waiting for Lina, who has almost made up her mind now; their best impulses and chances seem failing them; all about there seems to be only pain, and night, and trouble. But at last, when the night is blackest, the morning dawns, and Lina is saved.

Everything is then satisfactorily arranged, and Maurice is ruined, and Lina's old affection for him returns. The man of the world is also ruined, and determines to emigrate to some distant colony. Mr. and Mrs. Storn retire to an old-fashioned gabled house at Enfield, where they have no secrets from each other; and it is here that her husband one day tells Lina that he has brought an old friend to say good-bye to her, and then poor Herbert Clyne, the late man of the world, comes across the lawn, and says farewell for ever to both his friends in a very pathetic and touching scene.

Lina Storn is finally disposed of in ' Too Much Alone;' but Maurice Storn reappears in disguise, and under various assumed names, in almost all the author's subsequent novels. We are not sorry to meet him over and over again; for although we have never yet been able to realise this stern-cut personage as satisfactorily as we should have liked to do, yet we must confess to a partiality for him, and a respect for his astounding powers of application. Whether he turns his attention to chemistry, to engineering, to figures, to theology, the amount of business he gets through is almost bewildering. At the same time something invariably goes wrong, over which he has no control, notwithstanding all his industry and ability; and he has to acknowledge the weakness of humanity, and the insufficiency of the sternest determination, to order and arrange the events of life to its own will and fancy. To the woman or women depending upon him he is invariably kind, provokingly reserved, and faithfully devoted. He is of good family and extremely proud, and he is obliged for various reasons to live in the city. All through the stories one seems to hear a suggestive accompanying roll of cart-wheels and carriages. Poor Lina's loneliness seems all the more lonely for the contrast of the busy movement all round about her own silent, sad life. ' At first it seemed to give a sort of stimulus to her own existence, hearing the carts roll by, the cabs rattle past, the shout and hum of human voices break on her ear almost before she was awake of a morning. . . . But wear takes the gloss off all things, even off the sensation of being perplexed and amused by the whirl of life.'

In ' City and Suburb,' this din of London life, and the way in which city people live and strive, is capitally described; the heroine is no less a person than a Lady Mayoress, a certain Ruby Ruthven, a beauty, capricious and wayward and impetuous, and she is perhaps one of the best of Mrs. Riddell's creations. For old friendship's sake, we cannot help giving the preference to 'Too Much Alone;' but 'City and Suburb' is in many respects an advance upon it, and 'George Geith' is in its way better than either.

It seems strange as one thinks of it that before these books came out no one except Mr. Dickens had ever thought of writing about city life. There is certainly an interest and a charm about old London, its crowded busy streets, its ancient churches and buildings, and narrow lanes and passages with quaint names, of which we dwellers in the stucco suburbs have no conception. There is the river with its wondrous freight, and the busy docks, where stores of strange goods are lying, that bewilder one as one gazes. Vast horizons of barrels waiting to be carted, forests of cinnamon-trees and spices, of canes, of ivory, thousands and thousands of great elephant tusks, sorted and stored away, workmen, sailors of every country, a great unknown strange life and bustle. Or if you roam from the busy highway, you find silence, solitude, grass growing between the stones, old courts, iron gateways, ancient squares where the sunshine gathers quietly, a glint of the past, as it were, a feeling of what has been, and what still lingers among the old worn stones and bricks, and traditions of the city. Even the Mansion

House, with its kindly old customs and welcome and hospitality, has a charm and romance of its own, that is quite indescribable, from the golden postilion standing behind the Lord Mayor's high chair of state, to the heavy little mutton-pies, which are the same as they were hundreds and hundreds of years ago. All this queer sentiment belonging to old London, and the author feels and describes with great cleverness and appreciation.

'George Geith'[1] is the latest and the most popular of Mrs. Riddell's novels, and it deserves its popularity. It is the history of the man whose name it bears—a man 'to work so long as he has a breath left to draw, who would die in his harness rather than give up, who would fight against opposing circumstances whilst he had a drop of blood in his veins, whose greatest virtues are untiring industry and indomitable courage, and who is worth half-a-dozen ordinary men, if only because of his iron frame and unconquerable spirit.' Here is a description of the place in which he lived, on the second floor of the house which stands next but' one to the old gateway on the Fenchurch Street side :—

'If quietness was what he wanted, he had it ; except in the summer evenings when the children of the Fenchurch Street housekeepers brought their marbles through

---

[1] Written in 1865.

the passage, and fought over them on the pavement in front of the office-door, there was little noise of life in the old churchyard. The sparrows in the trees or the footfall of someone entering or quitting the court alone disturbed the silence. The roar of Fenchurch Street on the one side, and of Leadenhall Street on the other, sounded in Fen Court but as a distant murmur; and to a man whose life was spent among figures, and who wanted to devote his undivided attention to his work, this silence was a blessing not to be properly estimated save by those who have passed through that maddening ordeal which precedes being able to abstract the mind from external influence. . . . For the historical recollections associated with the locality he had chosen George Geith did not care a rush.'

George Geith lives with his figures, 'climbing Alps on Alps of them with silent patience, great mountains of arithmetic with gold lying on their summits for him to grasp;' he works for eighteen hours a day. People come up his stairs to ask for his help—

'Bankrupts, men who were good enough, men who were doubtful, and men who were (speaking commercially) bad, had all alike occasion to seek the accountant's advice and assistance; retailers, who kept clerks for their sold books, but not for their bought; wholesale dealers, who did not want to let their clerks see their books at all; shrewd men of business, who yet could not balance a ledger; ill-educated traders, who, though they could make money, would have been ashamed to show their ill-written and worse-spelled journals to a stranger; unhappy wretches, shivering on the brink of insolvency; creditors, who did not think much of the cooking of some dishonest debtors' accounts;—all these came and sat in George Geith's office, and waited their turn to see him.'

And among these comes a country gentleman, a M. Molozane, who is on the brink of ruin, and who has three daughters at home at the Dower House, near Wattisbridge.

There is a secret in George Geith's life and a reason for which he toils; and although early in the story he makes a discovery which relieves him from part of his anxiety and need for money, he still works on from habit, and one day he receives a letter from this M. Molozane, begging him to come to his assistance, and stating that he is ill and cannot come to town. George thinks he would like a breath of country air, and determines to go. The description of Wattisbridge and the road thither is delightful; lambs, cool grass, shaded ponds and cattle, trailing branches, brambles, roses, here a house, there a farm-yard, gently-sloping hills crowned with clumps of trees, distant purple haze, a calm blue sky and fleecy clouds, and close at hand a grassy glade with cathedral branches, a young lady, a black retriever and a white poodle, all of which George Geith notices as he walks along the path, 'through the glade, under the shadow of the arching trees, straight as he can go to meet his destiny.'

Beryl Molozane, with the dear sweet kindly brown eyes that seemed to be always laughing and loving, is as charming a destiny as any hero could wish to meet upon a summer's day, as she stands with the sunshine streaming on her nut-brown, red golden hair. She should indeed be capable of converting the most rabid of reviewers to the modern ideal of what a heroine should be, with her April moods and her tenderness and laughter, her frankness, her cleverness, her gay innocent chatter, her outspoken youth and brightness. It is she who manages for the whole household, who works for her father, who protects her younger sister, who schemes and plans, and thinks, and loves for all. No wonder that George loses his heart to her; even in the very beginning we are told, when he first sees her, that he would have

'Taken the sunshine out of his own life to save the clouds from darkening down on hers. He would have left her dear face to smile on still, the guileless heart to throb calmly. He would have left his day without a noon to prevent night from closing over hers. He would have known that it was possible for him to love so well that he should become unselfish. . . .

One cannot help wondering that the author could have had the heart to treat poor pretty Beryl so harshly, when her very creation, the stern and selfish George himself, would have suffered any pain to spare her if it were possible.

It is not our object here to tell a story at length, which is interesting enough to be read for itself, and touching enough to be remembered long after the last of the three volumes is closed. To be remembered, but so sadly, that one cannot but ask oneself for what reason are such stories written. Are they written to cheer one in dull hours, to soothe, to interest, and to distract from weary thoughts, from which it is at times a blessing to escape? or is it to make one sad with sorrows which never happened, but which are told with so much truth and pathos that they almost seem for a minute as if they were one's own? Is it to fill one's eyes with tears for griefs which might be, but which have not been, and for troubles that are not, except in a fancy, for the sad, sad fate of a sweet and tender woman, who might have been made happy to gladden all who were interested in her story?

A lady putting down this book the other day, suddenly burst into tears, and said, ' Why did they give me this to read ? ' Why, indeed ! Beryl might have been more happy, and no one need have been the worse. She and her George might have been made comfortable together for a little while, and we might have learnt to know her all the same. Does sorrow come like this, in wave upon wave, through long sad years, without one gleam of light to play upon the waters ? Sunshine *is* sunshine, and warms and vivifies, and brightens, though the clouds are coming too, sooner or later ; but in nature no warning voices spoil the happiest hours of our lives by useless threats and terrifying hints of what the future may bring forth. Happiness remembered is happiness always ; but where would past happiness be if there was someone always standing by, as in this book, to point with a sigh to future troubles long before they come, and to sadden and spoil all the pleasant spring-time and all the sport and youth by dreary forebodings of old age, of autumn, and winter snow, and bitter winds that have not yet begun to blow ? ' So smile the heavens upon that holy act,' says the Friar, ' that after sorrow chide us not.' ' Amen, amen,' says Romeo ; ' but come what sorrow can, it cannot countervail the exchange of joy that one short minute gives me in her sight.' And we wish that George Geith had been more of Romeo's way of thinking.

A tragic ending is very touching at the time, and moves many a sympathy; but who ever reads a melancholy story over and over and over as some stories are read? My father used to say that a bad ending to a book was a great mistake; that he never would make one of his own finish badly. What was the use of it? Nobody ever cared to read a book a second time when it ended unhappily.

There is a great excuse in the case of the writer of ' George Geith,' who possesses in no common degree the powers of pathos. Take for instance the parting between George and Beryl. She says that it is no use talking about what is past and gone; that they must part, and he knows it.

' Then for a moment George misunderstood her. The agony of her own heart, the intense bitterness of the draught she was called upon to drink, the awful hopeless-ness of her case, and the terrible longing she felt to be permitted to live and love once more, sharpened her voice and gave it a tone she never intended.

' " Have you grown to doubt me ? " he asked. " Do you not know I would marry you to-morrow if I could ? Do you think that throughout all the years to come, be they many or be they few, I could change to you? Oh, Beryl! do you not believe that through time and through eternity I shall love you and none other ? "

' " I do not doubt; I believe," and her tears fell faster and her sobs become more uncontrollable.

'What was she to him at that moment? More than wife; more than all the earth; more than heaven; more than life. She was something more, far more, than any poor words we know can express. What he felt for her was beyond love; the future he saw stretching away for himself without her, without a hope of her, was in its blank weariness so terrible as to be beyond despair. Had the soul been taken out of his body, life could not have been more valueless. Take away the belief of immortality, and what has mortality left to live for?

'At the moment George Geith knew, in a stupid, dull kind of way, that to him Beryl had been an earthly immortality; that to have her again for his own had been the one hope of his weary life, which had made the days and the hours endurable unto him.

'Oh! woe for the great waste of love which there is in this world below; to think how it is filling some hearts to bursting, whilst others are starving for the lack thereof; to think how those who may never be man and wife, those who are about to be parted by death, those whose love can never be anything but a sorrow and trial, merge their own identity in that of one another, whilst the lawful heads of respectable households wrangle and quarrel, and honest widows order their mourning with decorous resignation, and disconsolate husbands look out for second wives!

'Why is it that the ewe-lamb is always that selected for sacrifice? Why is it that the creature upon which man sets his heart shall be the one snatched from him? Why is it that the thing we prize perishes? That as the flower fades and the grass withereth, so the object of man's love, the delight of his eyes and the desire of his soul, passeth away to leave him desolate?

'On George Geith the blow fell with such force that he groped darkly about, trying to grasp his trouble; trying to meet some tangible foe with whom to grapple. Life without Beryl; days without sun; winter without a hope of summer; nights that could never know a dawn. My reader, have patience, have patience with the despairing grief of this strong man, who had at length met with a sorrow that crushed him.

'Have patience whilst I try to tell of the end that came to his business and to his pleasure; to the years he had spent in toil; to the hours in which he had tasted enjoyment! To the struggles there had come success; to the hopes fruition; but with success and with fruition there had come likewise death.

'Everything for him was ended in existence. Living,

he was as one dead. Wealth could not console him; success could not comfort him; for him, for this hard, fierce worker, for the man who had so longed for rest, for physical repose, for domestic pleasures, the flowers were to have no more perfume, home no more happiness; the earth no more loveliness. The first spring blossoms, the summer glory on the trees and fields, the fruits and flowers, and thousand tinted leaves of autumn, and the snows and frosts of winter, were never to touch his heart, nor stir his senses in the future.

'Never the home he pictured might be his, never, ah, never! He had built his dream-house on the sands, and, behold, the winds blew and the waves beat, and he saw it all disappear, leaving nought but dust and ashes, but death and despair! Madly he fought with his sorrow, as though it were a living thing that he could grasp and conquer; he turned on it constantly, and strove to trample it down.'

No comment is needed to point out the power and pathos of this long extract. The early story of George Geith is in many respects the same as the story of Warrington in 'Pendennis,' but the end is far more sad and disastrous, and, as it has been shown, pretty bright Beryl dies of her cruel tortures, and it is, in truth, difficult to forgive the author for putting her through so much unnecessary pain and misery.

One peculiarity which strikes us in all these books is, that the feelings are stronger and more vividly alive than the people who are made to experience them. Even Beryl herself is more like a sweet and tender idea of a woman than a living woman with substance and stuff, and bone and flesh, though her passion and devotion are all before us as we read, and seem so alive and so true that they touch us and master us by their intensity and vividness.

The sympathy between the writer and the reader of a book is a very subtle and strange one, and there is something curious in the necessity for expression on both sides: the writer pouring out the experience and feelings of years, and the reader, relieved and strengthened in certain moods to find that others have experienced and can speak of certain feelings, have passed through phases with which he himself is acquainted. The imaginary Public is a most sympathising friend; he will listen to the author's sad story; he does not interrupt or rebuff him, or weary with impatient platitudes, until he has had his say and uttered all that was within him. The author perhaps writes on good and ill, successes, hopes, disappointments, or happier memories, of unexpected reprieves, of unhoped-for good fortunes, of old friendships, long-tried love, faithful sympathies enduring to the end.   All this, not in the words and descriptions of the events which really happened, but in a language of which he or she alone holds the key, or of which, perhaps, the full significance is scarcely known even to the writer.   Only in the great unknown world which he addresses there surely is the kindred spirit somewhere, the kind heart, the friend of friends who will understand him.   Novel-writing must be like tears to some women, the vent and the relief of many a chafing spirit.   People say, Why are so many novels written? and the answer is, Because there are so many people feeling, thinking, and enduring, and longing to give voice and expression to the silence of the life in the midst of which they are struggling.   The necessity for expression is a great law of nature, one for which there is surely some good and wise reason, as there must be for that natural desire for sympathy which is common to so many.   There seems to be something wrong and incomplete in those natures which do not need it, something inhuman in those who are incapable of understanding the mystical and tender bond by which all humanity is joined and bound together.   A bond of common pain and pleasure, of common fear and hope, and love, and weakness.

Poets tell us that not only human creatures, but the whole universe, is thrilling with sympathy and expression, entreating, uttering, in plaints or praise, or in a wonder of love and admiration. What do the sounds of a bright spring day mean? Cocks crow in the farm-yards and valleys below; high up in the clear heavens the lark is pouring out its sweet passionate thrills; shriller and sweeter, and more complete as the tiny speck soars higher and higher still, 'flow the profuse strains of unpremeditated art.' The sheep baa and browse, and shake their meek heads; children shout for the very pleasure of making a sound in the sunshine. Nature is bursting with new green, brightening, changing into a thousand lovely shades. Seas washing and sparkling against the shores, streaks of faint light gleam in distant horizons, soft winds are blowing about the landscape; what is all this but an appeal for sympathy, a great natural expression of emotion?

And perhaps, after all, the real secret of our complaint against modern heroines is not so much that they are natural and speak out what is in them, and tell us of deeper and more passionate feeling than ever stirred the even tenour of their grandmothers' narratives, but that they are morbid, constantly occupied with themselves, one-sided, and ungrateful for the wonders and blessings of a world which is not less beautiful now than it was a hundred years ago, where perhaps there is a less amount of pain than at the time when Miss Austen and Miss Ferrier said their say.

Jane Austen's own story was more sad and more pathetic than that of many and many of the heroines whom we have been passing in review and complaining of, and who complain to us so loudly; but in her, knowledge of good and evil, and of sorrow and anxiety and disappointment, evinced itself, not in impotent railings against the world and impatient paragraphs and monotonous complaints, but in a delicate sympathy with the smallest events of life, a charming appreciation of its common aspects, a playful wisdom and kindly humour, which charm us to this day.

Many of the heroines of to-day are dear and tried old friends, and would be sorely missed out of our lives, and leave irreparable blanks on our bookshelves; numbers of them are married and happily settled down in various country-houses and parsonages in England and Wales; but for the sake of their children who are growing up round about them, and who will be the heroes and heroines of the next generation or two, we would appeal to their own sense of what is right and judicious, and ask them if they would not desire to see their daughters brought up in a simpler, less spasmodic, less introspective state of mind than they themselves have been? Are they not sometimes haunted by the consciousness that their own experiences may have suggested a strained and affected view of life to some of their younger readers, instead of encouraging them to cheerfulness, to content, to a moderate estimate of their own infallibility, a charity for others, and a not too absorbing contemplation of themselves, their own virtues and shortcomings? 'Avant tout, le temps est *poseur*,' says George Sand, 'et toi qui fais la guerre à ce travers, tu en es pénétré de la tête aux pieds.'

LITTLE SCHOLARS.[1]

If no better can be done,
Let us do but this,—endeavour
That the sun behind the sun
Shine upon them while they shiver
On the dismal London flags.
Through the cruel social juggle,
Put a thought beneath the rags
To ennoble the heart's struggle.—E. B. BROWNING.

YESTERDAY morning, as I was walking up a street in Pimlico, I came upon a crowd of persons issuing from a narrow alley. Ever so many little people there were streaming through a wicket: running children, shouting children, loitering children, chattering children, and children spinning tops by the way, so that the whole street was awakened by the clatter. As I stand for an instant to see the procession go by, one little girl hops an impromptu curtsey, at which another from a distant quarter, not behindhand in politeness, drops another; and presently an irregular volley of curtseyings goes off

[1] Written in 1859.

in every direction. Then I blandly enquire if school is over? and if there is anybody left in the house? A little brown-eyes nods her head, and says, 'There's a great many people left in the house.' And so there are, sure enough, as I find when I get in.

Down a narrow yard, with the workshops on one side and the schools on the other, in at a low door which leads into a big room where there are rafters, maps hanging on the walls, and remarks in immense letters, such as, 'COFFEE IS GOOD FOR MY BREAKFAST,' and pictures of useful things, with the well-thumbed story underneath; a stove in the middle of the room; a paper hanging up on the door with the names of the teachers; and everywhere wooden benches and tables, made low and small for little legs and arms.

Well, the schoolroom is quite empty and silent now, and the turmoil has poured eagerly out at the door. It is twelve o'clock, the sun is shining in the court, and something better than schooling is going on in the kitchen yonder. Who cares now where coffee comes from? or which are the chief cities in Europe? or in what year Stephen came to the throne? For is not twelve o'clock dinner-time with all sensible people? and what periods of history, what future aspirations, what distant events are as important to us—grown-up folks, and children, too—as this pleasant daily recurring one?

The motherly schoolmistress who brought me in tells me that for a shilling half-a-dozen little boys and girls can be treated to a wholesome meal. I wonder if it smells as good to them as it does to me, when I pull my shilling out of my pocket. The food costs more than two-pence, but there is a fund to which people subscribe, and, with its help, the kitchen cooks all through the winter months.

All the children seem very fond of the good Mrs. K——. As we leave the schoolroom one little thing comes up crying, and clinging to her, ' A boy has been and 'it me!' But when the mistress says, ' Well, never mind, you shall have your dinner,' the child is instantly consoled; ' and you, and you, and you,' she continues; but this selection is too heartrending; and with the help of another lucky shilling, nobody present is left out. I remember particularly a lank child, with great black eyes and fuzzy hair, and a pinched grey face, who stood leaning against a wall in the sun: once, in the Pontine Marshes, years ago, I remember seeing such another figure. ' That poor thing is seventeen,' says Mrs. K——. ' She sometimes loiters here all day long; she has no mother; and she often comes and tells me her father is so drunk she dare not go home. I always give her a dinner when I can. This is the kitchen.'

The kitchen is a delightful, clean-scrubbed place, with rice pudding baking in the oven, and a young mistress, and a big girl, busy bringing in great caldrons full of the mutton broth I have been scenting all this time. It is a fresh, honest, hungry smell, quite different from that unwholesome compound of fry and sauce, and hot, pungent spice, and stew and mess, which comes steaming up, some seven hours later, into our dining-rooms, from the reeking kitchens below. Here a poor woman is waiting, with a jug, and a round-eyed baby. The mistress tells me the people in the neighbourhood are too glad to buy what is left of the children's dinner. ' Look what good stuff it is,' says Mrs. K——, and she shows me a bowl full of the jelly, to which it turns when cold. As the two girls come stepping through the sunny door-way, with the smoking jar between them, I think Mr. Millais might make a pretty picture of the little scene; but my attention is suddenly distracted by the round-eyed baby, who is peering down into the great soup-jug with such wide wide open eyes, and little hands outstretched— such an eager, happy face, that it almost made one laugh, and cry too, to see. The baby must be a favourite, for he is served, and goes off in his mother's arms, keeping vigilant watch over the jug, while four or five other jugs and women are waiting still in the next room. Then into rows of little yellow basins our mistress pours the broth, and we now go in to see the company in the dining-hall waiting for its banquet. Somehow, as the children say grace, I feel as if there was indeed a blessing on the food: a blessing which brings colour into these wan cheeks, and strength and warmth into these wasted little limbs. Meanwhile, the expectant company is growing rather impatient, and is battering the benches with its spoons, and tapping neighbouring heads as well. There goes a little guest, scrambling from his place across the room and back again. So many are here to-day, that they have not all got seats. I see the wan girl still standing against the wall, and there is her brother—a sociable little fellow, all dressed in corduroys—who is making droll faces at me across the room, at which some other little boys burst out laughing. But the infants on the dolls'-benches, at the other end, are the best fun. There they are—three, four, five years old—whispering and chattering, and tumbling over one another. Sometimes one infant falls suddenly forward, with its nose upon the table, and stops there quite contentedly; sometimes another disappears entirely under the legs, and is tugged up by its neighbours. A certain number of the infants have their dinner every day, the mistress tells me.   Mrs. Elliot has said so, and hers is the hand which has provided for all these young ones ; while a same kind heart has schemed how to shelter, to feed, to clothe, to teach, the greatest number of these hungry, and cold, and neglected little children.

As I am replying to the advances of my young friend in the corduroys, I suddenly hear a cry of ' Ooo ! ooo ! ooo !—noo spoons—noo spoons—ooo ! ooo ! ooo !' and all the little hands stretch out eagerly as one of the big girls goes by with a paper of shining metal spoons.   By this time the basins of soup are travelling round, with hunches of home-made bread.   ' The infants are to have pudding first,' says the mistress, coming forward; and, in a few minutes more, all the birds are busy pecking at their bread and pudding, of which they take up very small mouthfuls, in very big spoons, and let a good deal slobber down over their pinafores.

One little curly-haired boy, with a very grave face, was eating pudding very slowly and solemnly—so I said to him :

' Do you like pudding best ? '

Little Boy. ' Isss.'

' And can you read ? '

Little Boy. ' Isss.'

' And write ? '

Little Boy. ' Isss.'

' And have you got a sister ? '

Little Boy. ' Isss.'

' And does she wash your face so nicely ? '

Little Boy, extra solemn. ' No, see is wite a little girl; see is on'y four year old.'

' And how old are you ? '

Little Boy, with great dignity. ' *I* am fi' year old.'

Then he told me Mrs. Willis ' wassed ' his face, and he brought his sister to school.

' Where *is* your sister ? ' says the mistress, going by.

But four-years was not forthcoming.

' I s'pose see has walt home,' says the child, and goes on with his pudding.

This little pair are orphans out of the workhouse, Mrs. K—— told me. But somebody pays Mrs. Willis for their keep.

There was another funny little thing, very small, sitting between two bigger boys, to whom I said—

' Are you a little boy or a little girl ? '

' Little dirl,' says this baby, quite confidently.

' No you ain't,' cries the left-hand neighbour, very much excited.

' Yes, she is,' says right-hand neighbour.

And then three or four more join in, each taking a

different view of the question. All this time corduroys is still grinning and making faces in his corner. I admire his brass buttons, upon which three or four more children hastily crowd round to look at them. One is a poor little deformed fellow, to whom buttons would be of very little use. He is in quite worn and ragged clothes: he looks as pale and thin almost as that poor girl I first noticed. He has no mother; he and his brother live alone with their father, who is out all day, and the children have to do everything for themselves. The young ones here who have no mothers seem by far the worst off. This little deformed boy, poor as he is, finds something to give away. Presently I see him scrambling over the backs of the others, and feeding them with small shreds of meat, which he takes out of his soup with his grubby little fingers, and which one little fellow, called Thompson, is eating with immense relish. Mrs. K—— here comes up, and says that those who are hungry are to have some more. Thompson has some more, and so does another rosy little fellow; but the others have hardly finished what was first given them, and the very little ones send off their pudding half eaten and ask for soup. I did not hear a sharp tone. All the children seemed at home, and happy, and gently dealt with. However cruelly want, and care, and harshness haunt their own homes, here at least there are only kind words and comfort for these poor little pilgrims whose toil has begun so early. Mrs. Elliot told me once that often in winter time these children came barefooted through the snow, and so cold and hungry, that they have fallen off their seats half-fainting. We may be sure that such little sufferers—thanks to these Good Samaritans—will be tenderly picked up and cared for. But, I wonder, must there always be children in the world hungry and deserted? and will there never, out of all the abundance of the earth, be enough to spare to content those who want so little to make them happy?

Mrs. Elliot came in while I was still at the school, and took me over the workshops where the elder boys learn to carpenter and carve. Scores of drawing-rooms in Belgravia are bristling with the pretty little tables and ornaments these young artificers design. A young man with a scriptural name superintends the work; the boys are paid for their labour, and send out red velvet and twisted legs, and wood ornamented in a hundred devices. There is an industrial class for girls, too. The best and oldest are taken in, and taught housework, and kitchen-work, and sewing. Even the fathers and mothers come in for a share of the good things, and are invited to tea sometimes, and amused in the evening with magic lanterns, and conjurors, and lecturings. I do not dwell at greater length upon the industrial part of these schools, because I want to speak of another very similar institution I went to see another day.

On my way thither I had occasion to go through an old churchyard, full of graves and sunshine : a quaint, old suburban place, with tree tops and old brick houses all round about, and ancient windows looking down upon the quiet tombstones. Some children were playing among the graves, and two rosy little girls in big bonnets were sitting demurely on a stone, and grasping two babies that were placidly basking in the sun. The little girls look up and grin as I go by. I would ask them the way, only I know they won't answer, and so I go on, out at an old iron gate, with a swinging lamp, up 'Church Walk' (so it is written), and along a trim little terrace, to where a maid-of-all-work is scrubbing at her steps. I tell her that I am looking for a house where girls are taken in, and educated, and taught to be housemaids. At which confidence she brightens up, and says, 'There's a 'ouse round the-ar with somethink wrote on the door, jest where the little boy's a-trundlin' of his 'oop.'

And sure enough, following the hoop, I come to an old-fashioned house in a courtyard, and ring at a wooden door on which ' Girls' Industrial Schools ' is painted up in white letters.

A little industrious girl, in a lilac pinafore, let me in with a curtsey.

'May I come in and see the place?' say I.

'Please, yes,' says she (another curtsey). 'Please, what name?—please, walk this way.'

'This way' leads through the court, where clothes are hanging on lines, into an office-room, where my guide leaves me, with yet another curtsey. In a minute the mistress comes out from the inner room. She is a kind, smiling young woman, with a fresh face and a pleasant manner. She takes me in, and I see a dozen more girls in lilac pinafores reading round a deal table. They look mostly about thirteen or fourteen years old. I ask if this is all the school.

'No, not all,' the mistress says, counting, 'some are in the laundry, and some are not at home. When they are old enough they go out into the neighbourhood to help to wash, or cook, or what not. Go on, girls!' and the girls instantly begin to read again, and the mistress, opening a door, brings us out into the passage. 'We have room for twenty-two,' says the mistress; 'and we dress them, and feed them, and teach them as well as we can. On week-days they wear anything we can find for them, but they have very nice frocks on Sundays. I never leave them; I sit with them, and sleep among them, and walk with them; they are always friendly and affectionate to me and among themselves, and are very good companions.'

In answer to my questions she said that most of the children were put in by friends who paid half-a-crown a week for them, sometimes the parents themselves, but they could rarely afford it. That besides this, and what the girls could earn, 200*l.* a year is required for the rent of the house and expenses. 'It has always been made up,' says the mistress, 'but we can't help being very anxious at times, as we have nothing certain, nor any regular sub-scriptions. Won't you see the laundry,' she adds, opening a door.

In the laundry is a steam, and a clatter, and irons, and linen, and a little mangle, turned by two little girls, while two or three more are busy ironing under the superinten-dence of a washerwoman with tucked-up sleeves; piles of shirt collars and handkerchiefs and linen are lying on the shelves, shirts and clothes are hanging on lines across the room. The little girls don't stop, but go on busily.

'Where is Mary Anne?' says the mistress, with a little conscious pride.

'There she is, mum,' says the washerwoman, and Mary Anne steps out blushing from behind the mangle, with a hot iron in her hand and a hanging head.

'Mary Anne is our chief laundry-maid,' says the

mistress, as we come out into the hall again. 'For the first year I could make nothing of her; she was miserable in the kitchen, she couldn't bear housework, she wouldn't learn her lessons. In fact, I was quite unhappy about her, till one day I set her to ironing; she took to it instantly, and has been quite cheerful and busy ever since.'

So leaving Mary Anne to her vocation in life, we went up-stairs to the dormitories. The first floor is let to a lady, and one of the girls is chosen to wait upon her; the second floor is where they sleep, in fresh light rooms with open windows and sweet spring breezes blowing in across gardens and courtyards. The place was delightfully trim, and fresh, and peaceful; the little grey-coated beds stood· in rows, with a basket at the foot of each, and texts were hanging up on the wall. In the next room stood a wardrobe full of the girls' Sunday clothes, of which one of the girls keeps the key; after this came the mistress's own room, as fresh and light and well kept as the rest.

These little maidens scrub, and cook, and wash, and sew. They make broth for the poor, and puddings. They are taught to read and write and count, and they learn geography and history as well. Many of them come from dark unwholesome alleys in the neighbourhood—from a dreary country of dirt and crime and foul talk. In this little convent all is fresh and pure, and the sunshine pours in at every window. I don't know that the life is very exciting there, or that the days spent at the mangle, or round the deal table, can be very stirring ones. But surely they are well spent, learning useful arts, and order, and modesty, and cleanliness. Think of the cellars and slums from which these children come, and of the quiet little haven where they are fitted for the struggle of life, and are taught to be good, and industrious, and sober, and honest. It is only for a year or two, and then they will go out into the world again; into a world indeed of which we know but little—a world of cooks and kitchen-maids and general servants. I daresay these little industrious girls, sitting round that table and spelling out the Gospel of St. John this sunny afternoon, are longing and wistfully thinking about that wondrous coming time. Meanwhile the quiet hour goes by. I say farewell to the mistress; Mary Anne is still busy among her irons; I hear the mangle click as I pass, and the wooden door opens to let me out.

IN THE YEAR 5619.

Deep in the heart of the City—beyond St. Paul's— beyond the Cattle Market, with its countless pens —

beyond Finsbury Square, and the narrow Barbican, travelling on through a dirty, close, thickly-peopled region, you come to Bell Lane, in Spitalfields. And here you may step in at a door, and suddenly find yourself in a wonderful country, in the midst of an unknown people, in a great hall sounding with the voices of hundreds of Jewish children. I know not if it is always so, or if this great assemblage is only temporary, during the preparation for the Passover, but all along the sides of this great room were curtained divisions, and classes sitting divided, busy at their tasks, and children upon children as far as you could see; and somehow as you look you almost see, not these children only, but their forefathers, the Children of Israel, camping in their tents, as they camped at Succoth, when they fled out of the land of Egypt and the house of bondage. Some of these here present to-day are still flying from the house of bondage; many of them are the children of Poles, and Russians, and Hungarians, who have escaped over here to avoid conscription, and who arrive destitute and in great misery. But to be friendless, and in want, and poverty-stricken, is the best recommendation for admission to this noble charity. And here, as elsewhere, anyone who comes to the door is taken in, Christian as well as Jew.

I have before me now the Report for the year 5619

(1858), during which 1,800 children have come to these schools daily. 10,000 in all have been admitted since the foundation of the school. The working alone of the establishment—salaries, repairs, books, laundresses, &c.—amounts to more than 2,000*l.* a year. Of this a very considerable portion goes in salaries to its officers, of whom I count more than fifty in the first page of the pamphlet. '12*l.* to a man for washing boys,' is surely well-spent money; '3*l.* to a beadle; 14*l.* for brooms and brushes; 1*l.* 19*s.* 6*d.* for repair of clocks,' are among the items. The annual subscriptions are under 500*l.*, and the very existence of the place (so says the Report) depends on voluntary offerings at the anniversary. That some of these gifts come in with splendid generosity, I need scarcely say. Clothing for the whole school arrives at Easter once a year, and I saw great bales of boots for the boys waiting to be unpacked in their schoolroom. Tailors and shoemakers come and take measurings beforehand, so that everybody gets his own. To-day these artists having retired, carpenters and bricklayers are at work all about the place, and the great boys' school, which is larger still than the girls', is necessarily empty, —except that a group of teachers and monitors are standing in one corner talking and whispering together. The head master, with a black beard, comes down from a

high desk in an inner room, and tells us about the place
—about the cleverness of the children, and the scholarship
lately founded; how well many of the boys turn out in
after life, and for what good positions they are fitted by
the education they are able to receive here;—' though
Jews,' he said, ' are debarred by their religious require-
ments from two-thirds of the employments which Christians are able to fill. Masters cannot afford to employ
workmen who can only give their time from Monday to
Friday afternoon. There are, therefore, only a very
limited number of occupations open to us. Some of our
boys rise to be ministers, and many become teachers here,
in which case Government allows them a certain portion
of their salary.'

The head mistress in the girls' school was not less
kind and ready to answer our questions. During the
winter mornings hot bread-and-milk are given out to
any girl who chooses to ask for it, but only about a hundred come forward, of the very hungriest and poorest
When we came away from —— Square a day before, we
had begun to think that all poor Jews were well and
warmly clad, and had time to curl their hair and to look
clean and prosperous, and respectable, but here, alas!
comes the old story of want, and sorrow, and neglect.
What are these brown, lean, wan little figures, in loose

gowns falling from their shoulders—black eyes, fuzzy, unkempt hair, strange bead necklaces round their throats, and earrings in their ears? I fancied these must be the Poles and Russians, but when I spoke to one of them she smiled and answered very nicely, in perfectly good English, and told me she liked writing best of all, and showed me a copy very neat, even, and legible.

Whole classes seemed busy sewing at lilac pinafores, which are, I suppose, a great national institution ; others were ciphering and calling out the figures as the mistress chalked the sum upon a slate. Hebrew alphabets and sentences were hanging upon the walls. All these little Hebrew maidens learn the language of their nation.

In the infant-school, a very fat little pouting baby, with dark eyes and a little hook-nose and curly locks, and a blue necklace and funny earrings in her little rosy ears, came forward, grasping one of the mistress' fingers.

'This is a good little girl,' said that lady, 'who knows her alphabet in Hebrew and in English.'

And the little girl looks up very solemn, as children do to whom everything is of vast importance, and each little incident a great new fact. The infant schools do not make part of the Bell Lane Establishment, though they are connected with it, and the children, as they grow up, and are infants no longer, draft off into the great free-school.

The infant-school is a light new building close by, with arcaded playgrounds, and plenty of light, and air, and freshness, though it stands in this dreary, grimy region. As we come into the schoolrooms we find piled up on steps at either end, great living heaps of little infants, swaying, kicking, shouting for their dinner, beating aimlessly about with little legs and arms. Little Jew babies are uncommonly like little Christians; just as funny, as hungry, as helpless, and happy now that the bowls of food come steaming in. One, two, three, four, five little cook-boys, in white jackets and caps, and aprons, appear in a line, with trays upon their heads, like the processions out of the Arabian Nights; and as each cook-boy appears the children cheer, and the potatoes steam hotter and hotter, and the mistresses begin to ladle them out.

Rice and browned potatoes is the manna given twice a week to these hungry little Israelites. I rather wish for the soup and pudding certain small Christians are gobbling up just about this time in another corner of London; but this is but a halfpenny-worth, while the other meal costs a penny. You may count by hundreds here instead of by tens; and I don't think there would be so much shouting at the little cook-boys if these hungry little beaks were not eager for their food. I was introduced to one little boy here, who seemed to be very much looked up to by his companions because he had one long curl right along the top of his head. As we were busy talking to him, a number of little things sitting on the floor were busy stroking and feeling with little gentle fingers the soft edges of a coat one of us had on, and the silk dress of a lady who was present.

The lady who takes chief charge of these 400 babies told us how the mothers as well as the children got assistance here in many ways, sometimes coming for advice, sometimes for small loans of money, which they always faithfully repay. She also showed us letters from some of the boys who have left and prospered in life—one from a youth who has lately been elected alderman in some distant colony. She took us into a class-room and gave a lesson to some twenty little creatures, while, as it seemed to me, all the 380 others were tapping at the door, and begging to be let in. It was an object-, and then a scripture- lesson, and given with the help of old familiar pictures. There was Abraham with his beard, and Isaac and the ram, hanging up against the wall; there was Moses, and the Egyptians, and Joseph, and the sack and the brethren, somewhat out of drawing.

All these old friends gave one quite a homely feeling, and seemed to hold out friendly hands to us strangers and Philistines, standing within the gates of the chosen people.

Before we came away the mistress opened a door and showed us one of the prettiest and most touching sights I have ever seen. It was the arcaded playground full of happy, shouting, tumbling, scrambling little creatures: little tumbled-down ones kicking and shouting on the ground, absurd toddling races going on, whole files of little things wandering up and down with their arms round one another's necks: a happy, friendly little multitude indeed : a sight good for sore eyes.

And so I suppose people of all nations and religions love and tend their little ones, and watch and yearn over them. I have seen little Catholics cared for by kind nuns with wistful tenderness, as the young ones came clinging to their black veils and playing with their chaplets;—little high-church maidens growing up rosy and happy amid crosses and mediæval texts, and chants, and dinners of fish, and kind and melancholy ladies in close caps and loose-cut dresses;— little low-church children smiling and dropping curtseys as they see the Rev. Mr. Faith-in-grace coming up the lane with tracts in his big pockets about pious negroes, and broken vessels, and devouring worms, and I daresay pennies and sugar-plums as well.

Who has not seen and noted these things, and blessed with a thankful, humble heart that fatherly Providence which has sent this pure and tender religion of little children to all creeds and to all the world?

OUT OF THE SILENCE.

Only the prism's obstruction shows aright
The secret of a sunbeam : break its light
Into the jewelled bow from blankest white;
   So may a glory from defect arise.
Only by Deafness may the vexed Love wreak
Its insuppressive sense on brow and cheek;
Only by Dumbness adequately speak,
   As favoured mouth could never, thro' the eyes.

R. BROWNING.

THERE is a certain crescent in a distant part of London
—a part distant, that is, from clubs and parks and the
splendours cf Rotten Row—where a great many good
works and good intentions carried out, have taken refuge.
House-rent is cheap, the place is wide and silent and
airy; there are even a few trees to be seen opposite the
windows of the houses, although we may have come for
near an hour rattling through the streets of a neighbourhood dark and dreary in looks, and closely packed with
people and children, and wants and pains and troubles of

every tangible form for the colonists of Burton Crescent to minister to.

We pass by the Deaconesses' Home : it is not with them that we have to do to-day ; and we tell the carriage to stop at the door of one of the houses, where a brass-plate is set up, with an inscription setting forth what manner of inmates there are within, and we get out, send the carriage away, and ring the bell for admission.

One of the inmates peeped out from a doorway at us as we came into the broad old-fashioned passage. This was the little invalid of the establishment, we were afterwards told ; she had hurt her finger, and was allowed to sit down below with the matron, instead of doing her lessons with the other children upstairs.

How curious and satisfactory these lessons are, any-one who likes may see and judge by making a similar pilgrimage to the one which F. and I undertook that wintry afternoon. The little establishment is a sort of short English translation of a great continental experi-ment of which an interesting account was given in the ' Cornhill Magazine,' under the title of ' Dumb Men's Speech.' Many of my friends were interested in it, and one day I received a note on the subject.

' Dumb men *do* speak in England,' wrote a lady who

had been giving her help and countenance to a similar experiment over here; and from her I learnt that this attempt to carry out the system so patiently taught by Brother Cyril was now being made, and that children were being shown how to utter their wants, not by signs, but by speech, and in English, at the Jewish Home for Deaf and Dumb Children in Burton Crescent.

The great difference in this German system as opposed to the French, is that signs are as much as possible discarded after the beginning, and that the pupils are taught to read upon the lips of others, and to speak in words, what under the other system would be expressed in writing or by signs. The well-known Abbé de l'Epée approved, they say, of this method, and wrote a treatise on the subject, and his successor, the Abbé Sicard, says (I am quoting from a quotation), 'Le sourd-muet n'est donc totalement rendu à la société que lorsqu'on lui a appris à s'exprimer de vive voix et de lire la parole dans les mouvements des lèvres.' This following very qualified sentence of his is also quoted in a report which has been sent me : 'Prenez garde, que je n'ai point dit que le sourd-muet ne peut pas parler, mais ne sait pas parler. Il est possible que Mapuiz apprît à parler si j'avais le temps de le lui apprendre.'

Time, hours after hours of patience, good-will, are

given freely to this work by the good people who direct
the various establishments in the Netherlands where the
deaf and dumb are now instructed.

How numerous and carefully organised these institutions are may be gathered from a little pamphlet
written by the great Director Hirsch of Rotterdam, who
first introduced this system into the schools, and who
has lately made a little journey from school to school,
to note the progress of the undertaking he has so much
at heart. Brussels and Ghent and Antwerp and Bruges,
he visited all these and other outlying establishments,
and was received everywhere with open arms by the good
brothers who have undertaken to teach the system he
advocates. Dr. Hirsch is delighted with everything he
sees until he comes to Bruges, where he says that he is
struck by the painful contrast which its scholars present
as compared to the others he had visited on his way.
'They looked less gay (moins enjoué) than any of those
he had seen.' But this is explained to him by the fact
that in this school the French method is still partly
taught, and he leaves after a little exhortation to the
Director, and a warning that public opinion will be
against him if he continues the ancient system as
opposed to the newer and more intelligible one. It is
slower in the beginning, says the worthy Doctor; it

makes greater demands upon our patience, our time, our money, but it carries the pupil on far more rapidly and satisfactorily after the early steps are first mastered, until, when at last the faculty of hearing with the eyes has been once acquired, isolation exists no longer, the sufferer is given back to the world, and everyone he meets is a new teacher to help to bring his study to perfection.

1873. The Jewish Home for Deaf and Dumb Children in Burton Crescent was only started as an experiment. The lady who wrote to me guaranteed the rent and various expenses for a year, after which the experiment was to stand upon its own merits. Since the opening of the home modifications have taken place in its arrangements, and finally it has been determined to open a second school for the education of any little Christians who, as well as the little Jews, might come as day-scholars there, to be taught with much labour and infinite patience and pains what others learn almost unconsciously and without an effort.

F. and I have been going upstairs all this time, and come into a back-room or board-room, opening with folding-doors into the schoolroom, where the children are taught. As we went in the young master, M. von Praagh (he is a pupil, I believe, of Dr. Hirsch's) came forward to receive us, and welcomed us in the **most** friendly way. The children all looked up at us with bright flashing eyes—little boys and little girls in brown pinafores, with cheery little smiling faces peeping and laughing at us along their benches. In the room itself there is the usual apparatus—the bit of chalk, the great slate for the master to write upon, the little ones for the pupils, the wooden forms, the pinafores, the pictures hanging from the walls, and, what was touching to me, the usual little games and frolics and understandings going on in distant corners, and even under the master's good-natured eye. He is there to bring out, and not to repress, and the children's very confidence in his kindness and sympathy seems to be one of the conditions of their education and cure.

He clapped his hands, and a little class came and stood round the big slate—a big girl, a little one, two little boys. 'Attention,' says the teacher, and he begins naming different objects, such as fish, bread, chamois, coal-scuttle. All these words the children read off his lips by watching the movement of his mouth. As he says each word the children brighten, seize the idea, rush to the pictures that are hanging on the wall, discover the object he has named, and bring it in breathless triumph. 'Tomb,' said the master, after naming a variety of things, and a big girl, with a beaming face, pointed to the ground and nodded her head emphatically, grinning from ear to ear.   But signs are not approved of in this establishment, and, as I have said, the great object is to get them to talk.   And it must be remembered that they are only beginners, and that the home has only been opened a few months.   One little thing, scarcely more than a baby, who had only lately come in, had spoken for the first time that very day—'â, â, â,' cried the little creature.   She was so much delighted with her newly-gotten power that nothing would induce her to leave off exercising it.   She literally shouted out her plaintive little 'â'.   It was like the note of a little lamb, for, of course, being deaf, she had not yet learnt how to modulate her voice, and she had to be carried off into a distant corner by a bigger girl, who tried to amuse her and keep her still.

'It is an immense thing for the children,' said M. von Praagh, 'to feel that they are not cut off hopelessly and markedly from communication with their fellow-creatures; the organs of speech being developed, their lungs are strengthened, their health improves.   You can see a change in the very expression of their faces, they delight in using their newly-acquired power, and won't use the finger-alphabet even among themselves.'   And, as if to corroborate what he was saying, there came a cheery vociferous outbreak of ' â's ' from the corner where the little girl had been installed with some toys, and all the other children laughed.

I do not know whether little Jew boys and girls are on an average cleverer than little Christians, or whether, notwithstanding their infirmity, the care and culture bestowed upon them has borne this extra fruit; but these little creatures were certainly brighter and more lively than any dozen Sunday-school children taken at hazard. Their eyes danced, their faces worked with interest and attention, they seemed to catch light from their master's face, from one another's, from ours as we spoke; their eagerness, their cheerfulness and childish glee, were really remarkable; they laughed to one another much like any other children, peeped over their slates, answered together when they were called up. It was difficult to remember that they were deaf, though, when they spoke, a great slowness, indistinctness, and peculiarity was of course very noticeable. But these are only the pupils of a month or two, be it remembered. A child with all its faculties is nearly two years learning to talk.

One little fellow with a charming expressive face and eyes like two brown stars, came forward, and ciphered and read to us, and showed us his copy-book. He is beginning Hebrew as well as English. His voice is pleasant, melancholy, but quite melodious, and, to my surprise, he addressed me by my name, a long name with many letters in it. M. von Praagh had said it to him on his lips, for of course it is not necessary for the master to use his voice, and the motion of the lips is enough to make them understand. The name of my companion, although a short one, is written with four difficult consonants, and only one vowel to bind them together, and it gave the children more trouble than mine had done; but after one or two efforts the little boy hit upon the right way of saying it, and a gleam of satisfaction came into his face as well as his master's. M. von Praagh takes the greatest possible pains with, and interest in every effort and syllable. He holds the children's hands and accentuates the words by raising or letting them fall; he feels their throats and makes them feel his own. It would be hard indeed if so much patience and enthusiasm produced no results to reward it.

'What o'clock is it?' M. von Praagh asked.

'Four o'clock,' said the little boy, without looking up.

'How do you know?' asked the master.

'Miss —— is come,' said the little fellow, laughing. This was a lady who came to give the girls their sewing lesson so many times a week.

I need not describe the little rooms upstairs, with the usual beds in rows, and the baths, the play-room—the arrangements everywhere for the children's comfort and happiness. If the school is still deaf and dumb for most practical purposes, yet the light is shining in; the children are happy, and understand what is wanted of them, and are evidently in the right way. For the short time he has been at work as yet, M. von Praagh has worked wonders.

Babies, as I have just said, with all their faculties are about two years learning to speak. There is a curious crisis, which anyone who has had anything to do with children must have noticed, a sort of fever of impatience and vexation which attacks them when they first begin to find out that people do not understand what they say. I have seen a little girl burst into passionate tears of vexation and impatience because she could not make herself immediately understood. I suppose the pretty croonings and chatterings which go before speech are a sort of natural exercise by which babies accustom themselves to words, and which they mistake at first for real talking. Real words come here and there in the midst of the baby-language—detaching themselves by degrees out of the wonderful labyrinth of sound—real words out of the language which they are accustomed to hear all about them, and something in this way, to these poor little deaf folks, the truth must dawn out of the confusion of sights and signs surrounding them.

This marvellous instinctive study goes on in secret in the children's minds. After their first few attempts at talking they seem to mistrust their own efforts. They find out that their pretty prattle is no good; they listen, they turn over words in their minds, and whisper them to themselves as they are lying in their little cribs, and then one day the crisis comes, and a miracle is worked, and the child can speak.

When children feel that their first attempts are understood they suddenly regain their good temper and wait for a further inspiration. They have generally mastered the great necessaries of life in this very beginning of their efforts: 'pooty,' 'toos,' 'ben butta,' 'papa,' 'mama,' 'nana' for 'nurse,' and 'dolly,' and they are content. Often a long time passes without any further apparent advance, and then comes perhaps a second attack of indignation. I know of one little babe who had hardly spoken before, and who had been very cross and angry for some days past, and who horrified its relations by suddenly standing up in its crib one day, rosy and round-eyed, and saying *Bess my soul* exactly like an old charwoman who had come into the nursery.

A friend of mine to whom I was speaking quite bore out my remarks. He said his own children had all passed through this phase, which comes after the child has learned to think and before he is able to speak. One's heart aches as one thinks of those whose life is doomed to be a life of utter silence in the full stream of the mighty flow of words in which our lives are set, to whom no crisis of relief may come, who have for generations come and gone silent and alone, and set apart by a mysterious dispensation from its very own best blessings and tenderest gifts.

I was thinking of this yesterday as we went walking across the downs in the Easter-tide. I could hardly tell whether it was sight or sound that delighted us most as we went along upon the turf: the sound of life in the bay at the foot of the downs, the flowing of the waves just washing over the low-ridged rocks with which our coast is set: the gentle triumphant music overhead of the lark, soaring and singing in the sunshine. The sea and the shingle were all sparkling, while great bands like moonlight in daylight lay white and brilliant on the horizon of the waters. The very stones seemed to cry out with a lovely Easter hymn of praise; and sound and sight to be so mingled that one could scarcely tell where one began or the other ended.

If by this new system the patient teachers cannot give everything to their pupils, the ripple of the sea, the song of the lark, yet they can do very much towards it, by leading the children's minds to receive the great gifts of nature through the hearts and sympathy of others, and give them above all that best and dearest gift of all in daily life, without which nature itself fails to comfort and to charm, the companionship of their fellow-creatures and of intelligences answering and responding to their own.

———

P.S. 1873. M. von Praagh is now the director of an institution in Fitzroy Square, for teaching teachers, as well as the children themselves, the art of lip-reading. This institution is not for Jews, but for anyone who likes to come. The system is absolutely the same as that already described in the article. The children seemed very eager, good, and attentive; they could speak to one another, and evidently greatly preferred this plan to the finger-sign system to which we are all accustomed. M. von Praagh told us that his pupils came from various parts of the country—from Ireland, from Birmingham, from Scotland. He is very much against their boarding together in one establishment, thinking it far better for them to live as other people do, and to mix with others habitually. The children are therefore only day scholars;

they board out in the neighbourhood. The room is large; there is plenty of light, and sound too; they are taught all the usual branches of education, in addition to the habit of utterance. Those children I saw five years ago, he told me, are some of them already out in the world, and earning their living. One is a watchmaker, another a line-engraver. They have a certificated drawing mistress in the school to teach them, who showed us a really admirable drawing by one of them, and pointed with pride to a tall boy in the window, a pupil a head and shoulders taller than herself, who had gained a prize at the South Kensington Museum.

Our conversation, it must be confessed, was somewhat laborious, but some allowance must be made for the natural shyness of a visitor confronted with so many pairs of bright and eager eyes.

'Côme a-gain,' said the children, in voices and accents as different as though they could hear. It was indeed very difficult to realise that they did *not* hear; they gave one more the impression of little foreigners imperfectly acquainted with English than of victims of so sad a fate; and I think the best testimony we can bear to the success of M. von Praagh's system is that it did not occur to us to pity anyone of them, except, perhaps, a boy and girl who did not come forward nor attempt to speak.

Teachers begin upon 50*l.* a year, and, if the system were once established, might make a comfortable livelihood. The director told us, however, that he had great difficulty in finding such pupils.

In a very interesting lecture given at the Society of Arts, Dr. Dasent speaks of the great superiority of the system practised by M. von Praagh over the French course, in which children were 'taught by signs, and consequently unfitted to enter upon the duties of life and tc communicate freely with their fellows. If all the world were an institution for educating the deaf and dumb, one might be satisfied with such a result; but as it is not, we must necessarily pronounce any system which contents itself with educating its pupils for life in the institution, and in the institution alone, self-condemned.'

Elsewhere Dr. Dasent says:

'So perfectly has this process of education been carried out in individual cases, that persons thus educated are able to carry away with them a sermon or a speech by only observing the motion of the lips and the play of the countenance of the speaker or preacher, and in one case that I have heard of, the preacher, ignorant of the infirmity under which a regular attendant at his church was suffering, sent to beg that so and so would not stare at him so hard as it put him out in his sermon.'

LITTLE PAUPERS.[1]

Patient children—think what pain
  Makes a young child patient!—ponder
Wronged too commonly, to strain
  After right, or weep, or wonder.

Wicked children, with peaked chins,
  And old foreheads! there are many
With no pleasure except sin,
  Gambling with a stolen penny.

Sickly children, that whine low
  To themselves and not their mothers—
From mere habit never so—
  Hoping help or care from others.—E. B. BROWNING.

A FEW old-fashioned lanes still run, a little way out of the thoroughfares—some of the great London dear old zigzag lanes and winding passages, that are fast falling before the inspirations of Improvement with her parallel lines. There is one corner still left undisturbed, with some trees casting their shade over a few old rambling houses and

[1] *A Practical Guide to the Boarding-out System.* By Colonel E. W. GRANT, C.E. Knight & Co., Fleet Street. *Children of the State: The Training of Juvenile Paupers.* By FLORENCE HILL. Macmillan & Co.

garden walls, where you may hear a crowing and clucking of poultry, a chirruping of birds in the branches, and where you may still recall, if you will, a bygone country tradition.   It was here I once met a procession I shall not easily forget.   Wearily it toiled along, dragging and lagging and slowly advancing up the lane, a stricken little company of 'workhouse children out for a half-holiday,' so I was told, and returning to the workhouse from whence it had come.   They were not Kensington children, who are well looked after, but orphans from another parish, of which the Union stands in Kensington.   Poor little wretches in pinafores and poke-bonnets and fustian, with heavy yellow faces and lagging steps.   One or two of the passers-by stopped to look after them.   A maid-servant came to a garden-gate.   'They *do* look bad,' she said.   As they went by I saw heavy heads tied up; a sling or two; dull indifferent faces; lame and shuffling feet.   There was a taint in the air.   Some of the smaller children were draggling at the arms of the elder girls.   I do not remember any one of them looking up as they passed. The very youngest of all was in a perambulator, slowly pushed along at the head of this doomed and battered little column.

I was told afterwards that these particular children were soon to be sent to a country school, where it is to be hoped the bandages may be loosened, and the weary burden of life lightened from their poor little backs. Perhaps it may be removed altogether; for when I remember how crushed and how hopeless they looked, it seems difficult to think that for these little creatures much youth or strength or life can be in store in any country place, no matter how pleasant.

Since seeing these children go by, and exchanging looks of sympathy with the maid-servant, the writer of this article has fallen in with one or two persons interested in the welfare of these poor little prisoners of fate.

As for their previous history there is not much variety in it. Some of them have come from outside, from some dismal slum; others are the baby-paupers of paupers' children—*l'onde sous l'onde dans une mer sans fond.*

We all of us know the look of the slip-shodden squaws and gins whose gaunt faces line our London bricks. Who has not watched them now and again as they come shuffling up some narrow passage, out of a mystery of rags and darkness, into the bustling thoroughfare? They hobble a few paces; they look round a little bewildered; and presently they stop, for they have come to a swing door, by which, alas, no angels with flaming swords stand ready to thrust them out. It is only at the gates of paradise that the repelling angels wait; these doors open

wide at a touch, and within them are warmth and life and strength—three pennyworth at a time. What does it matter ' that the children are cowering in the ashes at home, the boy lying naked on the vermin bed ? '—the swing-doors open wide, and the wretched creatures shuffle in and pay away their pence, their mothers' love, their self-respect, for the fatal little glassfuls of comfort in their life-trouble. One day it is their life they give, and then their trouble is over ; for the parish will bury them, and the relieving-officer comes, and the neighbours stand round the door of the empty cellar from whence the children are carried off to the workhouse. . . .

Henceforth the State—a sort of Jupiter-like parent—is the only one they have to look to for love, or sympathy, or care. It is not unkind, perhaps kinder than the real one, but then it has no eyes or voice, and knows not its children apart. It does not refuse them the cup of cold water—a tin cup, so that they shall not break it. It clothes them, all alike, in blue stripe and poke-bonnets, and fustian caps and coats. It feeds them—on gruel and suet-pudding. It takes them in—by hundreds in a dormitory. The children grow up in a place where one day is like another, where dull hour follows hour, where they watch yards upon yards of blue stripe, basons after basons of water-gruel passing through the wards from year's end to year's end. It cannot be helped ; these are not individuals, but children of the State, machine-made paupers growing up for the market. They can only be marshalled by rule. They have book-learning, but life-learning is unknown to them ; and the best learning of all, love and usefulness, and the faith of home, its peaceful rest and helpful strength, is a mystery as little dreamt of by them as the secret of heaven itself is by us. How can they love this abstract parent of theirs ? can they honour and succour it? That is for the nobility and ratepayers perhaps, but not for them. If they have one dream, it is a dream of liberty and escape from the rigid rule that confines them ; of going out into the world and seeing for themselves.

The day comes at last that they have looked for, and they are set free; happy if they have escaped the contagion of evil talk and ways that spreads like a curse in the workhouse. They are handed over to some mistress who has come to ask for a drudge, and then they discover that liberty means the run of some wretched lodging-house, a struggle, late at night and early in the morning, over the commonest things of life. They break the crockery; they have been used to wooden bowls, and they do not know how to handle brittle things. They lose themselves if they are sent on a message, and come home wild and frightened. They scarcely understand what is said to them; they scarcely try to listen. Everything is new, everything is terrible and difficult, and the harried mistress of three flights of discomfort and struggle bears with them for a time perhaps, and one day in despair gives them warning and turns them away. Warning! who is there to give them a warning and a helping hand? Do the good Lion and Unicorn come to protect these poor little Unas on their way through the sorrowful forest where wild beasts are prowling—hyænas, wild cats, serpents, and poisoned reptiles. Alas and alas! the Lion and the Unicorn are up in their places on the organ-lofts and the shop-fronts and public offices; and the fate of these poor children is almost too sad to speak of.

When you meet the little maid-of-all-work again it is a hardened and callous creature, whom you may vainly try to interest or touch. Social influence cannot reach her. What is there to touch? Who has ever loved her? Who is the worse for her offending? What has she got to lose or to hold by? It is too late now to hope that she can be a child again.

Miss Hill, in her admirable little book, quotes a letter from the Secretary of the Rescue Society, accounting for the small proportion of workhouse girls admitted into the Society's homes. 'It must be borne in mind,' she says, ' that our judgment is always opposed to the reception of

workhouse cases, from their comparative hopelessness.'
Workhouse they are—to workhouse they return. 'The
young women who have grown up in a workhouse ' (I am
again quoting from ' Children of the State ') ' form a class
proverbial for audacity and shamelessness. The chaplain
rarely visits them, conscious that they are beyond his
influence ; although it must be admitted that there are
instances in which the most obdurate have yielded to the
appeals and judicious sympathy of benevolent women.
Punishment only renders them more defiant. A year or
two ago an outburst of the noisiest insubordination (and
those only who have heard can realise its horror) was
apologetically accounted for by the master, who said,
" You see, sir, they are the girls who have been brought
up in the house." '

Miss Twining's words, quoted by Miss Hill, are very
earnest and melancholy to read. She speaks, as the
characteristics of paupers, of a total want of gratitude and
affection towards individuals. ' They are perfectly well
acquainted,' she says, ' with their " rights " as to main-
tenance by their parishes and reception into the workhouses. Above the age of sixteen they are completely
their own mistresses, and can go in or take their discharge
whenever and for whatever cause they choose. . . . An
officer connected with the large pauper-school at Swinton,

in Lancashire, being asked what proportion of the girls sent forth from that establishment, as compared with the daughters of artisans, had taken to bad courses, answered, "Do not ask me. It is so painful that I can hardly tell you the extent to which evil will predominate in those proceeding from our institution." And a similar statement was made by the officer of Kirkdale separate school.'[1]

The best solutions to the most complicated problems are always the most simple ones. The system which Miss Hill and her friends are advocating is merely a return to the first rudiments of Divine political economy. Instead

---

[1] Not long ago an appeal from the Rev. Thomas Quick was published in the 'Tablet.' He had put out about fifty orphans, who were going on well and satisfactorily; when the Manchester guardians, by refusing to extend further relief to orphan children, compelled half of them to be sent to Swinton workhouse. 'Out of these fifty orphans, about one-half belong to the Chorlton Union. With these I have little difficulty, as the board of guardians, in their desire to advance and improve the condition of these poor orphans—and to lessen the rates—allow me a reasonable support. Would that the Manchester guardians would act in like manner! It seems strange that they prefer sending an orphan to Swinton, where it will cost them from 6s. to 7s. per week, rather than give me 3s. or a relative 2s.; to say nothing of the advantages, nay the natural obligation of giving a child, if possible, a home or domestic training and education, where its affections will be developed, its self-reliance strengthened, and feelings of independence implanted in its mind. Of these fifty orphans twenty are at work, but not earning as yet their entire support; thirty are attending our day-school. Morning and evening they are taught domestic duties in the homes in which they reside, thus the sooner to qualify them for work or service.' 'It would seem such an easy solution,' says the lady who sends me the extract, 'of the difficulty of bringing up Roman Catholic children in the faith of their parents

of massing children together and allowing them to grow up in communities, the advocates of the boarding-out system urge the great advantages of individual care and interest. A small local committee is formed, the guardians are applied to for permission to put the children out to homes approved of by them as well as by the association. Each member of the committee undertakes to befriend one or more of the little boarders, and to send in a regular report; a list is kept, a small subscription paid. This is all the machinery that is required. The money which the children would cost the State in the Union is given to some respectable person, who undertakes to be foster-parent to the orphan. From all experience, the plan seems to answer admirably, and the child appears to be usually treated as a member of the family, to cast its lot with the protectors who have been found for it. I was speaking, the other day, to a relieving-officer at Eton, who evidently had the scheme at heart. He told me that the plan was first tried at Slough, some years ago (it seems to have sprung up almost simultaneously in different parts of the country). He said that the guardians had found that the boys and girls they sent out from their schools invariably returned to them again: that they were totally unfitted for earning a respectable livelihood; it was in vain that outfits were given, situations found—the chil-

dren were too ignorant and *scared* to retain them; and
after trying the experiment of sending them to some distant district school, from whence they were withdrawn
after a time, having all been attacked with a contagious
disease of the eyes, it was determined by the guardians to
board them out with any respectable persons who would
be willing to undertake them.

'The cost of the children in the house (including the
salaries of the officials, &c.) can scarcely be less than 6*s.*
or 7*s.* a week,' said Mr. ———. 'We allow 3*s.* 6*d.* a week
to the foster-parents, and also 6*s.* 6*d.* a quarter for
clothes, &c.'

This is a higher rate of payment than that which
I believe is made at Bath and Bristol, where 3*s.* a
week only is allowed. But people are willing to take
the children without pecuniary profit, and come forward—
childless couples, old maids, widows. One can imagine a
hundred silent homes that the presence of a child would
brighten, and where the helplessness of the poor little
pauper, and the lonely regrets of the foster-parent together, might make a happiness for both. Nature certainly intended children to be the vent for many and
many a sorrow and remorse. Among them lies most especially the dominion of women. Are we dull, ugly, shabby,
neglected—what does it matter to them? No queen is

more paramount than a mother in her nursery. Even foster arms may close with a tender all-satisfied clasp. It seems as if children were made naturally and unconsciously selfish and trustful to complete the parent's gift of tender devotion. Miss Hill, and Mr. Archer, and Colonel Grant, who have all written on the subject, unite in saying that the very greatest care should be taken in the selection of these homes and foster-parents. But when these are carefully chosen, and when, in addition to official machinery, there are superintending ladies, one to each child, it cannot often happen that anything should go very seriously wrong. 'You can almost tell by the children's faces if anything is amiss,' the relieving-officer said, to whom I applied. In Colonel Grant's 'Practical Guide' there are some excellent rules for the guidance of lady visitors : among other things he warns them against very frequent visits. Miss Hill gives several illustrations of the way in which foster-parents attach themselves to the orphans under their care. In Glasgow, a child who had been put to board with a woman in that district was found to have its settlement in Edinburgh, whither the parochial board directed that it should be removed. 'The foster-mother, hearing that the child was to be taken away from her, repaired in the greatest distress to Mr. Beattie, and besought him to obtain a reversal of the order. He explained to her that this was impossible : when, with tears streaming down her cheeks, she implored him to let her keep the child as her own, without payment, for part from it she could not ; and it was accordingly adopted by her.'

The author then goes on to give a clear and carefully elaborated history of the efforts that are being made to relieve these children of the State. Her story is told forcibly and simply. It comes home with all the eloquence of true sympathy for the weak and the ill-used, and her little book almost seems like a window thrown open in a dark and bewildering and over-crowded place, where everybody is talking at once, and running about and tumbling over everybody else. There is a pure breath of the fresh air, of common sense and rational charity. I ought in common fairness to quote the contrary opinion of a lady in Cornwall on whose judgment all those who know her must perforce rely. Mrs. F. told me that after some personal experience she had fully satisfied herself that small industrial schools were on the whole more free from possible abuse than private adoption.

One of Miss Hill's readers, who had no acquaintance with her at the time, wrote to her, and some weeks after went, at her suggestion, to see two friends, who promised to show her the working of the system as it has been started in a certain district not many hours distant from London. The person in question is accustomed to see facts and theories turning into print, but it was a newer experience to find print and theories starting back again into life; theories working in flesh and blood, sentiments changing into kind words and doings—vague 'foster-parents' with eyes and noses, and 'pauper children' becoming Lizzies and Katies, running across the garden. Parochial supervision is,—'Mr. Woods looked in—last Monday were it, Lizzie? He said he should be round again in a week; but he didn't say nothing about schooling money.' 6s. 6d. a quarter for repair of clothes becomes in reality,—'It's the boots, Miss. Why, Lizzie, she du wear them out in no time; this is her Sunday pinbefore. She sewed at it herself, but gels, why, they would like to be runnin' in and out all day long.' This was from a funny, clever, goggle-eyed old lady whom we drove to see, over a green round hill, beyond the streets of the old city. It was a place not unlike the old Hogarth etchings of outdoor life. The streets were wide, stone-paved, be-gabled, alive with busy people. The women wear flapping bonnets, drive their donkeys to market, carry their fish-baskets, and stride out freely as the figures do in the old-fashioned pictures.

We had left it all behind us and climbed another hill

and turned into some by-lane again. The carriage rolled along between two rows of small tenements with front gardens, in which dogs and cats and children seemed growing and climbing everywhere. These latter were hanging to the rails, peeping over walls, straggling across the street. A carriage, a little baby in a blue hat, three ladies inside:—all this, no doubt, was a sight worth running for. I remember one little creature starting out into the middle of the road to look after us with two dark eyes. She had a little dark curly head, and a black frock, and one small black leg: the other foot was bare, and came patting fat and pink over the stones. As we drove away, she held up one little black stocking to us. There was also a pale curl-paper child, with horns sticking out all over its head, who came running to a garden gate at the end of the street. But curl-papers are not to be despised if my theory of life is a true one; and if facts gain in significance as they are the types and images of higher things, even curl-papers may be a distorted development of maternal affection

Mrs. Pearman did not live in a street, but in a cottage, with a garden full of snapdragons. She was like an old woman in a fairy tale, living on the edge of a common, with her one little orphan-girl for her maid. She was sitting working at her door as we drove up, with aureoles

of nice bright saucepans hanging up all round her head.
The usual old man in the smock was sitting silent in the
corner of the chimney; the little girl came and peeped at
us and ran away tossing her hair. The old woman looked
hard at my companion, suddenly brightened up and came
out to meet us, with knobby hand-shakes, and led the way
out of the kitchen into the state parlour. It was a homely,
sunny little place; the Dutch clock with the bunch of
flowers painted on its nose was ticking in the corner; an
embroidered cat was hanging up, framed and glazed
against the wall, faded, but grinning still at the opposite
sampler, like the celebrated Cheshire cat in 'Alice.'
There was a lattice window with geraniums, an old oak
chest of drawers, a round oilcloth table with work and
workboxes piled upon it. The old lady smoothed her
apron and made us sit down on her broad mahogany chairs.
She was a clever-looking old woman, as I have said, with
a frill cap and grey hair, and a hook nose and bright-blue
goggle eyes. My friend went to the point at once.

'Here is a lady, Mrs. Pearman, who is interested in
this plan of ours for boarding out the children, so I
brought her to talk to you. How is Elizabeth, and how is
she going on ?'

'You shall see her, Miss,' the old lady said myste-
riously; 'that was herr you see along o' uncle. She is

getting on, thank you; but dear me! she is a deal of trouble at times' (confidentially).

'I am sorry to hear you say this, Mrs. Pearman,' said her visitor.

'Thank ye, mum,' said Mrs. Pearman, instantly mollified. 'Gels they all du answer sarce at times. Uncle, that were uncle in the kitchen, he can speak sharp too; but I ses to 'Lizabeth (one finger up), "When he speaks to you, don't you say nothin' at all." Why, she oughter be a good gel when she is took and cared for' (many expressive nods and shakes). 'I says to her, "'Lizabeth, who do you suppose would ha' took and cared for *me* if I hadna' had a good father and mother when I was a little lass?" She should remember such.'

This impressive bit of morality being delivered, Mrs. Pearman calls Elizabeth, and the little girl instantly pops her head in at the door.

'Come in, Lizzie,' says her protectress; 'the ladies would like to see you. You can show them your copy and your brother's letter. They teaches her at school,' says Mrs. Pearman, while Elizabeth is getting her copy-book out of a clean apron in the drawer; 'but, bless you, I have had to learn her everything about the house. My word, Miss, they teach them nothin' at that there Union. When she come to me' (impressively) 'they had not so much as learnt her to peel a potato. If I sent her out when first she come, she wer' like a wild child. Now, 'Lizabeth, fetch your slate and your new pinbefore, and don't forget the letter.'

Mrs. Pearman nodded and winked delightedly as soon as ever the little girl's back was turned, and made many approving signs. She was evidently as proud as possible of her attainments, but anxious that Elizabeth herself should not suspect them.

Poor little pauper! She was a dark-faced, half-wistful, half-tamed little creature, with a sullen look and then a bright one. The story of many a bygone trouble and dreary tramp was written in her face—the hardships and troubles of other lives than her own. She had thick black hair and stunted broad shoulders.

'Do you see any change in her since she came to you?' I asked once, when she was out of the room.

'Why, she have all wakened up like,' said the old woman; 'she du sing now o' mornings, and she begins to curl her hair. She's terrible fond o' children, too.' Then turning to Miss ——, 'She took to Mrs. Parks' little gel from the first, Miss; that were a *dear* child, and I do feel amiss without her, that I do—on'y three year old, but such a good child: she were a darling little one. And Lizzie she du love children. I took her to a prayer-meeting out a-field the other day, and there she gits a baby in her lap, and nurses it a' the time. The people they laffed to see her' (some more expressive nods and winks at us. We are to show no admiration).

Mrs. Pearman was also evidently very much pleased with the brother's letter, which she read, holding it out at arms' length.

'It come last April,' said she, 'and we never thought as how he wanted us to write. Bristol—it be written from Bristol.'—

'"My dear Sister,—I hope you are well" (said the brother) "and obedient to your mistress—for you should be always obedient" (says Mrs. Pearman at a venture)— "and you must remember that your mistress knows what you should do. You must be obedient and try to please your mistress. And I hope to hear you are a good and obedient child. So no more.

'"Your affectionate brother,

'"Wm. Dobbs."'

'So we understands her name is Dobbs, not Stubbly,' Mrs. Pearman prattled on. 'They told us Stubbly at th' Union. Her brother he signs Dobbs, Miss, as you see. Elizabeth, your name must be the same o' his.'

'Can you write your name down on the slate, Elizabeth?' said Miss ——.

Elizabeth set to work at railway pace, while Mrs. Pearman finished her little story.

How was it Elizabeth came to her? She felt lonesome, she said, after her first girl married, and she heard of this new plan, and thought as how she should like to take a little gel. ' 'Tis a kindness,' she said, ' to take the children and larn them. Elizabeth she don't talk much about the Union; if she speaks sarce, I say' (shakes of head and other reassuring signals to us), ' Elizabeth, I shall take you back.'

Elizabeth grinned, not looking much alarmed, and showed all her white teeth : she had covered the slate with ' Elizabeth Dobbs' meanwhile.

Our visit was nearly at an end. Miss ——'s little nephew was brought in from the carriage, where he had been winking his blue eyes and making believe to pull the reins all this time. Good old Mrs. Pearman brightened up brighter still to welcome the little blue and white visitor. Elizabeth looked pleased and shy : the baby was living in a world where there are no differences of estate as yet, and where the little pauper girl coming up and clapping her hands before him, was as welcome a companion as a princess in her right.

I have described this visit at length, because it seems to me a fair average example of the working of the system. My friends took me to see some more children before I left, and for another drive the next day through the green park that spreads for miles all round about the busy old city—bright commons, sheltering trees, valleys, and hills up which the horses climb. We stopped at a post-office by some cross-roads.

'This is not my district,' my friend explained; 'but I know that some children are boarded out somewhere near this, and I must find out here.'

Then she came out again, and led the way by a narrow sort of back-passage place, with low thresholds, and geraniums, and children. We peeped into the open doors, and saw churns and pails and country appliances, and a man sitting like a pre-Raphaelite picture, adding up his books in an inner room. Then someone came to a door-way, and called to us to go on straight to the end house. This little *cul-de-sac* finished with a garden gate. There was a garden full of roses beyond it, and a stout elderly grey-headed woman watching us as we came up the alley. Was she Mrs. Bennet? No. Mrs. Bennet was her mother. Had they any little boarders? Yes; but they were at school. Then—for she was a friendly-minded woman— she gave a second glance at the party.

'Won't you walk in?' said she, and she flung wide open the little gate of the rose-garden. There were cabbages and vegetables, and all along the box-edged pathway were roses grafted, white and pink, upon their stems. The white roses were specially sweet and beautiful. Out of the garden we stepped into the house, passing through the kitchen, where, as usual, the old man in the smock was sitting in the chimney-corner. Then we came into a little square dim parlour, with a window wide open on the garden. There was an old-fashioned couch pushed up to the window, and on the couch a woman was lying, looking up with a grave face. 'This is my sister,' said the other.

There was a certain likeness between them; but the education of pain and silent suffering had given a strange sweet look to the sick woman's face. Her voice, too, was very low and clear. I thought that they were happy little paupers who had found such a friend. The sick woman seemed to be their foster-parent from the way she spoke, although she often quoted 'mother,' and what mother said and did for them. Mother was ill upstairs, and the grey-headed sister must have had a handful, for the invalid could not move her limbs. She told us that the children were at school, but they would be home directly. It was some six months since they first came. They had thought they would as soon take two as one. They would be happier together, and mother had gone up to the Union to choose them ; and one evening after dark Mr. Reynolds brought them down. Kitty she was not frightened, but the little one cried bitterly, and so they put them both to bed; and then the next morning there was such a piece of fuss as never was when the time came for them to go to school. 'But mother said, "If we give in the first day, maybe we shall ne'er hear the end of it." So to school they went, and there has never been a word since then. They are quite at home. Little Kitty has her sister up at Mrs. Peterson's. She do say she have five aunts, and an uncle, and a grandfather and grandmother tu. That is mother and father, and all of us, you know,' said the woman, gently smiling: 'I heard her tell Mr. Peterson so t'other day, Mary' (to the sister). 'Phœbe laughs, and says *she* ain't no relations, she was picked up in the street and taken to the Union—"that old Union," she calls it. It's nicer like for the little things to have some-one to go to, ma'am,' the foster-aunt went on, appealing to Miss ——, 'and they get better places afterwards. In th' Union they see the big girls coming in and out, and they do get set up to tricks. Now, Phœbe here can help my sister nicely—she scours and runs for errands. Little Phœbe had a big lump in her neck when first she came, and little Kitty's ear were bad, and so was her arm, and Phœbe's too: 'twere in the blood, I think ; but they are doing nicely now. We give them nothing, only feed them like ourselves, and cold water to bathe. They be good children,' said the aunt, smiling. 'Little Kitty do have her tantrums; then she is but a little maid.'

Little Kitty and Phœbe came running home just then past the windows and the rose-trees. They had clean fresh faces and pinafores, and their aunts had made them some little hats, and tied up their hair. Kitty was a sweet-looking little girl of four, with great blue eyes. Little Phœbe was about eight, and she looked like the descendant of a hundred tramps. She had the same stunted grown look that had struck me in Elizabeth the day before, the narrow head and Chinese eyes; her face seemed to tell the same piteous story of the past. But here she was fresh and clean and wholesome, and watched with kindly care; her bad arm was healing, and her swollen glands were cured: she lived in this little rose-garden house, she went to school, she helped her 'aunts,' she played with Kitty, and she sewed. Phœbe's stitches were displayed all along Kitty's pinafore. Poor little stray waif of a vagrant race, apparently doomed to a like hopeless fate; 'found in the street,' she had drifted into a tranquil and happy home, among good people and peaceful things. We bestowed the small benefaction of a threepenny piece upon them (it was put into a special drawer for their benefit), as we said good-by. As we came away I looked back: the last sight I had was of the children standing by the sick woman's couch; she had hold of Kitty's hand, and was looking into their faces with her kind eyes. It is not much to tell, but the sight touched me. After this we went to see two more little lilac pinafores boarding with the schoolmaster and his wife. They were about twelve, and had just been christened Susy and Sally. The little pinafores dipped curtseys at every other word. Susy was going into school, Sally stopped at home on Fridays to help aunt; they, too, had swollen glands (dip Susy, dip Sally), and the schoolmaster asked Miss —— about sending Susy to the doctor. Sally was much better than when she came; she helped 'aunt' with the house and the baby (dip Sally, and beam all over). Susy was the little kitchen-maid (dip Susy). 'Sally was a good useful little girl, but a terrible hand at breaking crockery' (here poor Sally's face fell); 'she had never been used to anything but wooden bowls at the Union.'

'Sally must learn,' said kind Miss ——, 'for the time when she goes into a place.' Sally here gave a melancholy and remorseful curtsey, so it seemed to me; but she brightened up before we left.

Our last visit was to 'Kitty's little sister, at Mrs.

Peterson's.' We came to an old-fashioned-looking house, with a straggling garden, and someone standing watching us as we drove up. The kitchen door was wide open, and we could see a deep high-roofed fireplace, a wooden dresser and tables, milk-bowls and jerkins, and great bunches of vegetables heaped up. It looked something like an old Dutch interior; Mrs. Peterson, who stood in the doorway, had a striking dark-eyed face, with smooth black hair; she was not unlike one of those solemn ladies that Vandyke has painted in frills and in black velvet and gold chains. She knew Miss ——, and welcomed her warmly. 'She is very bad, Miss,' she said; 'she is worse since you saw her last. Won't you come in? Milly will be glad to see you.'

In a back parlour out of the old kitchen sat a little child humped up in a wooden chair, with two poor little swelled legs in white stockings, resting on a wooden stool. It was dressed with a pinafore. There it sat in the window, waiting placidly, with great eyes smouldering in its pale face, and with thick brown hair, brushed back. Every now and then it gave a little cough. It didn't speak, it only sat quite still, watching us. Two smart dolls were toppling unheeded against the window-sill, in pink and blue finery and feathers; there was a box of toys half open.

' Are they good?' said Miss ——, pointing to the

dolls. Little Milly did not answer; she only looked a great wide far-away look. Mrs. Peterson answered, ' I never hears them quarrel,' she said, smiling, and looking back at the little girl. ' That one you was kind eno' to send was to have been called Rose, and this one Rosyblue; but poor Mill she don't care for them now. She ha'f ondressed Rosyblue the day before yesterday; but she were not strong enough to dress herr again. So there is the poor creature left standin' in her shimmy.' Little Milly still sat watchful and speechless while Mrs. Peterson sat down and went on with her little monologue. ' Peterson he has to carry her upstairs at night; we got her little bed on the floor in our room. She used to sleep down here, but, bless you, I was up and down ha'f the night. I've not had a right sleep for a week, and my back do ache holdin' her; she do sleep so badly. It's " O dear!" and " O my!" and " O how can I!" T'other morning she was still complainin' like, and I says, " Milly, that's the night's litan'," and she left off directly. She is a good little girl, Milly is. One day she got out into the passage, and we thought she was going to be well; but 'twas no use. I often says to her, " Milly, if ye should be dying, what should you like your little sister to have?" Milly says she should like to go to heaven if Mrs. G—— is there. I asked her t'other day, if she should like to go back to the Union to be nursed; but she don't want to go —do ye, Milly?' said her foster-mother with a tender look. The child gave a faint smile, and shook her dark shaggy head. 'The doctor says her heart and her liver, and her stomach is all in bits,' said Mrs. Peterson. 'He didn't mention her lungs, but no doubt they'll go too.' She spoke openly and simply, as people do who have not learnt artificial paraphrases for the inevitable truths of life, but Peterson had walked I don't know how many miles to get a doctor for the 'poor little maid;' all the strawberries in the garden were for her; all the best they had to give—their night's rest, their kind hearts' overflow. I don't think there is any comment needed to the little story. Mrs. Peterson followed us out to say the Doctor, when he came last, had told them they must not hope to save the child. If Milly had been their very own they could not have been more tender.

What does it mean? Does it mean that the world is a happier, kinder, better world than we have been brought up to acknowledge? I have just heard someone say that perfection does exist in this life, though we are too timid to believe it. Is this true? The elements are to be found scattered everywhere. To each one of us the harmonies which might be are so near at times; the possibilities of happiness, the wild possibilities of perfection, so deep stirring in our hearts that we cannot help believing in them, even though we put out our hands again and again only to grasp whole dust-heaps of disappointment, of ashes, and dead leaves; and if we start from our fancies with a thrill of keen regret, the very pain with which we realise that they were but dreams, not realities, seems to speak to us of the truth of some actual realisation somewhere else, some other day, for others, perhaps, if not for ourselves. Is it sad to let the fancy go? It would be worse a thousand thousand times if it had not come; for rainbows, and bubbles, and dreams are realities, flashes that brighten the twilight of life, in radiations from the great Light of a clearer truth.

At all events, it is no dream that there are children dying and utterly wrecked for want of homes, homes sad for want of children; that there are kind souls ready, out of the abundance of their hearts, to pour out upon others the love that is but a pain and a regret when it is constrained within bonds that it longs to burst. Of all the well-meant failures of life, the busy about nothingnesses, the honest endeavours after confusion and ill-success, it is not necessary to speak. We have had most of us to acknowledge our mistakes again and again; but even in the midst of it all, here and there comes a success and a more complete achievement. Of course this may not always be the case : now and then the most careful plan may fail from one reason or another. The visitor may be deceived, the homes ill-chosen : the boarding-out system cannot pretend to infallibility any more than any other of the makeshifts of life ; but it is out of doors and open to daily inspection, and not enclosed within four walls : it has nature and human sympathy upon its side ; and it seems to the writer one of those endeavours of which their good sense and simplicity are the best recommendations.

I will conclude by quoting the following extract from Colonel E. S. Grant's ' Practical Guide.' Colonel Grant says : ' The rules on this subject, submitted by Mr. Henley, in his report on the boarding-out system in Scotland, are so sensible, and so similar in almost every respect to those already adopted in the Bath Union, that they are given here *in extenso :* '—

The following classes should under no circumstances be boarded out :—

(*a.*) Illegitimate children of widows still living.

(*b.*) Other illegitimate children whose mothers are still living.

(*c.*) Children deserted by one parent.

(*d.*) Children whose parents are living.—*Note.* These classes are not excluded in Scotland, but are so in

England by the present Poor Law regulations. How far some of them might be modified is deserving of consideration.

2. Deserted children should not be boarded out till they have been for some time in the workhouse.

3. Children should not usually be boarded with relations.—*Note.* In some English unions this is extensively practised; but although, as a general practice, it is believed to give rise to imposition and other evils, there are cases in which it seems very desirable.

4. No child should be boarded with a person who is, or otherwise would be, in receipt of parochial relief.—*Note.* This has been done in some cases, and with apparent good results.

5. A child, before it is boarded out, should be passed by the medical officer, and a certificate given that it is in a proper state, mentally and bodily, to be sent out.—*Note.* This is a most necessary rule, as otherwise cutaneous and other diseases might be carried into and spread in villages; and any physical defect, such as the loss of one eye, partial deafness, or any deformity, should be noticed in the certificate.

6. Not more than two children, except in the case of a family, should be sent to one house.—*Note.* This should depend whether the foster-parents have any

children of their own, and upon the amount of accommodation, as three children can be well cared for in one family.

7. Brothers and sisters should usually be kept together.

8. The sexes should, as far as possible, be separated in the sleeping-rooms.

9. Children over seven years of age should not sleep in the same room with married people.

10. Children should be boarded out as young as possible.—*Note.* And may be kept until they are eligible to be placed out in service, which in some unions is considered to be the case at the age of thirteen; but at the district school at Hanwell no *girl* is sent out to service until she is fourteen, and the writer thinks there are obvious reasons for extending it to this latter age for the case of girls.

11. Children should be removed—1st. If they are kept away from school, Sunday-school, or place of worship; 2nd. If lodgers are put in the same room with the children; 3rd. If children are taken in to board from other unions or parishes; 4th. Or from private people.—*Note.* The 2nd rule regarding lodgers is particularly necessary to be observed, especially where there are girls.'

I would only add to this extract the opinion of a

person who has thoroughly and devotedly studied the subject, and who is, perhaps better than anybody else, qualified to speak. The danger of abuse is very great, says this lady, but the more she sees of the working of the system *under proper supervision*, the more convinced she is of its benefit. It can, however, only be applied to orphans; the number of homes is limited, and the influence of parents removing their children from time to time is fatal to the success of the scheme.

A CITY OF REFUGE.

This said, his powerful wand he waved anew ;
  Instant a glorious angel-train descends—
The Charities to wit, of rosy hue ;
  Sweet love, their looks a gentle radiance lends,
And with seraphic flame compassion blends.
  At once delighted to their charge they fly,
When lo ! a goodly hospital ascends,
  In which they bade each lenient aid be nigh
That could the sick-bed soothe of that sad company.
                                          THOMSON.

To be well, to be ill, to be sad, to be cross ; to feel jars that shake, pains that tear and burn, and weary nerves that shrink and flutter, or that respond so strangely and dully to the will that it seems almost as if we were scarcely ourselves, at times, when, longing to feel and to sympathise with the emotion of others, we are only conscious of a numb cold acquiescence in their gladness or pain : all this is in the experience of us all, of the most happy as well as of the least happy alike, of the softest and hardest hearted. Only with some it is the experience of an instant and with others of a lifetime.

The range of this mysterious gamut teaches us, perhaps, something of the secret of what others are feeling; and in the same way that the sick and unhappy may imagine what vigour, hope, love, the fervour of life and youth mean, the fortunate may guess now and then at the sorrows of years, understand the hopelessness, the patience, the disappointment of a lifetime—guess at it for an instant as they stand by a sick-bed or see the poor wayfarer lying by their path. There is a group I have now in my mind that many of us may have noticed of late—some tired people resting on the roadside, a sunset marsh beyond; they have lighted a fire of which the smoke is drifting in the still air, and the tired eye looks out at the spectator and beyond him in the unconscious simplicity of suffering. We all understand it, though we have perhaps never in all our lives rested for the night, wearied, by a ditch-side. It is so true to life that we who are alive instinctively recognise its truth and uncomplaining complaint.

The persons of whom I am going to write just now, are most wise in these sadder secrets of life, which they have learnt by long years of apprenticeship. Poor souls! We have all come across them at one time or another. Sometimes we listen to their complaint, sometimes we don't; sometimes we put out a helping hand to pull them along, sometimes we get weary, and let them go. But although it is easy enough to help our brothers and sisters seven times—more easy than to forgive them, it is difficult enough for us individually to help them seventy times seven times, and in this must lie the great superiority of institutions over individual effort, of which the kindness is left to chance and to good-natured impulse, instead of being part of a rule that works on in all tempers and at all times.

It seemed to me the other day that it was real help that was being given to some afflicted persons whom I was taken to see, at the Incurable Hospital on Putney Common, a few of the afflicted out of all those that are stricken and in trouble, and in numbers so great that, for the most part, we might pass on in despair if it were not for the good hope of present and future help such places afford.

We crossed Putney Bridge one bright spring day, and drove up through the quaint old Putney High Street. The lilacs were beginning to flower in the gardens and behind the mossy old walls. When we had climbed the hill we came out upon a great yellow gorsy common, where all the air was sweet with the peach scent of the blossom. Its lovely yellow flame was bursting from one bush and from another, and blazing against the dull

purple green of the furze. We had not very far to go.
The carriage turned down a green lane, of which the trees
and hedges did not hide glimpses of other lights and other
blossoming commons in the distance; and when we
stopped it was at a white lodge, of which the gate was
hospitably open, and from whence a shady green sweep led
us to a noble and stately house, which was once Melrose Hall, but which is now the Hospital for Incurables.

A little phalanx of bath chairs was drawn up round
the entrance, and in each a patient was sitting basking in
this first pleasant shining of summer sun. The birds were
chirping in the tall trees overhead, the little winds were
puffing in our faces, and those of the worn, wan, tired
creatures, who had been dragged out to benefit by the
comforting freshness of the day. Some of them looked
up—not all—as we drove to the door.

M. sent a small boy with a card to ask for admission
for some friends of Mr. H.'s, and we waited for a few
minutes until the answer came. All the time that we
were waiting, an eager, afflicted young fellow was trying
hard to make himself intelligible to the sick man in the
bath chair next to his own. The poor boy could only
make anxious uncouth sounds; the sick man to whom he
was speaking listened for a while, and then shook his head

and turned wearily away. So it wasn't all sunshine even
in the sunshine in the lovely tree-shaded garden, with the
chirruping birds and lilac buds coming out. There
were some attendants coming and going from chair to
chair. There were other little carriages slowly progressing along the distant winding paths of the garden,
and presently the message came that we might be
admitted. The matron was away, but the head-nurse said
she would show us over the place; and she led the way
across the vestibule with its pretty classical ornamentation, opening the tall doors and bringing us into the
stately rooms where a different company had once
assembled, and yet it was not so very different after all,
for pain and ill-health are no excessive respecters of
persons. The Duke of Argyll, who was chairman at the
last anniversary dinner, spoke of some of the persons who
used to meet in these very rooms once upon a time, before
they were turned to their present uses; among the rest
Sir Walter Scott and Lockhart, and Sir Humphry Davy.
I could almost fancy the kind and familiar face of Sir
Walter looking on with gentle interest and compassion at
the pathetic company which is now waiting in the big
drawing-room of Melrose Hall, with the stately terrace
and lofty windows that let in the light so bountifully—
lame, blind, halt and maimed, from London highways and

the distant country by-ways. They sit in groups round the tables and windows, busy, somewhat silent. At the end of the room there is a golden-piped organ, the gift of the treasurer. A governess, who is one of the patients, often plays to the others upon it, and so do the ladies who visit the place. Once when I was there someone opened the instrument and began to play. As the music filled the room we all listened, beating a sort of time together. It seemed like a promise of bett:r things to those who were listening, for themselves and for others. This sitting-room is a lofty, stately place, as I have said, with columns and mouldings. All about there are comfortable chairs and tables, and spring sofas for aching spines that cannot sit upright, tables for work, over which all these patient creatures are bending. They have still tranquil faces for the most part, quiet and pale, and resting for a time in the refuge into which they have escaped out of the weary struggle and crowd of life. The privilege is sad enough, heaven knows, and the price they have paid for it is a heavy one.

The head-nurse went from one to another, and the faces all seemed to light up to meet hers. It is a very simple and infallible sign of love and of confidence. 'It would not do for me to pity them too much,' the kind nurse said; 'I always try to speak cheerfully to them.'

We who only come to look on may pity and utter the commonplaces of compassion and curiosity. How tired the poor things must be of the stupid reiteration of adjectives and exclamations. There was one old woman, so nice and with such sweet eyes, that I could not help sitting down by her and saying some one of those platitudes that one has recourse to. She didn't answer, but only looked at me with an odd long look.

'She cannot speak,' the nurse whispered, beckoning me away.

A few of the patients were reading, but only a few. 'Good Words' seemed to be popular, and the story in it is particularly liked, they told me. Some of the patients do plain work, and as I was speaking to one of them the door opened, and a good-natured-looking man came in.

'Any of the ladies like to go out for a drive to-day?' he said in a brisk business-like tone.

Two or three voices answered, 'Only Miss ——,' and then Miss —— began beckoning and waving her hand from the other end of the room, and was rolled off accordingly for her drive in the garden-chair.

It was not my first visit to the hospital; but though a year had passed, there were many of the faces as I remembered them sitting in the same corners, stitching and hooking, blind women knitting, the clever, patient fingers weaving an interest into their lives with threads of cotton and wool; one gentle-looking old lady, in a frill cap, was working a pair of slippers, dull red with bright green spots. She had but two fingers to work with, and only, I think, this one painful crippled hand; but she was working away on a frame to which her canvas was fixed.

'I *cannot* like your colours this time, Mrs. ——,' the nurse said; 'your last slippers were so pretty, and your work is so beautiful, that it is quite a pity you should not have pretty-coloured wools to set it off.'

The old lady shook her head; she wouldn't be convinced. 'These are lovely wools, my dear,' she said. 'I shall certainly go on with them. It's all your want of taste, that is what I think.' And she nodded her head and laughed and stitched on with fresh interest.

As we went upstairs we were shown lifts and pulleys and all sorts of comfortable appliances for the use of the patients. I could not help admiring the extreme order and neatness of all the arrangements, and the freshness and ventilation of all the places we went into.

In one of the rooms upstairs a funny old fellow, in a tall night-cap, was stitching away at his torn shirt-sleeves. He was sitting quite by himself in a big ward, with many empty beds in it. He laughed when he saw us, winked, waved his night-cap with an air, and then informed us he was the oldest patient, and was doing a bit of work; he didn't like to trust his shirt to others—not he—he was a poor old bachelor, he had to sew his own buttons on—and he was then very mysterious and confidential about a shirt which had been lost at the wash a year ago. Dark suspicions evidently were still haunting him on the subject, but he cheered up, winked, laughed, waved his night-cap again to us when we went away out of the room. 'She is my greatest joy and comfort,' he said, with a bow to the nurse, who could not help laughing. The men have much more courage than the women, they keep about until the last, this lady told us; women would be in bed and refuse to get up, when the men crawl downstairs day after day, and insist upon making the effort.

And yet in the men's sitting-room there is a much sadder, duller, and more helpless community than in the women's. The numbers are fewer, and in most cases the brain seems more hopelessly affected. One boy was making paper fly-catchers, but I don't think any of the others were doing anything. I have a vision of an old man sitting at a table, while we were there, trying to take up a broken piece of bread. His hand passed beyond it again and again; it was by a sort of chance that he feebly clutched it at last and carried it to his mouth.

It didn't seem much to be able to walk away, to look back, to remember what we had seen ; and yet how is it that we are not on our knees in gratitude and thankfulness for every active motion of the body, every word we speak, every intelligent experience and interest that passes through our minds ?

There was a great scampering of children's feet in one of the passages as we came up the wooden stairs, and some bright eyes peeped at us, and three little girls in the short kilts and plaid ribbons of middle-class London retreated into a room of which the door was wide open, and fled to a bedside, where they all stood shyly in a row until we could come up. Our guide led the way and we followed her in, and there from the bed a pair of big bright brown eyes, not unlike the childrens', were turned upon us, and a handsome young girl, lying flat on her back, greeted us with a good-humoured smile. 'Aunt Mary' the children called her. Big and handsome and strong though she looked, this poor bright-looking Aunt Mary was completely paralysed as far as the head : she could not move hand or foot ; it was a dead body with this bright bonny living face to it. She did not look more than six or seven and twenty ; she had nice thick brown hair and even white teeth. With these this brave girl had imagined for herself that with practice she should be able to hold a pencil and guide it, tracing the words against a little desk that was so contrived as to swing across her bed when wanted. She was perfectly enchanted with the contrivance, and said it was the greatest delight to her to be able to write for herself. The doctor, she told me, not without pride, had been quite surprised to receive a letter from her one day, and could not imagine how she had written it for herself.

Leaving her we crossed a passage and came to a room not far off, where two women were lying; one of them had got something in her bed that she was caressing and talking to in a plaintive pitying voice, patting as if it was some animal or living thing. M., wondering what it could be, went up to see; she found that it was a watch of which the glass was broken. In the other bed a gentle-faced very old woman was lying, afflicted with palsy. Her poor body shook and trembled painfully as I stood beside the bed, and her hands, in attempting to meet, crossed and passed each other again and again. I said to her that I could not think how she bore her affliction so patiently, for the head-nurse had told me that her sweetness was quite touching; she never complained, never said an impatient word.

'When I am not well,' I said, 'I grumble and complain to everybody, even for little trifling ailments. You make me feel ashamed.'

' Ah,' the old woman answered gently, ''tis good to be still.'

She said it so simply and quietly that it came home to me then and there, the gentle remonstrance coming from the weary bed where so many long hopeless hours had passed for her, where she lay patiently enduring while we walked away. The other woman was still talking to her watch, and did not notice us as we passed.

The room, which was formerly the library, makes a delightful room for one or two of the patients. It has tall windows, opening on a broad terrace-like balcony, and beyond are the same elm-trees and glimpses of sky and common that we see from the big room down below. There is one great sufferer here who does not often get down. She cannot sit up, from spine disease, and when I saw her last she was lying by the window, with her face wrapped in cotton wool, poor soul, for she had been suffering tortures from neuralgia ; and though the dentist had come and taken out two of her teeth she was still in pain. The head-nurse pitied her, and recommended a little blister to draw away the inflammation. The patient shrank and laughed and shook her head. She couldn't bear any more pain, she whispered imploringly; she wanted so to get down for a change. A little belladonna plaster where nobody would see it, under her cap, so that it shouldn't show and look ugly, and where nobody would see it, please. There were two good-sized baskets standing on a table near this patient. They were literally piled and packed with tracts. 'We get a great many,' she said, seeing me look at them; 'more than we can read.' Poor soul! I hope her belladonna plaster has done her good. As we came away, the nurse stopped for a moment to speak to quite an elegant old lady, who was sitting up, extremely nicely dressed, in a chair, with a grand cap and ribbons, and a knitted lace shawl.

It was getting late, and we began to pass blue-garbed under-nurses carrying little trays with teas. The patients who are well enough to get down have their meals in the big dining-room, but these little trays looked very nice and appetising; the whole order of the place is perfectly appointed. Some of the rooms upstairs were like little bowers, with pots flowering round the windows, bird-cages hanging up, pictures on the walls of the friends or the sick people. One pale face looked at us as we passed a white bed. Her room was like a little chapel, with light streaming in from through the flowers and bird-cages and the climbing greens upon the casement, and the poor martyr, alas! lying on her rack.

There was another pale face that looked out, too, as we passed; but as we were going in the nurse stopped us, and said she feared the patient was dying; and so we moved away. I asked to be taken to a sick woman I remembered a year before—a kind, merry person, who had gone through a terrible operation. She was in bed still in the same room, still looking the same, bright, friendly, with smart little curls, and a friend gossiping by her bedside.

To see such a place as this as it is, to be sorry enough and tender enough to continue to sympathise with all its suffering, would need, I think, a mind scarcely human in its powers. The whole subject is so vast, so mysterious, and utterly beyond our comprehension, that it is easier to dwell upon the comforting kindness, the helps to endurance and courage, that are to be found here more than in any place I ever saw. There was one poor girl who had been lying for seven years upon her side. All the lines of those seven years seemed to me in her white wan face. She did not complain, though her eyes complained for her; but she said she had a nice water bed—that was a great comfort; and her cup of milk and toast for tea were beside her, so nicely served and prepared that it was a pleasure to see the little meal; and there was a great bunch of spring lilac buds in a glass

that another patient had brought to her out of the garden
—the first of the year.

And so with all its endless combination of pain and
of sorrow this hospital does not send us away sad and
rebellious at heart, as do many refuges for sorrow and
trouble : for instance, a workhouse ward, where there are
cases often enough that might be admitted here if there
was room for them; or a sick close room, in a narrow
street, where the healthy and unhealthy are shut up together for days and for nights. Here, where there is
such great suffering, there is also great comfort and
tender nursing and companionship; there are trees, and
grasses, and sweet lilac and gorse-blown winds, close at
hand. There is a certain liberality in all the arranging
and economy of the place that seems to disprove the
practical notion of Charity being a grinding, snubbing
sort of personage, who would like to get the scales into
her own hand if she could, and to weigh out her kind-
nesses by the ounce. Such a plan as this would defeat
its own object if the inmates were not well and generously
tended. Perhaps I should in fairness confess to having
heard of the bitter complaints of one of the patients, who
had a fancy for lobsters every day, and who was denied
this delicacy; but she is not the first to long for the
unattainable, and certainly, to some of us, grumbling is
almost as great a privilege as eating lobsters every day.

It seems fitting and seemly that in a great country like ours there should be munificent charities, comforting and liberal in their dealings; one only longs that their doors should be set open more widely, if possible, to the crowds that are waiting about them for admission. Here is a paper before me: it is two years old, and I know not how many have succeeded in their efforts; but looking at it, it would indeed appear as if the wayfarers were lying all along the road, and the Samaritan passing by has only one ass to carry them away upon.

These biographies are not very long in writing, and I may quote one or two that I have copied off the list :—

Paralysis, loss of speech . . .	. Captain of a Steam-vessel.
Disease of the Brain and Debility .	. Governess.
Disease of the Spine and Joints, Paralysis.	Governess.
Paralysis	. Captain of a Mail Steamer.
Disease of Spine and Throat . .	. Schoolmistress.
Injury to Spine	. Working Engineer.
Paralysis and Asthma . . .	. Master Tailor.

These are seven out of 160—a whole sad life of labour and suffering told in a few words. There are laundry-women, servants, journeymen, dressmakers. It is a comfort to turn back to those who are safely within reach of kind hands, helpful appliances, and friendly words such as those which I heard the head-nurse speaking to her patients as I followed her about from one room to another.

It has been proposed lately to establish a hospital on somewhat similar principles for children, with this one comforting proviso that the children are to be cured if possible. A doctor of very great experience and reputation, who once superintended a children's hospital in Paris, and for whose opinion his friends have a great and just regard, was speaking on the subject to a friend, and saying that there are many chronic cases in childhood deemed incurable which are in reality perfectly curable, but which require a doctoring of fresh air, of regular diet, of cleanliness, &c., that it is impossible they should receive at home. I believe it was in this way the idea originated, and now the hospital really seems in a fair way to being established. Four or five people have each promised a hundred a year towards it, of their own accord, without solicitation. When a thousand a year is assured the hospital will be begun. A big garden is the first thing wanted, for the children to play in and to exercise their limbs. The children's hospitals, admirable as they are, cannot keep the little things always, and are obliged to change their patients constantly. Anybody who has seen the piteous crowd waiting at the doors in Great Ormond Street will understand the necessity there is for more and more such help and assistance to the good work which is done there.

Only yesterday there was a little patient who had been discharged almost cured from what seemed a hopeless and chronic illness, after only two months of care in the children's hospital, who was begging and praying to go back from his home in the back kitchen with the mangle. One patient! A hundred—a thousand, to-morrow, if one searched for them, and knew what to do with them when one had found them, or where to send them. This incurable children's hospital has, however, good friends among people who love their own children, and who are willing to come forward with generous hearts and great sums to assist it, and there is great hope of its speedy establishment.

But one of the greatest difficulties that have to be contended against at present in the management of anything of the sort is the extraordinary system which has grown up all about us, and which seems to be almost impossible to contend with.

I have the reports before me now of two hospitals, conducted by different people, each doing a great and important work. How much the help might be extended if the machinery were more simple and the manner of administering aid less complicated and costly, it would be hard to say. A great country like ours should have noble charities ; niggardliness seems to me a far more deprecable fault than excess of generosity in the help afforded. But what people complain of, and with reason, I think, is that part of the money they subscribe, instead of going to the objects of their charity, the attendance, the food, the comfort of the patients, is by the mere fashion and necessity of the day put to strange and vexing purposes—to printing little books that nobody reads, to sending circulars that go straight into the fire, to arranging an elaborate machinery of admission that in no way benefits the patients. The postage and advertising and printing of two hospitals comes to 1,300*l.* in the course of a year; of which 100*l.* a year for the postage of each hospital represents something like, say, 240,000 letters. I don't know how many hard days' work 240,000 letters would mean, and how many of them are mere circulars, or how many might be spared; but it seems as if so much of our energy went into advertising and crying our good intentions that, in time, there will be no strength or time left for anything else.

An experiment has been partially tried at an institution where no canvassing is allowed, and no public election. The votes—so a friend to whom I had spoken on the subject writes—are quietly 'counted at the office, and the result is announced.' He, however, goes on to say that this plan is not successful in a pecuniary point of view; and a charity in which all the power was vested in a committee would have still less chance of success. I had spoken to him on the subject of this incurable hospital, and asked why the most pressing cases were not elected by a competent board instead of those people having the best chance who had most friends, and whose friends were most active in their behalf. 'You do not know,' he said, 'all the outcry and discontent that such a proceeding would give rise to. We should be accused of unfairness, of partiality. We ourselves dislike the system as much as you do, but we cannot help ourselves; we are obliged to give in to the common cry and common weakness of human nature, and to take the good and the bad as they come together.' And so it is, and we must be content to accept things as they are; but with the bad and the good there is certainly given to each one of us an instinct for better things, and is it quite impossible that any effort should ever be made to disembarrass good and noble things from the cumber of selfish interest and patronage which weight them so heavily? Is there no divine indignation left among us strong enough to over- turn the tables of the money-changers, to chase away those that sell doves in the temple?

What a horrible complication it seems looking at it honestly with unbiassed eyes! Is it possible that we are sunk so low that we cannot give freely and with generous, tender, and grateful hearts, without this hideous system of patronage, of rules, of complimentary clapping, of bad dinners and wines, of subscription lists and names affixed to little miserable scraps of crumbs from our table that should make us ashamed instead of complacent, as we turn to B or A or whatever our initial may be, and see our honest name set down with a shabby price to it like the cheap rubbish in a huxter's shop?

I think Mr. Froude, in his essay on 'Representative Men,' has put words to a difficulty which a great many have felt, but which few people have put words to before. It is a difficulty of words in itself: and concerns the constant cry of the age, the advice of the preachers, which comes to us from every side, calling and urging us to be good, and bidding us be noble, crying that to us is entrusted a mission of love and of charity. 'Go forth,' so they say, 'Go forth and fulfil it.' And then the difficulty occurs to some of us, where are we to go forth? how are we to be good? when are we to be noble? Passive charity is useless without a practical use for it, and so the teachers acknowledge. But have you no neighbours to tend? they cry, no sufferers to comfort by the way? Are there no wayfarers who have fallen by the roadside? And all this is true enough—too true, alas!—for the wounded wayfarers may be counted by thousands.

And yet as I write I feel that the preacher is right in the main, though his talk is vague, and he has not sufficiently applied the science of the truth he instinctively feels, to the daily facts of life. Life, I suppose, must for most of us be a rule of thumb—if I may be allowed so to speak ; and to go forth must mean to take a cab and call upon a dull friend, or to protest, when we see occasion, against wrong-doing of any sort, or to take trouble about things that do not interest or concern us very much. There are some noble and honest natures to whom instinctively the impulse comes for action, and for right and great action, too—some lives whose love and example are benedictions to those who are about them—one noble tender heart leavening the dough by its unconscious generous tenderness and example. These people need ask no questions, for theirs are the voices that answer, not in preaching, but by their simpleness, their truth, their tender impulse. As a rule we who ask are not the people who work and achieve.

A woman died not long ago who had lived some twenty-six or twenty-seven years one of those lives that do not question for themselves, but that seem like answers to the vague aspirations of others. I do not know if I may write her name, but those who have loved this lady will know how it is that I quote her as one of the examples of this bright and resolute devotion, that shines like a beacon in the storm to those who are wandering about in search of a way. She was the head-nurse of the hospital at Lincoln, where in time a terrible mortality and illness overtaxed her strength, and her strength of life being gone, she died.

I have drifted away from the incurables a little; any-one who likes to go and see the place is welcome, and no one can go without coming away touched and humbled, and perhaps a little the better for the visit.

The privilege is a sad one, heaven knows, that belongs to all these poor people; but sad as it is, when one looks at these gentle and tranquil faces, it is hard to think of those still outside, in a world that looks peaceful enough, and pleasant and green to-day from these open windows, but which is a weary, illimitable place for those who, with paralysed limbs and racked bodies, are hopelessly and helplessly trying to escape from the overwhelming tramp of the legions by which they are overwhelmed: legions that advance upon them, as one has sometimes dreamt in dreams, by every road, by every turn of life. I can imagine poor wearied, hunted souls trying to fly from want, from anguish, from loneliness, from neglect and cruel words, but their limbs will not carry them; they cannot work, they are too weak even to beg, friends weary,

subsistence fails, their own hearts fail. The Duke of
Argyll says that nearly 6,000 people annually leave the
London hospitals suffering from incurable disease. Of
these how many must there be in miserable condition.
One's own heart might indeed fail at the thought of such
tremendous calamity; but for 6,000 incurables, how many
hundreds of thousands are there not among us who are
well and strong, and who have enough to live and enough
to give to others, and asses and pennies to spare for others
in their need ?

I cannot help mentioning one or two other small
enclosed cities of refuge, one in Queen Square, Blooms-
bury, which was founded by two ladies for children
afflicted by hip disease, an illness so tedious and so long
that other hospitals are obliged to refuse them admittance.
Anyone who has an hour to spend on sick children may
see the wards, the November twilight, the patient little
creatures under their crimson blankets, lying waiting—
for health let us hope.   One small patient jumped up
when she saw the lady superintendent, and caught her
round the waist with those dear little outstretched children's arms so ready to love, so wide open to kindness.
This little girl had a bed near a window. 'I see ever
so many people walking in that garden,' she told me ,
'look! look! there's someone now.   *I* can walk now;

that little boy got up one day, but he's had to go to bed again.' This little patient has been ill for many years, but is recovering at last. There was another little thing who had learnt to talk in the hospital; it was a baby when it came. I think I must have seen nearly fifty little patients lying in their cribs. Their poor little wrists are sometimes affected as well as their hips and knees. Many of them were singing little songs to themselves, others were shouting out to the nurses, some of them were thoughtfully staring at their tea-things and waiting for their tea. 'Do you like eggs for your tea?' I asked a little boy who gave a little silent confidential nod. The lady in charge took me out of the ward of children into a large room with great pleasant windows and some ten little empty cots. 'It is melancholy, isn't it, to see all these empty beds,' she said. 'There is another ward down below also empty. We have more than twenty empty beds and nearly forty children on the books waiting for admission; one does long to see the ward open.'

And so by the loving perversion of helpful charity, it comes to pass that illness, trouble, and cruel disease are made welcome guests within the walls of the old houses where these kind ladies live, their stricken little flock lying prostrate all around them. In town and country villages, and seaside places, people are at work, and sisters of charity of some sort or another (for it is not the quilled cap which makes the difference) are nursing and tending their little patients, stirred by the same gentle, natural impulse, which makes real mothers love their little ones with an anxious pain and love and fear, in which some women find the greatest happiness which this world can bestow.

I cannot help mentioning here that I have seen yet another quiet city of refuge down by the river-side. A newly-planted garden spreads before its narrow windows, a terrace, along which carriages and omnibuses are rolling, and then again the waters with their drifting freight gleam in long lines beyond the terrace. This pretty old-fashioned house is at No. 46 Cheyne Walk. It has an old staircase and deep window sills, and an open space at the back. It is called Cheyne Home for Sick Children, and it is indeed a real home, and one from which the little family need not fear that it will be sent away. As the children lie in their cots they watch the steamers and the barges float by, and the carriages as they roll along the great embankment. The other day when I came I heard the childish voices calling in great excitement to one another, 'There's a 'orse, and a man on him.' 'Oh, he'll tumble off,' from one little fellow.

'No, he won't,' cries the opposite crib, and then the only crutch among all these little bed-ridden babies stumps up in a great hurry just as the man on the prancing horse disappears.

But a 'funny carriage' drives by to make up for the disappointment. These windows are live picture-books of which the leaves turn every moment as the people go by. The changes on the river never cease, and the opposite shores gleam with light. 'It is such a pretty colour over there in the mornings,' says a pale boy, called Arthur, lying on his back, and looking up from a slate upon which he is busy drawing something under the direction of a young lady who seems proud of her pupil's attainments. She shows me a slate-pencil river with a slate-pencil bridge, and a neatly-ruled frame to enclose it all, which Arthur has just completed. The children here are very ill indeed, they are mostly suffering from hopeless complications of disease, and the nurses of the institution in Queen Square are thankful that there should be some one place, where these poor little martyrs may at least be left in peace to rest upon their beds and to wait the end. The nurse showed me a folded little bed from which one childish sorrow and pain had passed away for ever.

I remember once hearing of a poor little child, sent from hospital to hospital, and from nurse to nurse, wearied with pain, frightened by strangers, having found at last one faithful tender friend out of all the strange men and women through whose hands it passed. This friend said to me, ' You think it sad that poor little Lizzie should die —to me death appears to be the only home for these poor little hunted creatures, for whom there seem no resting places here.'

In this little home by the river the little ones once admitted may remain, and need not fear being driven from the kind sheltering walls.

IF some mighty spirit were to give us the gift of seeing into the lives of the people who are passing like ourselves through the slush and mud and dim vapours of a London winter, we might well be scared, we middle respectable classes, hurrying along from one comfortable firelit world to another,—worlds closed in by curtains and shutters, warmed by fires and carpets, steaming with the flavour of good things. We go out into the streets, and hurry back again to our snug paradises, where white-robed houris are singing and playing upon grand pianos with golden strings, where ministering butlers and waiters and parlour-maids are pouring claret into thin glasses that sparkle, where tables are spread *à la Russe* with fruit and with flowers, and the faithful are feasting in companies of six, eight, and ten at this season of the year. As they feast they are reclining upon seats of mahogany and rosewood, and discoursing of past and future deeds. Shining is the broadcloth, spotless the

P

white linen; veils and crowns are set on the heads of the matrons, and wreaths lie on the maiden's heavy tresses that are plaited and stained to gold; and soft words are uttered; and smoking viands pass round between the pauses of the conversation. But, speaking seriously, it seems almost impossible to some of us, living in a certain fashion, to realise the state of mind in which certain other people alongside are existing,—people whose chief possessions are a few rags perhaps, a body to hunger and weary with, aching feet to tramp along the pavement, the fierce winds blowing at the corners, the gusts of rain, and the piled-up mud in the streets. The wet railings to lean against are theirs too, a kerbstone perhaps to rest upon, and the bitter fruits of the knowledge of hunger, of patience, of utter weariness, of the length of the night.

'I daresay you don't know what it is to walk about all night long,' a woman said to me one day not long ago; and her eyes filled up with tears as she spoke quietly in a sort of whisper. 'I walked about three nights this week,' she said, 'till a person I met took pity on me, and let me into her room. She was only a poor woman; not a lady,' the woman said. 'She told me to come here.' 'Here,' was the women's ward in the Newport Market Refuge, a long room, with slender iron pillars, and a double row of narrow beds on either side of the middle passage. The beds were wooden frames stretched with sacking, and fastened to the wall. By each bed a woman was standing, waiting while someone at the far end of the room was busily preparing bowls of hot coffee and dividing hunches of white bread. One or two of the women looked scared and sad; but not all. Till this person spoke to me, I should never have guessed how the week had passed for her nor what straits she was in. I had even wondered to see her there, for her appearance was decent and respectable, and her face looked quiet and cheerful; only when she answered me her eyes filled with tears, and her voice failed. This was the only woman to whom I spoke; but I suppose there were some thirty of them in the long room, who had just been let in out of the rain.

I had come a long way, and the horse had struggled and stumbled through the black, twinkling mud, for it was dark and wet with rain this London winter's evening; dim crowds were flitting and hurrying along shadowy pavements that all the flaming gas-becks in the shop-fronts were not enough to lighten,—no sky overhead, no tops to the houses, but a dense Christmas vapour dripping upon the heads of the passers-by. We turned from gas to utter blackness, out of the long street which had put me in mind of some foreign street for odd stores, tobacco, bird-cages, jewellery-shops; and then we jolted into dark and lonely places where no lights were shining, and no one passed. The cab stopped, and the man asked me which was the way to go. A small shrill ghost appearing in a doorway, and hearing us talk of the Newport Refuge, screamed out to us to 'go ba-ack, turn to the roight, and then to the lef' agin;' and then, in another gloom, the stumbling horse stopped once more, and the driver opened the door of the cab. The rain was beginning to cease, but the drops still dripped as I stood in the middle of a muddy sheet, to which I could see no shore. As well as I could make out, we were in a narrow sort of court-passage, opening into a wider court, with tall tenements enclosing it. One or two people were standing round about something that looked like a big barn-door, half-open. 'In there, missus,' said a man with a pipe; and so out of the darkness I stumbled through the barn-door.

I was a little bewildered after my long drive by what seemed at first a dazzle of light, a din of voices, a sudden strumming of distant music. . . . . . I think I went up some steps. I saw a staircase, a passage, in which was a lighted window, and a man's face looking out over some books. A woman was standing at the window, a great round clock was ticking, and its hands were pointing to ten minutes past five. I asked the porter if this was the Refuge, and if the people were all in for the night? Yes, they were all come; some sixty of them, out of the street. 'We let them in early to-night,' said the man at the window, 'because of the rain.'

I myself was glad enough to get under shelter. I don't know how I should have felt if I had been walking about all day and all the night before, and all the day before that, and the night before that again, in the slough without, as some of the people had done who were just admitted. If I had come to ask for a night's lodging, the man at the window would have asked me my name, what I worked at, where I slept the night before. The other woman standing beside me said she made envelopes, had been turned off some weeks, meant to go to this place and that in the morning to ask for work; had tried all day long, and all the shops, and didn't know what she should do.

'There is no reason why you should not find employ-ment,' said the man at the window. 'People write as many letters in winter as in summer. You should ask at the manufactories instead of going to the shops. There is a man here to-night who had given up asking in des-pair. I sent him to Messrs. ——, and he got work im-mediately. You can go up.'

One of the committee, who had come in with a dripping umbrella, asked if the woman had ever been there before?

'No,' she said anxiously. 'Mrs. So-and-so in the court had took her in last night, and the neighbours told her to come.'

The porter nodded, and at this sign of Watchful's the poor Christiana, nothing loth, trudged up to her supper by the wooden stairs that led to the women's dormitories. It was a very simple affair, soon settled, and the man shut up his book for the night, for the people were all in. There they were, two long lines of names all the way down the page.

I followed Mr. C. through the men's ward, which was on the ground-floor. It was like the women's ward, more beds, more suppers preparing, and more weary folks waiting to eat, and rest a little while, before they started again on their rounds. As I walked after my friend down this narrow passage the many eyes fixed upon us made us glad to escape. I was surprised by the respectable self-respecting look of most of the refugees. They did not look as people often do in workhouses, with that peculiar half-hopeless, half-cunning face, which is so miserable to see. There were some workmen and others, shabbily dressed, but still respectable, and they had the appearance of shopmen or clerks or servants out of place. One boy, I remember, glanced up with a bright, handsome Lord Byron face as we passed, and I also carried away the vision of a melancholy old man with a ragged beard, sitting staring before him with his hands on his knees. After we left the ward, Mr. C. began telling me something of the people who came to it. They were of all trades and callings; clergymen, officers, schoolmasters, a well-known radical reformer, a billiard-marker, a surgeon. In last year's list I see fifty-one tailors and sixteen waiters were admitted. They come in for a night or two, or stay on longer if there seems any reason for it, or chance of employment. To some of us it may seem sad to read that no less than sixty-five soldiers took refuge in the ward last year, and that no other calling has sent so many applicants for relief. 'Of all who come,' said Watchful, 'they are the most difficult to provide for. We got one a situation in a county gaol the other day; but it is not always that we can help them.' Men of war, mulcted of their arms, discharged before they have served their time, knowing no trade, sick, helpless. It seems a hard fate enough. I heard of some poor invalided fellows coming back from India the other day, discharged, in high spirits at the prospect of getting away and seeing their friends and homes again. 'Good-by, you Asiatics!' one of them shouted, waving his cap as the train set off. The farewells are cheerful perhaps, but the welcomes awaiting these poor men at their journeys' end are not cheering to contemplate. I could not help wondering the other night, as I talked to my guide, who there was among the men of peace ready to fight their battles.

Here, in the Newport Refuge, many get helped, one way and another. Trouble and time are given ungrudgingly by the committee, by the people upon the establishment, and by the kindest of sisters, in her nice grey dress and white cap. This lady is in charge of the women's department. She sits in her quaint dark room, leading out of the women's sleeping-ward, with its glass doors opening every instant to admit one or other person,— application, complaint, enquiry, petition. The women come, the boys come, the committee comes, and its wives, and stray outsiders like myself; but there is a method in all these comings and goings, a meaning and an unaffected kindness and good-fellowship that impress one irresistibly. The sister told me to go and see the boys' refuge, and the kitchen, where all the suppers were preparing. It was a large kitchen on the ground-floor, with cocoa-nut matting and generous-looking pans and coppers, and a white cook watching the coffee-pots that were just beginning to boil.

The Newport Refuge not only takes in people to sleep for the night, and cooks their supper for them, but there are also some small folks whom it keeps altogether,— certain homeless boys, who live in the old house, and who are taught and fed, and finally started in life from this curious busy hive of a home. A painter dealing in lights

and sudden glooms might have found more than one
subject for his art, among the dark passages of this
ancient and high-roofed barn this foggy, flaring, winter's
night. Through an open door I caught sight of a little
group of tailors at work. They were in a long low play-
room, where I have been amused to see the boys darting
about in the twilight like imps at play, shouting, gallop-
ing, gambolling. Now the little imps were hard at work
in a bright corner of the dark room, squatting cross-legged
in a circle on the floor, round a tall lamp, and demurely
stitching at the rents and patches in their various
garments. Grey walls, grey boys, with their little brown
faces, a black master; strongly-marked shadows and
lights, a red handkerchief tied round a boy's neck,—it
does not take much to make up a harmonious picture.
The little fellows were unconscious of pictorial effect as
they sat cobbling and mending a few of the tears and
tatters that exist in this seam-ripped world. The triumph
of the tailors was a grand pair of trousers that one of the
little fellows had achieved, with all the buttons gleaming
brass. The conqueror himself, I believe, was despatched
to fetch the garment, which was displayed before us,—the
banner of the industrious little phalanx at our feet. The
master-tailor and the committee-man had a little talk
together, while I watched the boys' youthful fingers stick-

ing in stitches with much application, but some uncertainty. So-and-so was to be apprenticed, such an one had sent a good account of himself, another wanted to give up tailoring altogether; and when the little consultation was over we left the tailors, and climbed a winding stair. It seemed to lead us into the kingdom of boys. A cheerful jingle of sounds, scrapings, cheerful voices, met us from above, from below; small clumping steps and echoes; boys flying up and down, disappearing through doors. In one room, by the light of a blazing fire, a number of little fellows were trolling out a Christmas hymn, at the pitch of their childish trebles. In the intervals of this hymn came a brilliant accompaniment from above of I don't know what trumpets, trombones, flutes, executing some martial measure. The two strains went on quite independently of each other, and making noise enough, each in its own place, to deafen the auditors and drown every other sound.

One of the choristers was pointed to by the umbrella, and beckoned off to come and show us the sleeping-ward, where the boys each possess a box, a suit of Sunday-clothes, a bed, a grey blanket, and a red one, and a nice little pair of sheets, all doubled up like a rolypoly pudding, neatly cut through the middle.

The young chorister proceeded to make his bed very

nicely and expeditiously. While he was accomplishing this little task, I saw the grand pair of trousers being carefully put away in the box of their fortunate possessor.

Upstairs, in a sort of loft, where the bandsmen were practising, while the master beat time energetically the musicians pulled and blew at enormous instruments, by the music on the stands before them. The little fellows seemed to me like all the champions of Christendom manfully struggling with vomiting monsters and yawning dragons. One boy was solemnly puffing away at an ophicleide quite as big as he was, with an enormous proboscis that seemed ready to gobble him up each time it advanced; others gallantly grasped writhing brass serpents : a rosy-cheeked infant was playing on the flute, a boy on a bench was reading a song-book, a charwoman was scrubbing the floor. The sister, in her quaint grey gown, came up the stairs, and stood smiling at the overflowing music, and beckoning to us : for we could not hear her speak in the din of their youthful lungs and violent trumpets and trombones. She wanted us to come to the shoemakers, before they left off work.

So we left the musicians playing their triumphant march. Well may they play it, fortunate little musicians, rescued from the darkness without, where no stars are shining, and where monsters, not harmless and tameable such as these of brass and sound, are wandering ready to make a prey of children, and weakness, and helpless things, vainly struggling against the dark and deadly powers of ignorance and want.

The little shoemakers were finishing for the day. They lived at the other end of the building in a workshop all to themselves. There was a kind eager young master to direct them ; there were more gas-becks, more lights and shadows, more brown-faced boys, drills and lasts, very thick little boots on the floor, with nails, and shapes, and abundant energy. The sister laughed, seeing the little fellows' desperate efforts. ' Look at Carter,' she said, ' how hard he is working.' Carter grinned, but did not look up, and tugged away at his leather thongs more vigorously than ever. They offered to make me a pair of shoes. They had made some for the sister already. This very day a friend has consented to be measured for a pair of hobnailed boots. As we were finding our way downstairs back to the sister's room again, we began to meet trays of food, coming up apparently of their own accord. ' Go down, trays,' cried the sister, and the slices of bread, the mugs, &c., began slowly to descend again.

The sister told me that the little bandsman I had seen with the flute was the son of a soldier at the Cape, who had brought him to the Home before he left, and who regularly paid for him out of his earnings, and wished that he should be brought up a bandsman. Some children are drafted on to other institutions; some are apprenticed. Grown-up people are helped one way and another. And I must here gratefully acknowledge my own obligations for the kindness I have received in the home. I heard of a cook who had no clothes, but who knew of work. This man was given clothes, and allowed to live there long enough to save a few shillings out of his wages, so as to redeem his things and set up in a lodging for himself. The report tells of newspaper editors and musicians helped to employment. Servants come in great straits, and they, too, are assisted.

I have not space to set down all the ways and means, and people, and wants, and supplies that are brought together here.

It is some comfort to come away from these refuges and hospitals with a remembrance of children's laughter in the twilight, and voices at play, of troubles quieted, of the sick and wounded made whole, of a light of hope shining upon the arid and blighted vineyard, and cheering the failing labourers at work among the vines.

THE NEW FLOWER.

So the Prince grew up to be a man,
  Oh! the bonny bud 's blowing!
And ever the same fair course he ran,
  Oh! the bonny bud 's blowing!—T. WESTWOOD.

IT is like a story in a fairy book to hear how there was once a prince with a beautiful glass palace of his own, in which wonders of every lovely form and colour were to be seen, all blooming and flowering and scenting the air— great palms making triumphal arches with their beautiful leaves, and ferns springing up high overhead, throwing a green network against the crystal; and flowers of every sweetest perfume and colour. The story goes on to say that the prince, although the possessor of such lovely things, was not content; for he had not yet got the wonderful tree without a name, of which travellers had brought back histories from distant lands beyond the sea —a tree, they told him, that was more beautiful than anything he had in all his palace, and which it was almost impossible to procure. But the prince, nothing daunted, determined to possess it, and after taking information he despatched a mission to a distant empire, where a wise doctor of his own country had said that the tree was to be found. Some flowers had been given to him by a learned traveller, who had gathered them in a garden belonging to a monastery ' around the hill of Kogua, in the Saluen river, in the far-away kingdom of Birmah.' There the traveller had seen handfuls of the flowers of the tree thrown as offerings in the caves, before the images of Buddha. And meantime, while the mission was still absent on its travels, the prince caused a beautiful pot to be prepared to receive the tree when it should arrive—a wooden tub, all carved and kyanised, for greater security; and, in case the hearers of this fairy tale should not know what kyanising meant, they were told that it was a peculiar process by which wood was prepared and steeped, so that it should last for years, nor decay nor rot away.

And in time the mission returned to the prince, bringing back a specimen of the tree in triumph from the other end of the world. With great pomp and ceremony it was planted in the pot, and the prince and all the doctors hoped to see it grow and flourish, and give out the beautiful shining flowers of which they had heard so much.

But they hoped and waited in vain. Years and years went by, and the plant made no progress: no flowers grew upon it, and the doctors said it was because they had not yet waited long enough that the blossoms did not come. At last one of the doctors, more impatient than the rest, bethought him that perhaps the magnificent tub which had been prepared at such pains and expense might be itself the cause that, notwithstanding all their science, the tree did not flourish; and that perhaps the poisonous preparation in which the wood had been steeped to prevent it from decay was affecting the too susceptible plant. And this wise doctor was right in his surmise; for no sooner was the tree taken out of the grand and special tub which had been made for it and put into a common one than it began to rally and recover itself, and to throw out shoots.

This wise doctor was no other than Sir Joseph Paxton; the prince was the Duke of Devonshire; the palace was the palace of Chatsworth; the travellers were Dr. Wallich and his friend Mr. Crawfurd; the flower is the famous *Amherstia nobilis*—the splendid Amherstia, of which all the world has heard; and as for the fairy tale, it was told on Tuesday afternoon in the council room of the Horticultural Gardens by Mr. Bateman, F.R.S., and Vice-President of the Royal Horticultural Society, to about 300 people who had assembled to hear it, and to 'see a specimen of the beautiful flower which had bloomed after thirty years; for, on the day when Mr. Gladstone brought forward his Reform Bill the flames of the splendid Amherstia burst forth at last.

It was decided after some days to send specimens of these flowers to London, to the Horticultural Gardens, for all the world to see; but it almost seemed as if some adverse fate still attended the long-expected blossom, for, although it had already been delayed some thirty years, the railway company kept it back an hour longer, and the lecturer had to begin without it. However, he had not proceeded very far when a big box was carried in in triumph, and the great bright blossom of the Amherstia was displayed at last to view.

Perhaps it will be best to give Dr. Wallich's own description of the plant. He says :—

'The leaves are ample, pinnate, and of a dark green colour; while young they are glaucous, purple, and hang down loosely, together with the tender shoots to which they are attached. The leaflets are large, oblong, tapering into a most slender point, very glaucous underneath, and furnished with slender prominent ribs and nerves, the latter reaching towards the margin in a very elegant manner. The flowers are numerous and very large, scentless, of a brilliant vermilion colour diversified with three yellow spots. They are arranged in gigantic ovate bunches, pendulous on their long peduncle, and partially hidden beneath the profuse and elegant foliage.'

We cannot also refrain from quoting his history of the discovery.

In March 1825 Doctor Wallich accompanied the British envoy to Ava, and in his official report of a journey on the river Saluen he thus writes :—

'In about an hour I came to a decayed kioum (a sort of monastery) close to the large hill of Kogua, distant about two miles from the right bank of the river, and twenty-seven from the town of Martaban. I had been prepared to find a tree growing here of which an account had been before communicated to me by Mr. Crawfurd, and which I had been fortunate enough to meet with for the first time a week ago at Martaban; nor was I disappointed. There were two individuals of this tree here. The largest, about forty feet high, with a girth at three feet above the base of six feet, stood close to the cave. They were profusely ornamented with pendulous racemes of large vermilion-coloured blossoms, forming superb objects unequalled in the flora of the East Indies. . . . . . The Birman name is Toha. Neither the people here nor at Martaban could give me any distinct account of its native place of growth, but there is little doubt but that it belongs to the forests of this province. The ground was strewed even at a distance with its blossoms, which are carried daily as offerings to the images in the adjoining caves.'

It was Dr. Wallich who named this tree the *Amherstia nobilis*, after the Countess Amherst and her daughter, Lady Sarah, who both took a great interest in his pursuits. To the latter lady, when the lecture was over, the specimens of the flower were despatched.

In 1849, one other specimen of the Amherstia was known to have flowered in England. It was in the possession of Mrs. Lawrence, of Ealing Park, to whom it had been given by Lord Hardinge some time after the original plant had first come to Chatsworth.

It is cheering and refreshing, amid storms and wars and rumours of wars and of famine and of pestilence, at a time when a day of national humiliation is appointed, to read of such harmless and delightful triumphs as these, of idylls still upon the earth, of three hundred people coming to see a flower. It was blooming bright and beautiful, although, owing to state arrangements, sackcloth and ashes were the order of the day.

FIVE O'CLOCK TEA.

For lo! the board with cups and spoons is crowned!
On shining Altars of Japan they raise
The silver lamp; the fiery spirits blaze;
From silver spouts the grateful liquors glide,
While China's earth receives the smoking tide.
At once they gratify their scent, and taste,
And frequent cups prolong the rich repast.

Rape of the Lock.

Five o'clock tea is rarely good. It is either strongly flavoured with that peculiar bitter taste which shows that the tea has been kept waiting and neglected too long, or else it is cold, weak, and vapid. These remarks apply strictly to the tea itself; for, as a general rule, it is the pleasantest hostess who provides the worst tea, and it would almost seem, notwithstanding a few noticeable exceptions, that a lively conversation and a pleasant wit are incompatible with boiling water, and a sufficient supply of cream, and sugar, and souchong. But, fortunately, the popularity of five o'clock tea does not depend upon its intrinsic merits. Five o'clock friendship, five o'clock gossip, five o'clock confidence and pleasant confabulation, are what people look for in these harmless cups; a little sugar dexterously dropped in, a little human kindness, and just enough pungency to give a flavour to the whole concoction, is what we all like sometimes to stir up together for an hour or so, and to enjoy, with the addition of a little buttered muffin, from five to six o'clock, when the day's work is over, and a pleasant, useless, comfortable hour comes round.

Everybody must have observed that there are certain propitious hours in the day when life appears under its best and most hopeful aspects. Five o'clock is to a great many their golden time, when the cares which haunt the early rising have been faced and surmounted; when the mid-day sun is no longer blazing down and exhibiting all the cracks and worn places which we would fain not see; when the labours of the day are over for many, and their vigils have not yet begun; and when a sense of soon-coming rest and refreshment has its unconscious effect upon our spirits. Whether for work or for play, five o'clock is one of the hours that could be the least spared out of the twenty-four we have to choose from. Two o'clock might be sacrificed; and I doubt whether from ten o'clock to eleven is not a difficult pass to surmount for many: neither work nor play comes congenially just after breakfast, but both are welcome at this special five o'clock tea-time. A painter told me once that just a little before sunset, at the close of a long day's toil, there comes a certain light which is more beautiful and more clear and still than any other, and in which he can do better work than at any other time during the day. It is so, I believe, with some people who make writing their profession, and who often find that after wrestling and struggling with intractable ideas and sentences all through a long and wearisome task, at the close, just as they are giving up in despair, a sudden inspiration comes to them, thoughts and suggestions rush upon them, words fall into their places, and the pen flies along the paper. Miss Martineau says in one of her essays that after writing for seven hours, the eighth hour is often worth all the others put together.

There is no comparison, to my mind, between the merits of luncheons and breakfasts and five o'clock tea, in a social point of view. People sometimes experimentalise upon the practicabilities of the minor meals, but pleasant as luncheons or breakfasts may be at the time, a sense of remorse and desolation when the entertainment is over generally prevents anything like an agreeable reminiscence. One has wasted one's morning; one has begun at the wrong end of the day; what is to be the next step on one's downward career? Is one to go backwards all through one's usual avocations, and wind up at last by ordering dinner just before going to bed? The writer can call to mind several such meetings, where persons were present whom it was an honour and a delight to associate with, and where the talk was better worth listening to than commonly happens when several remarkable people are brought together; and yet, when all was over, and one came away into the mid-day sunshine, an uncomfortable feeling of remorse and general dissatisfaction, of not knowing exactly what to do next or how to get through the rest of the day, seemed almost to overpower any pleasant remembrances. It was like the afternoon of a wedding-breakfast, without even a wedding. No such subtle Nemesis attends the little gathering round the three-legged five o'clock tea-tables. You know exactly the precise right thing to do when the tea-party is over. You go home a little late, you hurriedly dress for dinner with the anticipation of an agreeable evening, to which your own spirits, which have been cheered and enlivened already, may possibly contribute; and the knowledge that each other member of the party is also hurrying away with a definite object, instead of straggling out into the world all uncertain and undecided, must unconsciously add to your comfort.

Two o'clock is much more the hour of friendship than

of sentiment. Sentimental scenes take place (it would seem) more frequently in the morning and evening, or out of doors in the afternoon. One can quite imagine that after breakfasts or luncheons the stranded guests might fly to sentiment to fill up the ensuing blank vacancy. But although one has never heard of an offer being made at five o'clock tea, the story of the engagement—more or less interesting—and all the delightful particulars of the trousseau, and settlements, and wedding presents, are more fully discussed then than at any other time. What is *not* discussed at five o'clock tea, besides the usual gossip and chatter of the day? How much of sympathy, confidence, wise and kindly warning and encouragement it has brought to us, as well as the pleasure of companionship in one of its simplest forms! It is now the fashion in some houses to play at whist at five o'clock, but this seems a horrible innovation and interruption to confidence and friendship. If the secret which Belinda has to impart is that she happens to hold four trumps in her hand, if the advice required is whether she shall play diamonds or hearts; if Florio is only counting his points, and speculating on his partner's lead, then, indeed, all this is a much ado about nothing. Let us pull down the little three-legged altars, upset the cream jugs and sugar-basins, and extinguish the sacred flames of spirits of wine with all the water in the tea-kettle.

I do not know whether to give the preference to summer or winter for these entertainments. At this time of the year one comes out of the chill tempests without to bright hearths, warmth, comfort, and kindly welcome. The silver kettle boils and bubbles, the tea-table is ready spread, your frozen soul melts within you, you sink into a warm fireside corner, and perhaps one of the friends that you love best begins with a familiar voice to tell you of things which mutually concern and interest you both, until the door opens and one or two more come in, and the talk becomes more general. In summer time Lady de Coverley has her tea-table placed under the shade of the elm trees on the lawn. There is a great fragrance of flowering azaleas and rhododendrons all about; there are the low seats and the muslin dresses in a semicircle under the bright green branches; shadows come flickering, and gusts of summer sweetness; insects buzzing and sailing away, silver and china wrought in bright array, and perhaps a few vine-leaves and strawberries to give colour to the faint tints of the equipage. You may almost see the summer day spreading over the fields and slopes, where the buttercups blaze like a cloth of gold, and the beautiful cattle are browsing.

Five o'clock is also the nursery tea-time, when a little round-eyed company, perched up in tall chairs, struggles with mugs, and pinafores, and large slices of bread and butter. I must confess that the nursery arrangements have always seemed to me capable of improvement, and I have never been able to understand why good boys and girls should be rewarded with such ugly mugs, or why the bread and butter should always pervade the whole atmosphere as it does nowhere else. It is curious to note what very small things have an unconscious influence upon our comfort at times, and I could quite understand what a friend meant the other day when she told me that whenever anybody came to see her with whom she wished to have a comfortable talk, she was accustomed to move to a certain corner in her drawing-room, where there was a snug place for herself and an easy chair which her guest was certain to take. Those who have been so fortunate as to occupy that easy chair can certify to the complete success of the little precaution.

Of the sadder aspect of my subject, of the tea-parties over and dispersed for ever, of old familiar houses now closed upon us, of friends parted and estranged, who no longer clink their cups together, I do not care to write.

The readers of 'Pendennis' may remember Mrs.

Shandon and little Mary at their five o'clock tea, and the extract with which I conclude :—

'So Mrs. Shandon went to the cupboard, and in lieu of a dinner made herself some tea. And in those varieties of pain of which we spoke anon, what a part of confidante has that poor tea-pot played ever since the kindly plant was introduced among us! What myriads of women have cried over it, to be sure! what sick-beds it has smoked by! what fevered lips have received refreshment from out of it! Nature meant very gently by women when she made that tea-plant; and with a little thought, what a series of pictures and groups the fancy may conjure up, and assemble round the tea-pot and cup.'

THE DISASTROUS FASCINATIONS OF CROQUET.

Go! cries the nymph and strikes the flying ball.—CUNNINGHAM.

To the Editor of the Pall Mall Gazette.

SIR,—I am sorry to trouble you with the following remarks, and yet I feel that it is right that the attention of the public should be drawn to the spread of an infatuation which seems to me in its strange progress almost to resemble the well-known hysterical affections of the middle ages.

I have been staying for the last three days in a country house in Hampshire, belonging to some old friends whom I have been in the habit of visiting for many years. I arrived on Monday evening, driving up in a fly from the station in that half-satisfied, half-expectant state of mind in which people arrive at the hospitable houses where the friends are to be found whom they wish to see, and where a long-standing welcome awaits them. Not the least agreeable part of my pleasurable feeling in coming to Malleton Hall was the anticipation of the cordial welcome and friendly greeting of my host and hostess. I remembered arriving the time before, and how they came out into the hall to receive me, and while I drove along pleased myself by imagining the meeting.

As it was, the flyman rang twice before the door was opened by a stupid young country footman. I could not help thinking it a little strange that no one .appeared, as I had expected. I was shown into the library, and told that Mrs. F—— would be with me directly, and I accordingly waited for twenty minutes by the clock on the chimney. The place seemed to me a little less cared for than it used to be; the general aspect was less pleasing—newspapers lay about on the floor and on the chairs, the books were somewhat in confusion, and happening to look for a favourite volume in one of the book-cases—‘ Grote’s Antiquities ’—I found it was not in its place. The flowers too seemed to me faded, and no longer arranged with that taste and precision for which my hostess had been always remarkable. At last, however, the door opened and the daughter of the house came in. I must own that she was looking remarkably well; a bright colour was in her cheeks, her eyes shone, and her white dress was prettily looped up over a flowered petticoat. 'How do you do, dear Mr. Croker?' she said. 'I am so glad you are come. We wanted a fourth so badly for the second set. Mamma is in the middle of her game, and she says will you come out upon the lawn to her as she can't come to you.'

All my momentary ill-humour had vanished at the sight of the bright young face, and, though I did not quite understand her allusions, I followed her across the hall, and out through a little back room, of which the windows open into the garden. 'What has happened to this little boudoir?' I asked, when, instead of the trim and orderly retreat in which I remember having so many pleasant talks and quiet, happy hours, we passed through a sort of lumber-room—I can give it no other name. Two great wooden boxes were lying on the floor, so were a quantity of mallets and croquet balls, together with hats, cloaks, umbrellas, and india-rubber shoes. 'My dear child, what a pity to have unfurnished this room!' I exclaimed. 'How did you come to pull it to pieces?'

'Why, you see the balls spoil so if they are left out all night,' said Miss Lucy; 'the paint rubs off quite directly; and it was such a very long way to carry them all round the house, that by degrees we came to put them in here at the window. We are out so much that we really do not want the room.'

We were now approaching the croquet-ground; the distant report of the balls going off reached our ears, while the players were still concealed behind the bushes. As I came up, Mrs. F——, mallet in hand, came to meet me, with all her old kindly charm and cordiality. F—— himself waved his stick in the air, and called out, 'Welcome, welcome!' but he did not come up, and seemed immediately afterwards to forget my presence, and to be once more absorbed in the game. I never in all my life beheld such a sight: F—— and his wife, Frank the son, Lucy, two young men, and a strange middle-aged lady, were all tapping and rapping the wretched balls, pegging and unpegging, spooning—I think the expression is—crocketting, rocketting, as if their lives depended on it.

'Who plays next—blue?' said F——, who used to be a man of sense, of some conversation, and wit.

'Blue played before you,' said young Frank; 'yellow comes next. Look sharp, yellow!'

'Yes, yes!' says F——, in great excitement; '*then* green and then black. Who is black? Is it you, Smith?'

'I am the invincible green, said Smith; 'Jones is black.'

'And who wired black?' F—— went on.

'I did,' said Miss Lucy, who was standing in a pretty little attitude, with one foot on an iron hoop.

'I never saw such a fluke,' cried young Frank. 'You spooned in the most audacious manner; you know you did.'

'How could I spoon when I played sideways, Frank?' cried Lucy. 'Papa, did I spoon?'

This conversation went on for ever so long, my poor friends showing every sign of lively interest in it, until at last I confess I was quite wearied of the whole thing The sun was beginning to set by this time; the whole place was illuminated. It was in vain I called their attention to the lovely effects—not one of them had any idea beyond his or her hoop.

I had brought down a little piece of London gossip which I knew would amuse my hosts, and being somewhat curious to see the way in which it would be received, and to hear their opinion on the subject, I could not resist taking Mrs. F—— presently a little apart and telling her confidentially that I had a bit of news which would interest her.

Mrs. F—— looked surprised, as I expected, laughed, said the usual 'do tell me,' and I was accordingly beginning to recount the whole thing as I was told it by someone who was staying at Chatterton at the time, when suddenly F——roared out from the other end of the lawn, 'I say, Croker, just get out of the way, will you?' and Mrs. F—— beckoned me to another part of the field. 'The fact is,' I said, 'she was supposed to have a *tendresse* in another quarter, and being an heiress, you know, our friend would never have come forward if it had not been pretty clearly intimated by the lady's guardian that—a—that—' 'Pray, Mr. Croker, will you move a little more to *this* side?' said Mrs. F——, looking absently round and about her. Blue and black now flew past, and I received a violent blow on the shin from green. Of course there were apologies made, which I accepted, and seeing that Mrs. F—— was really interested in my story, I went on to tell her in a few words, that propositions were made in so many words, always supposing, you know, that the family was willing to come forward. 'Go back—go back!' shrieks Miss Lucy, springing forward, with her hair flying, in a state of very unbecoming excitement. 'Everything depends upon this move,' said F——, solemnly placing himself in an attitude and hitting a tremendous crack, while Mrs. F—— looked anxiously at a washed-out pink ball which was lying on a tuft of grass at our feet, and breathed a great sigh of relief when F——'s ball flew past it. 'Everything depended upon the way in which the proposition was taken,' I said, 'and now comes the extraordinary part of my story. It seems almost incredible that after the distinct assurance that was given ——' At this moment Mrs. F.—— suddenly exclaimed with great animation, 'Oh, Mr. Croker, now it's my turn to play. I will come back to you directly.' I need scarcely say that when she did return, elated and triumphant, announcing that she had hit the stick and croquetted her husband into the shrubbery, I was too much bewildered by all these evolutions to finish my story. I only enquired at what time dinner would be ready, and said I should go up to my room for the present. I abominate five-o'clock tea, and I am always glad when the dinner hour comes round, so that I could not help feeling a little annoyed to hear they did not dine before half-past seven, though my hostess smiled, and pointed very graciously, saying,—'You know your room, Mr. Croker; the windows look over the flower garden. I know that is the view you like best.'

There was nothing to complain of in my room: comfortable writing apparatus, four-post bed, prints— Her Majesty, the Duchess of Kent, the Duke of Wellington. One of the advantages of getting old is being promoted from the garrets to the first floor, with its various comforts, nicely-framed prints, arm-chairs, looking-glasses. &c., &c. I threw open my window. There was a pleasant view of the flower garden, of the hills all brightening, while close at hand the trees, and the glades, and the waters, were reflecting the sudden colours of the evening glow. After enjoying the prospect for some minutes, I lay down on the sofa and read a number of the 'Pall Mall Gazette,' which I happened to have brought with me, and over which I took a comfortable little nap. I only woke up at a quarter-past seven, when someone came in with some hot water. Although I dressed quickly, I was sorry to find myself just two minutes behind the time Mrs. F—— had given me as the dinner hour. I hurried downstairs into the hall, where the family assembles, but not a soul was to be seen. I looked into the drawing-room, the library; they were both empty. I waited, I walked up and down the hall. I confess the delay was vexing to a man who had eaten nothing since breakfast. At eight o'clock precisely someone hastily rushed across from the garden and ran upstairs—then another—and then another. I could scarcely believe it possible, when finally Mrs. F—— herself appeared in complete garden costume, with 'Oh, Mr. Croker, I am afraid you will find us very unpunctual! The two last were such exciting games, we really could not tear ourselves away.'

We sat down to table at a quarter to nine. The dinner was cold, burnt, overdone. The fish was sodden, the soufflet came up like a pancake, the ice was in a soup. All dinner-time the young folks discussed the fortunate strokes of the afternoon, and the desirability of getting a new set of mallets heavier than the last. Captain Smith described at great length an ingenious device with a ball which greatly increased the length of the game and the difficulty of passing the middle hoop.

In the evening the ladies were too tired to give us any music, to which I am exceedingly partial. F—— went fast asleep in his chair until eleven o'clock, when they all parted for the night, making arrangements to get up early next morning and practise at the hoops before breakfast.

Sir, I do not exaggerate when I prophesy that this diversion, if carried to such extremes, will prove the bane of the rising generation. If I speak with force, it is because I feel deeply on the subject upon which I address you. Yesterday I refused to join the party, and sat in the library all the morning by myself; in the afternoon I took a solitary walk. I am now confined to my own room by a hurt in the foot proceeding from a violent blow I struck myself in my efforts to master the rudiments of the game. I was only induced to attempt to do so by the entreaties of my hostess and her friend who is staying with her—they wanted me, they said; they were going to try to play at night with lamps fastened to the hoops and the mallets. I weakly yielded to their solicitations: the result is that I am disabled by this accident, and also much shaken by a fall over one of the hoops. I do not complain, and I feel that it is only what I deserve for my foolish weakness in consenting to their wishes against my confirmed convictions; but under the circumstances I feel that I am justified when I entreat you, Sir, to lend the aid of your powerful columns to arrest the progress of this growing evil.—I remain your obedient servant,   CHARLES CROKER.

MONDAYS, TUESDAYS, WEDNESDAYS, ETC.

So here hath been dawning
    Another blue day;
Think, wilt thou let it
    Slip useless away?

Out of Eternity
    This new day is born;
Into Eternity
    At night will return.

Behold it aforetime
    No eye ever did:
So soon it forever
    From all eyes is hid.—T. CARLYLE.

To the Editor of the Pall Mall Gazette.

SIR,—Some months have elapsed since I last ventured to address you upon the subject of an annoyance which the inclemency of the weather has allayed for a time; although I have little doubt but that the summer ides will witness a return, with all its accompanying violent and alarming symptoms of the contagious and widely-extended infatuation which may not inaptly be termed the croquet pest.

Sir, I perceive that the evil is too deeply rooted for my feeble pen to battle with; all expostulation would now be useless. My country haunts are torn up and invaded, and I am driven from the lawns and green pastures where I had hoped to end my days by the wayward blow, the bewildering course of the ball, the iron hoop of fate.

I returned to London in the beginning of the winter, shattered in health and spirits, suffering from a severe injury to the leg, but hoping still among familiar haunts and in the social intercourse of an agreeable acquaintance, to forget the disheartening scenes of which I had been a reluctant spectator. I leave you to imagine with what feelings I discover another enemy springing up on every side—a fiend no less insidious than that *diable à deux mille bâtons* from whom I was escaping when I met with my unfortunate accident.

Sir, need I say after this that I allude to the Mondays, Tuesdays, Wednesdays, Thursdays, Fridays, Saturdays, and Sundays by which I am attacked, persecuted, and exasperated on every side? I am aware that one must consent to pay the penalties of being an agreeable and popular person. I am willing to put myself to a certain inconvenience for the sake of those upon whom—speaking without affectation or irrelevant modesty—I am well aware my prolonged absence entails considerable disappointment; but there are bounds to the utmost limits of good-nature.

I ask you, *how* is it possible to find one's self, as the clock strikes five on any given day, at Putney, at Clapham, at Brixton—I have old friends in that locality —in Eaton Place, Grosvenor Crescent, and Hertford Street, Mayfair? Hitherto I have taken my friends in districts; travelled quietly round from one well-known door to another, at my own leisure, and at my own inclination. If Lady Noddington was unfortunately from home, I consoled myself with her cheerful neighbour, Mrs. Dashmore, next door. If Mrs. Dashmore was out driving, I left my card with the satisfactory reflection that I was doing a good day's work, and travelled on to Miss Spitville's, whom I do not wish to offend, or to my old friend and relative, Lady Katherine Croker's, where I have always been sure of a chatty half-hour. The butler, a most excellent servant of my own recommending, knows me, and I am shown upstairs into the drawing room without demur. The house is dark and shabby, but what I call a thoroughly liveable house; and Lady Katherine, who is as good a creature as ever breathed, is always delighted to see one. One feels quite at home sitting in the corner while her ladyship sits and knits stockings, and we talk over the occurrences of the last few days— where she is going; who dined at —— House the night before, Madame de l'Etoile's strange mistake—I won't particularise it here, because the poor thing mightn't like it made public; in a word, we have been for years past in the habit of exchanging all those little minutiæ of conversation which go so far to make up the real value and interest of social intercourse.

Sir, these quiet meetings and oases in the deserts of London society are destroyed for ever. This execrable institution has annihilated some of the most agreeable reminiscences of my life. Lady Katherine now receives the whole rabble on Thursdays, and rushes off to kettle-drums every other day in the week. I give you my honour, I am worn to a skeleton trudging about from one end of the town to another. When I wake in the morning, my first thought is, ' This is Mrs. Ramsbotham's Tuesday,' or whatever the combination may be. My man brings me my letters—I loathe the very sight of them. I know by intuition that, instead of agreeable little summonses to rational entertainments, invitations to dinner, &c., &c., the usual formula will greet me—' Dear Mr. Croker, we have been so unfortunate, &c., &c.: other of our friends who kindly call upon us, &c., &c., have determined in future to stay at home on alternate Mondays and Tuesdays from a quarter-past four to twenty minutes to seven. Pray, if you should be in our neighbourhood, &c., &c., and so forth, and so on. Dear Mr. Croker, yours *most*,' &c., &c. One is invited to 'drop in,' as if one was for ever hovering over all the chimney-pots in London.

Saturday is a fearful day for me, no less than eight of my most intimate friends (all of whom I am particularly anxious to be well with) having chosen it for their especial property. The consequence is that I am able to see each of them once in two months with the utmost exertion. Even the poor old Miss Creepers in their impossible villa at Brompton are determined not to be behindhand with the fashion. 'Dr. Clapper has kindly promised to look in upon them,' they write, ' on his way to Madame Tussaud's next Friday. He is anxious to renew his acquaintance with an old and valued friend; will I come and meet him, and also look in on any other Friday, when I shall be *sure* of finding them and a few mutual acquaintances of " auld lang syne " ? '

The poor old things have no conception of what they are asking. Why, I am not even able to get to Lady Taplow's, at Upper Lower Lodge, Regent's Park, whose note comes in with Miss Creeper's—' Lazy Man! Why didn't you come to my last Tuesday? *Mind* you come to my Fridays. I have changed the day, and shall take no excuse. Ever yours, Emma Taplow.'

Ladies are privileged, of course, but I ask you, Sir, in the name of common sense, who is to remember or to keep count of all these combinations? One person I know of has changed her day no less than five times in the course of the last three weeks. Another, I am told, is gone out walking when I arrive panting at her door by special invitation. Besides, there are some combinations which are simply impossible. Take Lady Katherine's last Thursday, for example. I drop in as requested, though my heart misgives me. Old Mrs. Codlington, in her wraps and boas, is installed in my favourite corner, staring apoplectically at Lady Broadstairs, who reposes, terrible, impressive, and deadly calm, upon the sofa, grasping a screen like a sceptre. Mrs. Codlington persists in enquiring after my rheumatism, my deafness ; do I use spectacles? do I like the motion of a bath chair? Lady Broadstairs never sees me, never asks me to her parties, never notices any little remark I may make in the course of conversation. Sir, I ask you what possible pleasure can I find in their society? Instead of enjoying my social little chat with Lady Katherine, I have to sit silent or engage in a conversation more utterly vapid than you can have any idea of. It happened last Thursday that I had just heard a piece of news concerning young R. G., whose engagement is a subject of congratulation to all his friends. I made an attempt. 'Well, Lady Katherine,' I said, ' what do you say to a marriage? " Je vous le donne en dix, je vous donne en vingt," as Madame de Sevigné says.' Any other day in all the week I know Lady Katherine would have been delighted, and would have asked me a hundred questions; but what is she to do? Lady Broadstairs slowly turns her head away and examines an old cracked teacup. Mrs. Codlington is convulsed with an asthmatic fit of coughing. The door opens: enter Lady Taplow with a rush and a flutter— enter the Miss Spitvilles dressed alike, knowing nobody, with old Lady Grogan from Queen Anne Street. ' My dear Mr. Croker,' whispers Lady Katherine, bewildered, hastily pouring out a cup of lukewarm water, ' take this to Lady Grogan, and pray go and talk to those dreadful Miss Spitvilles if you can,' for the three were sitting on a round ottoman, back to back, in alarming silence. Lady Katherine goes on with forced cheerfulness. But I—I flee in consternation, leaving the poor lady to get out of it as best she can.

' Who is it who likes it?' said a friend of mine the

other day. Everybody grumbles. Sir, my disposition is a contented one, and I am not apt, without due cause, to express all that I feel upon certain subjects, but I cannot contemplate, silent and unmoved, the fatal infatuation which dooms our firesides to ruin, our life to toil and misery, and our finest feelings to be nipped and blighted in the bud—I am, Sir, your obedient servant,

CHARLES CROKER.

ROME IN THE HOLY WEEK.

Oh ! come to Rome, nor be content to read
  Alone of stately palace and of street
Whose fountains ever run with joyful speed,
  And never-ceasing murmur.   Here we meet
Great Memnon's monoliths, or, gay with weed,
  Rich capitals, as corner stone, or seat ;
The sites of vanished temples, where now moulder
  Old ruin, hiding ruin even older.
Ay ! come and see the statues, pictures, churches,
  Although the last are commonplace or florid.
Some say 'tis here that superstition perches,
  Myself I'm glad the marbles have been quarried.

F. LOCKER.

[LETTER I.]

THURSDAY was bright sunshine and blue, and as we
came downstairs all the marbles and stone carvings in
the courtyard were glittering in the light. A great
golden carriage went by (it was the hereditary Captain
of the Guard driving off to his post). That was the first
sign of the day's festive humiliation, except, by the way,
some guns and bells in the early morning. As we drove

along, we passed a whole procession of people walking along the narrow street towards St. Peter's. Black-veiled ladies, carriages, green, blue, red petticoats, coal-black tresses, children in little black veils tripping along, swaddled-up babies held up at the doors to see the sight. Then brown friars, white monks, black and white Dominicans, and some strange brown creatures, penitents in huge bonnets, and priests without number, all drifting in the same direction. As we neared St. Angelo the carriages came thicker, and all the pretty ladies (they did not, however, look so pretty as usual) drove by faster and faster. We drive on and on down the quaint beautiful streets, arched, and wrought, and carved; past fountains, where even on days like this the women are watching the water flow into their pitchers heedless of the crowd; past shrines, and Mater Dolorosas with sorrowful upturned eyes, past milk-merchants, lottery establishments, sausage shops, past Raphael's palace and the ancient Doge's barn, and iron-worked windows; by open shop arches full of light and darkness, and you come at last to the river and the great bridge of St. Angelo all alight in the wonderful dazzle. Someone points out the gonfalones streaming from the fort, and quotes the old saying about always meeting a soldier, a priest, and a beggar on the bridge. The saying is true enough to-day as far as priests and soldiers are concerned, but the beggars seem to have dressed themselves, and put on uniform and velvet gowns, and to be coming along with us to the piazza in front of St. Peter's. It is flowing with people; they are squatting on the steps; standing against the great columns in hundreds; and every minute the crowd is growing thicker and closer. There sits a row of peasant women with beautiful red sunny petticoats; there stand the monks talking together, with their umbrellas; here are shepherds coming up from the country with cross-barred Italian legs. In Rome itself common people don't dress up any more, unfortunately, and wear trousers instead of the familiar rags and ribbons we all admire. However, country people have not yet abandoned their traditions.

There are some dresses left, happily for us sightseers. There stands one of the Swiss guard in his grand-looking uniform. Michael Angelo designed it, it is said; yellow with stripes of red and black, with a beefeater's cap and halberd. As we come into St. Peter's one of these grand-looking creatures bars our passage and silently motions us to turn back to a place where everybody is crowding round a little sacristy door, protected by a young Zouave officer.

Great St. Peter's is strangely decorated for the occasion with crimson stages and hangings, and countless pens or raised stands full of the veiled ladies whom we have seen arriving by every winding street and piazza. Common people are strolling about hand in hand ; those are the Zouaves in their blue picturesque dress, and again more monks and priests. It is very like the scene outside, only the great dome is overhead and the carved walls and windows about us, and many people are on their knees, specially round the statue of the bronze St. Peter with his key and his shining toe. We persuade the officer of the guard at the turret-door to let us pass before the crush, and we climb the broad shallow steps. Figures out of the picture galleries meet us at every corner. Here is a plum-coloured clerk, slashed and square-toed, waiting to take the favoured yellow tickets ; and at the top of the stairs a Vandyke hero is gallantly standing, velvet cloak, ruffle, golden chain, with one hand on the sword's hilt, and black silk legs. This is a handsome American general, who has been appointed ' cameriere segreto,' and who takes us under his protection. He tells us that if we will wait in a certain narrow passage at the back of the pens, which are also here for the use of the veiled ladies, he will provide for us in time. In this little secret passage we wait patiently, and well amused. All sorts of strange figures flit past, the great Swiss guards bearing down upon us ; a

little uneasy violet priest, with a muslin petticoat, darting
here and there in an agony to find a corner, more Vandykes, then Raphaels and Titians in furred tippets and
red and violet caps, and then there is a pause ; we see a
little bustle at the far end of the passage ; three or four
priests in white fur capes attended by their acolytes hurry
by without noticing us ; some huge waving things appear
above the pens. 'There are the Pope's fans,' says my
companion ; 'he is coming to bless the people outside.
Listen !' And then in the dead silence which suddenly
seems to overpower all the sounds and glitterings and
echoings that are everywhere about, we stand listening as
a clear voice not far away repeats some few words, to
which comes a thundering amen from the priests. Again
the voice speaks. Again the amen fires off its boom, and
then a quavering old man's voice utters something—a
blessing—upon the patient crowds waiting down below.
It is with an odd feeling of touched bewilderment that
one stands silent, listening to the faded voice blessing the
kneeling multitude. As it ceases the guns begin to fire
and the bells to ring.

After the blessing came the curse : a crash, a scream,
all barriers broken down along our little secret passage,
a sudden overwhelming torrent pouring over everything,
charging the Swiss guard, setting aside the indignant

Vandykes. 'E una impertinenza!' I hear them crying in fierce indignation. The ladies don't care; they come on laughing and running with dauntless courage, and begin to hop and scramble into their places; the place echoes, then pens creak, and still the ladies pour in. Some have cavaliers, fine old gentlemen, with orders, some have tickets, some have none. We are installed in our places by this time, and watch them pass before us. The diplomatic corps now marches up, in swords and tights and embroidered coats, the white Austrian uniforms and the beautiful Hungarian dress. Little by little this human sea flows into the dykes and dams and locks which have been provided, and we begin to look at the spectacle we have come to see. In this beautiful light hall of the Vatican a stage has been raised upon which a table is spread; as well as I can make out all the cakes and puddings and fruit seem to be of gold, but now immediately a procession passes, damask and stately servitors bearing food and wine, and then come in thirteen white figures with tall white caps upon their heads; these are the priests whose feet have been washed down below by the Pope, and who are now to be served at table by him. They are surrounded by a stream of prelates and damask attendants. I see the old Pontiff bending as he serves; cold fish and cold vegetables is the fare provided. It is too far off to distinguish very plainly what is going on, only this, a long table glittering, quaint figures sitting at it, a Pope serving, and robed and splendid figures looking on. Paul Veronese, Raphael, and others, painted from their own time, and have left us records of what they saw round about them, and here is time going backwards and our curious critical and yet charmed eyes see as they saw, and the stately past rises before us. This was not the first collation of the day, at eight o'clock the camerieres and other officials had been treated to ices and coffee.

Later in the afternoon we went to the *Miserere* in the Sixtine Chapel, and still by favour of a kind cameriere segreto we were admitted, just before the lamentation began, to a dim arched place where many people were waiting, and some lights burning, and the daylight was streaming through the windows upon Michael Angelo's great prophets and sibyls, and upon the magnificent creation of man, a fresco high up in the roof with a mountain height feeling about it, that takes one away out of the chapel and beyond the angels and devils painted on the walls. We had all got quite used to our black veils by this time, and we listened, in our rows, to the chanting which at first seemed disappointing. The Pope did not come that afternoon, and his throne stood empty, but the

service went on and on, and presently some of the lights
were put out, and the chanting seemed to thrill a little
and then to go on and on once more, and then some more
lights went out, and with the last the chanting stopped
short, and now began a melody so strange, so sad, so carefully sweet, so utterly unlike anything I had ever in my
life listened to before, that I do not know how to write of
it; sad, still, strange, and shrill, it deepened and died
away, and seemed soaring to those very mountain heights
which were dimly reflected in the fresco overhead; the
secret of life seemed to be in its voice if one could only
understand it.   It did not sound like singing; it seemed
to change, to turn sadder and more sad in the grey of the
sunset, from which all the gold had died away.   At last
came one note of hope, one only, and as we all listened for
more the music stopped and the *Miserere* was over.   We
came out into the Sala Regia of the Vatican, dark figures
crowding, awestricken, and silenced by this wonderful
service.   Except in the sepulchres no lights are allowed in
the churches till Easter, nor do bells ring any more.

[LETTER II.]

Good Friday.

A LONG procession of red figures passed us this afternoon in the Felice; they were chanting, and bearing their veiled crosses high aloft. Their eyes gleamed out of their silk masks and pointed red caps. The coachman told us that these were Brothers of Consolation, but consolation would seem somewhat terrific thus muffled and mysterious. I saw another procession of ladies in black silk carrying a cross through the streets. All the brothers and sisters were out this afternoon; the Roman gentlemen and ladies come to St. Peter's or stand out in the piazza to see their penitent friends go by. The confraternities went wending along the streets, chanting and travelling from campo santo to campo santo; then during the vesper service they come wearily back across the piazza to St. Peter's to pray at the high altar and to receive absolution. I was in the chapel listening to the *Miserere*, so that I missed a great deal that was going on.

One rush of feet meant that the Pope had arrived in order to see the exhibition of relics from the balcony. Another turning and straining of heads, several processions of green, white, and black penitents were advancing up the great aisle together. While the chanting is peacefully thrilling in one chapel, in another a number of people are sitting waiting round a cardinal's chair, which stands by a certain altar. It is here that twice a year he listens to the confessions of the most unpardonable offenders, and gives absolutions for crimes which could at no other time be forgiven. People sit and wait to see the looks of the cardinal and of the offenders, and to guess at the horrible tragedies that are wiped out by this long-suffering tradition. I, seeing as I passed nice-looking young ladies and amiable-faced gentlemen waiting, imagined that these were the criminals, and passed on duly horrified, until I was told that they were merely spectators. Once, some-one assured me, a man was seen to rush wildly in like a madman, leap over the barriers, and in a desperate, excited way hiss out something in the cardinal's ear. The cardinal shrank back with a scared face, but all the same gave his absolution, and the man, with a shriek, rushed away as he had come, flying down the crowded aisle and out through the door into the piazza. I saw nothing more exciting than the rod working from the doors of the confession-boxes and the faithful passing meekly beneath its stripes. The sun was set by the time we left the cathedral, and all the people were slowly dispersing: the bridges, the streets, were crowded with loiterers; the moon was streaming her own peculiar benediction over-head, the churches were lighted, and the homeward bound faithful were pouring in. We went into one quiet place, dark, and with prostrate figures on their knees round a beautiful glowing shrine. Another church was packed so closely that we were glad to turn and come out into the moonlight again. As we went along we were amused to see the cheesemongers' shops, brilliantly illuminated and turned into chapels for the time being. Surrounded by strings of alternate sausages and burning candles, stands a holy figure; eggs in water float before it, hams hang from the ceiling, cheeses are ranged in ornamental rows, and then come more dips, wax tapers, candles of every sort; it is a quaint sight, and an old custom taken from a bygone religion, most probably.

In one crowded narrow street that we passed on our way home we saw a number of grand carriages waiting at the door of a barn-like building. These were the carriages of the Roman ladies who were washing the feet of the pilgrims within. These poor people come on foot for miles—forty miles at least are necessary to entitle a pilgrim to the privilege of board and lodging during these three great days. They are fed and housed, and the poor grand ladies come in their carriages and black silk dresses and red aprons to wait upon them. They wash their feet, they fold up their rags and tuck them under their arms, and take the pilgrims up to supper and then to bed. The poor ladies are often made ill by it, but they do their work charmingly, and smile over the dreadful garments, and don't falter, though the steam and the grime and the atmosphere are, I am told, something indescribably horrible. The grand ladies pray the whole time, and someone reads out of a holy book. In another part of the building some 200 men are waited on by the gentlemen of the town. What part of their suppers the pilgrims cannot eat there and then they carry up and put under their pillows.

Sunday.

Easter began this morning about five o'clock with bells and cannons for an Easter hymn. All the clanging and booming set the canaries singing in the next room, and I believe most people got up and dressed, for many were at St. Peter's by seven, and even earlier. The N——'s were there by six, and I heard of some people who dressed at four so as to be in time for the ten o'clock mass. After this one is ashamed to remember a nine o'clock breakfast; but though we came late there was a kind person present, with influence to turn the hard hearts of barrier-keepers and camerieres, and to get us admitted into an uncrowded place, from whence, by standing, we could see the great sight. A moment's dizziness and breathlessness, and then you see it there before you, a wonderful waving, shining sea beating against the rocks of St. Peter's; by degrees you feel that every wave is bright with colour; a sort of rainbow dazzle is in the air almost veiling the far depths of the great brilliant arches. High overhead are specks of people looking from galleries; the altar shines and glitters with shimmering smoke and light, and a sound of music and chanting begins. There, at the far end of the church, sits the Pope enthroned in white, with his officers of state around him, and all the long way from the throne to the altar is lined with the brass helmets of the guards, while every arch and nook is crowded; the uniforms are glittering, the knights, nobles, and diplomatists are each in their places. Upon the steps of the high altar crowd cardinals and bishops and attendant priests. I see a row of silver mitres on cushions, which their fortunate possessors will presently assume. One black motionless figure stands upon the high step of the altar. This is a young nobleman representative of the great families of Rome. Overhead the great figures in the dome hang silent over all this pomp and eager wide-spreading wave of life, and we dizzy spectators get down from the step on which we have been standing to make way for a Roman princess, who is going to take her seat in the privileged place which has been prepared for her. They look magnificent in their veils, these Roman ladies, as they sweep past us. The dress suits them better than it suits the pilgrim English and American ladies, who have not coal-black hair, and whose bright complexions are dimmed by the black. Someone tells me the names of some of the great ladies as they kneel side by side in the front of the box kneeling and bending lower. There is a thrill, the soldiers fall on their knees, and so do the camerieres, and the Pope and his holy mysteries pass by. Then the incense begins to mount, and the music swells; the Pontiff himself officiates, and elevates the host, and swings the silver censer. People who are used to the service kneel, and then have a little conversation, and then kneel again, so that Protestants find it difficult to follow the various phases; and I must here protest that though I have heard much complaint of the Protestants' behaviour, it has always been the Catholics who have most talked and made disturbance wherever I have been. Strange and brilliant creatures come into our reserved corner: M. de Charétte, the Captain of the Zouaves, in his splendid dress—the Hungarians in their Vandyke dresses—and the Captain of the Pope's Guard, a noble mediæval head, with a close frill and a grand suit of armour, which he wears with a sort of knightly grace. Nothing seems out of place in this curious glittering company, from the Roman princesses to the barefooted friars. Here is no actual thing, or time, or place. It seems like a mystical, typical multitude from all time and all places worshipping and wondering round the high altar of Catholicism. Splendour, devotion, and the fervent faith of the past, and the chill and doubting yet true-hearted spirit of these plain-speaking times are there, and long use and love and new fervours awakened. All centuries of feeling seem represented under this re-sounding roof, while the light of heaven shines through the windows of the dome alike upon the just and the unjust. And now, as we are waiting, suddenly all talking ceases, and once more the vast multitude bows low. The incense rises, and the censers clank, but the music has ceased; there is a pause, a sort of hushed silence, which is very impressive; and then clear above our heads sound the silver trumpets, musical, majestic, lovely in harmony; and the heads bend lower and lower, and the brilliant strain dies away. . . . . .

I have not attempted to describe the passing and repassing of cardinals, the mitres doffed and reassumed; the solemn state of the mass was so big and so brilliant that the details were almost beyond my ken. I saw the cardinals sitting in a splendid row by the throne. I had a glimpse of ambassadors in their places, and royalties, and of the hundreds gazing upwards, and then someone called me and told me to follow quickly, and a number of us, under the protection of a special and friendly cameriere, hurried down the centre of the church, between the two long lines of the people held back by ropes. We came at last to a side door and climbed steps and hastened along halls and passages and so came out upon the leads of the Vatican into a place partitioned off with an awning, and a view of the piazza, where another multitude was waiting for the benediction.

The cavalry stands in squares of grey and green, and the line in uniforms of yellow and red, and there are Zouaves glittering blue, with their prancing commanders, and the Household troops; then comes a group of country women and a file of Sisters of Charity in their white flapping caps; from all the distant windows heads are bending; on the distant hills stand people watching from a long way off; some cardinals and white and red robes are looking out of the windows of the Vatican, and all the leads are crowded. The sun comes out and shines on the bright great piazza, on the leads, on the

Vatican, on the distant hills, on the window with the tapestry, from whence the blessing is coming. The Pope's mitre is there already on a cushion, and half-a-dozen priests are waiting for his coming. Now the sun bursts bright and hot from rain clouds, and the lights come and go, and suddenly 'Ecco!' cry the people, for the fans appear under the awning, and the golden figure is carried to the window; and as the Pope appears there is a sort of murmur, and then the priests say something, and then once more the trembling hands are upheld, and the kind quavering voice is heard. At its first utterance the word of command rings out quick and sharp, and the army of soldiers kneel with a great clank and glitter among all the country people on their knees; and so the kind old Pontiff blesses his kneeling multitude; and as the blessing ends the peacock's feathers move, and the golden figure disappears, and with a cheer (it made our eyes fill somehow) the people spring to their feet.

We went home in a crowd of senators' and princes' and monsignores' carriages. The senators had ruffles, gold bodies with crimson arms, the little pages were peeping from the windows of the great coaches. I saw one great glass carriage with four delighted-looking little boys in ruffles and a monk to take care of them. I saw Monsignor Stonor in a brougham, and Cenci and Montecchi, and Visconti and Barberini, and all the historical names that one knows, in splendid mediæval dresses, driving in solemn state. It is rather depressing to come away, having seen this grand sight, and to reflect that there is probably nothing more of the sort to come in all one's life so golden and so magnificent, and that all of us, men and women, have done our utmost here, and can't go any farther.

CLOSED DOORS.

E'en tho' temptation press thee hard and sore,
  And strength is failing, and that prayer for **grace**
Was thy last effort, and thou canst no more.

Now, on some week-day, if thy heart be hot
  Within thee to thank Him for mercy given,
Towards His sanctuary go thou not!
  Its doors are shut, and back thou wilt be driven!

And if wide from thy gracious Lord thou'st erred,
  Yet late repentant to thine heart are cut,
Repent elsewhere; for here no vows are heard:
  God's ears are open, but His church is shut!

Closed Doors—HON. MRS. KNOX.

To the Editor of the Pall Mall Gazette.

SIR,—I am writing to you very early on a Sunday morning, and as I write the bell is ringing of a little whitewashed chapel standing by a wooden bridge and a rushing torrent, and down from the high green Alps, stream-crossed and pine-scented, the peasants are coming at its call. All round about this plateau are white, dazzling snow mountains and green slopes, where, on week days, the peasants are at work early and late reaping the grasses, and the grey oxen come down the precipitous sides of the mountains, dragging the sledges upon which the sweet dry hay is piled, or it may be the household goods of some little family flitting from its high Alpine home to its chalet in the village down below. The husband goes first, with his arm round the broad-horned head; the mother follows with steady step, through the pine trees, carrying a little Italian peasant baby in her arms. In the valley where we are staying there are perhaps three or four little wooden houses by the stream, but a good many seem to have flown up right out of the valley and perched upon the mountains, all about our low stone house with the stone-piled roof, which has been erected for those who come to drink the waters that flow from the iron spring in the valley.

Among the company are some Milanese ladies, convent-bred, who go often to the little whitewashed chapel, and whose many questions as to the ways of our Church, its beliefs, its consolations, I sometimes find it difficult to answer. To them their Church means religion itself, to us it is (or should be) but an expression of something higher. They ask me if it is to our Church we go for consolation in trouble, for daily sustainment and advice.

'Ah, no,' cries the youngest of the party, 'your Church is not a friend to you as ours is to us.' Practically, perhaps, she is in the right, if a Protestant may concede so much.

These are days of change, of eager debate of words that do not spare; on every side people are looking out for the fall of superstructures erected by our predecessors, at whose traditions this impatient age not unnaturally rebels, just as men of forty sometimes rebel at the professions made for them by men of twenty-three. We see beacons destroyed or tottering (in truth they are beacons no longer, for the harbour is closed and the tide is sweeping elsewhere), previsions are evaded, professions turned into protests. To some consciences, perhaps, Faith in spiritual matters may mean love; to others it may mean hope; but not to many, is it Faith any longer; and such as these, who would not willingly desert the ancient edifice, hear gladly on every side what is being done to open wide the ways, to enlarge the spirit of a grand old community, which may be narrow-minded and inconsequent at times, but which recognises honour as a part of its creed, and to which votaries cling from traditions that have almost become a part of their very natures. One point after another is stretched, one tenet after another is tacitly abandoned, things are cried in the market-place now which in my youth were scarcely whispered. I have been told of a sect now existing at Geneva so wide and comprehensive in its views that many who thought themselves excluded from all communities now find that they can conscientiously belong to this.

Some of the best and wisest spirits of our time are anxiously trying to do all they can to counteract the cry that the Church as a Church is no living institution, excluding as it does many of the most honest and scrupulous of its members from holy orders, and appealing to the uneducated in a very limited and partial degree; and while these reformers, preserving as far as they can the spirit of the creed of England, are attempting to enlarge the profession of its doctrines, and allowing to every man more and more liberty to determine for himself that inscrutable point of connection between the known and the unknown, the spiritual and the material, another class are in a very simple and effectual manner closing the doors of the Church (and I am speaking no metaphor) in the faces of its votaries, and doing more by that turn of the key in the too well-greased lock to abolish in the minds of those who are thus excluded all realisation of a living actual sympathy in the community, than all the doubts, expressed and non-expressed, of honest sceptics, or the railings of fanatics and scoffers have ever done. Why are church doors closed, bolted, and barred? why are pew-openers and sightseers the only people who are allowed to enter from one week's end to another? Why am I at this minute—it is about nine o'clock on Sunday morning —the member of an established church, which is shut up, with drawn blinds, into which there is no admittance for two hours at least?

Here in this little village, high up among the Rhœtian Alps, a bell is ringing, as I have said, and the peasants are coming over the mountains and down the green slopes that lead to the little chapel by the torrent. It is only a low white shed, a little larger than the neighbouring chalets, or baitas, as they call them here. It is quite shabby and humble, and whitewash is falling from its walls, but the bell rings evening after evening for the 'Ave,' the people go in and come out and walk away quietly by the torrent or along the narrow mountain paths that travel by rock and waterfall and by fragrant scent of thyme and through fresh pine woods to higher Alps near the snow peaks that encircle our valley; and all day long, on Sundays and week days, the worm-eaten door of the chapel is open, and one lamp burns dimly. Whenever you look into the humble little place the lamp is burning, and one or other kneeling figure is there, peasant or traveller. On Sundays the country people come in full dignity of knee-breeches, and wives and sweethearts, and huge red umbrellas, and streaming out after the mass sit in a row on the low wall in front of the establishment, while the little children run about and peep through the wooden planks of the bridge at the boiling waters below.

This seems a long round-about way of entering my protest, and petitioning for leave to enter the church to which I belong, but the contrast between our own system and that which I see here has struck me very much. Not long ago, at Oxford, one day I remember walking from one noble old chapel to another and wondering at the barred doors: in one place a shutter had been left a little open, showing a glimpse of aisle and lofty arch and peaceful light, but the outer gate was safely locked, for fear any passer-by should enter.

It seems a small thing to ask for—leave to go in now and then out of the busy street of life to a quiet place hallowed by association, and to stay there for a little while among surroundings which should bring peaceful and holy things before us. To some natures and temperaments such minutes, coming, maybe, at a moment of doubt or loneliness, would count more than even a whole three hours' service and sermon all complete, and perhaps unsuited to their need, and coming when the stress was over and help no longer of any avail.—I am, Sir, your obedient servant,

OUT OF SEASON.

SIR EDWIN LANDSEER.

WHEN he was a very little boy, Edwin Landseer used to ask his mother to set him a copy to draw from, and then —so his sisters have told me—complain that she always drew one of two things, either a shoe or a currant pudding, of both of which he was quite tired. No wonder that this was insufficient food for the eager young spirit for whose genius in after life two kingdoms were not too wide a range. The boy, when he was a little older, and when his bent seemed more clearly determined, went to his father and asked him for teaching. The father was a wise man, and told his son that he could not himself teach him to be a painter, that Nature was the only school, Observation the true and only teacher. He told little Edwin to use his own powers; to think about all the things he saw; to copy everything: and then he turned the boy out with his brothers—they were all three much of an age—to draw the world as it then existed upon

Hampstead Heath. There seem to have been then, as now, little donkeys upon the common, old horses grazing the turf and gorse, and children and chickens at play, though I fear that now, alas! no curly-headed boy is there storing up treasures for the use of a whole generation to come.

Day after day the children used to spend upon the Heath in the fresh air, at their sports and their flights, but learning meanwhile their early lesson. Their elder sister used to go with them, a young mentor to keep these frolicsome spirits within bounds. One can imagine the little party, buoyant, active, in the full delightful spring of early youth. Perhaps youth is a special attribute belonging to artistic natures, to those whom the gods have favoured, and the old fanciful mythology is not all a fable. When I last saw Sir Edwin Landseer, something of this indescribable youthful brightness still seemed to be with him, although the cloud which dimmed his later years had already partially fallen. But the cruel cloud is more than half a century distant at the time of which I am writing, and, thanks be to Heaven, the whole flood of life, and work, and achievement lies between.

Young Edwin painted a picture in these very early days, which was afterwards sold. It was called the 'Mischief-makers:' a mischievous boy had tied a log of wood to the tail of a mischievous donkey. The ass's head in the South Kensington Museum may have been drawn upon Hampstead Heath—a careful black-lead donkey, that cropped the turf and looked up one day, some sixty years ago, with a puzzled face. .Perhaps it was wondering at the size of the artist standing opposite, with his little sympathetic hand at work. The drawing is marked ' E. Landseer, five years old.' This little donkey, of the line of Balaam's ass, had already found out the secret and knew how to speak in his own language to the youthful prophet. Our prophet needs no warning on his journey ; he is not about to barter his sacred gift, and from Hampstead Heath, and from many a wider moor, he will honestly give his blessing to the tribes as they come up in turn. The tribe of the poor ; the tribe of the hard-working rich ; the tribe of Manchester ; the tribe of Belgravia. There are other sketches in the frame at the Kensington Museum ; a policeman pointed them out to me. '*He* knew Sir Edwin's pictures well, and his sketches, too ; why, he was only six years old when he drew that dog,' said the policeman, kindly. The dog is a pointer curling its tail ; there is the household cat, too, with broad face and feline eyes. There is a more elaborate sketch done at the age of fifteen, and probably representing the same pointer grown into an ancient model now, and promoted from black-lead to water-colour. The painter himself must have been starting in life by this time: born with his fairy gift, the time was come to reveal it.

Little Edwin was eight years old when he first engraved a plate of etchings; asses' heads, sheep, donkeys all were there, and then came a second plate for lions and tigers. He was always drawing animals. When he was thirteen he exhibited the portrait of a pointer and puppy, and also the portrait of Mr. Simpson's mule, by 'Master E. Landseer,' as mentioned in the catalogue. In this year his father took him to Haydon, the painter. There is a notice in Haydon's 'Diary':—

'In 1815 Mr. Landseer, the engraver, had brought me his sons, and said: "When do you intend to let your beard grow and take pupils?" I said, "If my instructions are useful or valuable, now." "Will you let my boys come?" I said, "Certainly." Charles and Thomas, it was immediately arranged, should come every Monday morning, when I was to give them work for the week. Edwin took my dissections of the lion, and I advised him to dissect animals as the only mode of acquiring a knowledge of their construction.

'This very incident generated in me the desire to form a school, and as the Landseers made rapid progress, I resolved to communicate my system to others.'

In 1817 Landseer exhibited a picture of 'Brutus,' the family friend. After 'Brutus' comes a picture called 'Fighting Dogs getting Wind,' which was his first real success. It was, I believe, bought by that friendly umpire of art, Sir George Beaumont. In 1818 Wilkie writes approvingly to Haydon, saying: 'Geddes has a good head, Etty a clever piece, and young Landseer's jack-asses are also good.' Most of these facts I have read in a helpful little biography in the South Kensington Museum, which contains a list of Sir Edwin's early works. The list is a marvel of length and industry. There are many etchings mentioned, and among them 'Recollections of Sir Walter and Lady Scott When Sir Edwin gave up etching, it was Thomas Landseer who engraved his pictures. And here I cannot help adding that, looking over the etchings of that early time, and of later date, my admiration has not been alone for Sir Edwin, but for his brother's work as well.

Haydon's advice about depicting lions seems to have stood the young student in good stead. There is mention made of roaring and prowling lions, of a lion disturbed at his meal, on a canvas six feet by eight. Haydon, as we know, was for extremes of canvas and other things. Leslie, in his autobiography, has his appreciative word for Haydon : 'I was captived with Haydon's art,' he writes, 'which was then certainly at its best, and tried, but with no success, to imitate the richness of his colour and impasto. . . . . . At a much later period I was struck with his resemblance to Charles Lamb's " Ralph Bigod, Esq.," that noble type of the great race of men—" the men who borrow." I even thought, before Lamb declared Fenwick to be the prototype of Bigod, that Haydon was the man, and I am not sure that Lamb did not think of him as well as of Fenwick.   All the traits were Haydon's.   Bigod had an *undeniable* way with him.   He had a cheerful, open exterior, a quick, jovial eye, a bald forehead, just touched with grey, *cana fides.*   He anticipated no excuse, and found none.   When I think of this man—his fiery glow of heart, his swell of feeling—how magnificent, how *ideal* he was, how great at the midnight hour, and when I compare him with the companions with whom I have associated since, I grudge the saving of a few idle ducats, and think that I have fallen into the society of *lenders* and *little* men.'

In 1822 Landseer received a premium from the British Institution for a picture called ' The Larder Invaded.' In 1842 he paints the celebrated ' Catspaw : the monkey's device for eating hot chestnuts.' It was sold for 100*l.*, and would fetch near 3,000*l.* now.   Then he is made A R.A. ; and in 1826 the scene changes from lions' dens

Monday 20th

My dear Thackeray

Old Rams look . . . usually innocent . . . What
am I to do ?

Turn over —

If. He will let me know what class of "Sheep you really want —— with the mystery to illustrate Page for the Mag:

and monkeys' pranks to the well-loved moors and lakes—to the misty, fresh, silent life of the mountain that he has brought into all our homes.

Some of his earliest paintings are illustrations out of Walter Scott's romances. He loved Scott from the beginning to the very end of his life, and kept some of his books and some of Shakespeare's plays by his bedside, to read when he could not sleep. One of his very first oil pictures, however, was not out of a book: it was the portrait of his sister as a little baby girl, toddling about in a big bonnet.

There is a pretty little paragraph in Leslie's autobiography, about Landseer after he became a student at the Royal Academy. 'Edwin Landseer,' he says, 'who entered the Academy very early, was a pretty little curly-headed boy, and he attracted Fuseli's attention by his talents and gentle manners. Fuseli would look round for him and say, " Where is my little *dog-boy?*"'

The few words tell their story, and at the same time reveal the kind heart of the writer, who all his life seems to have admired and loved his younger companion, of whom there is frequent mention in his books. 'Art may be learnt, but can't be taught,' says Leslie, as the elder Landseer had said. 'Under Fuseli's wise neglect Wilkie, Mulready, Etty, Landseer, and Haydon distinguished themselves, and were the better for not being made all alike by teaching, if indeed that could have been done.'

Fuseli's system seems to have been to come in with a book in his hand and to sit reading nearly the whole time he remained with the students; and here I cannot help saying that Leslie himself followed a very different method. It is true that when he taught young painters he used to say very little, but ' he would take the brushes and pallet himself and show them a great deal,' says his son George.

It is now about fifty years since the little *dog-boy* (who was only some nineteen years old) set up in life for himself, hired a tiny cottage with a studio in St. John's Wood. The district even now is silent and unenclosed in many places. In those days it must have been almost a country place. A garden paling divided the painter and his young household from friendly neighbours; and Mrs. Mackenzie, his sister and housekeeper in those youthful days, has told us of pleasant early times and neighbourly meetings; while the young man works and toils at his art, and faces the early difficulties and anxieties that oppress him, and that even his fairy gift cannot altogether avert.

In one of the notices upon his pictures it is said that as a boy and a youth he haunted shows of wild beasts with his sketch-book, and the matches of rat-killing by terriers. Cannot one picture the scene, the cruel sport; the crowd looking on, stupid or vulgarly excited, and there, among coarse and heavy glances and dull scowling looks, shines the bright young face, not seeing the things that the dull eyes are watching, but discerning the something beyond—the world within the world—that life within common life that genius makes clear to us?

What are the old legends worth if this is not what they mean? Our Sir Orpheus plays, and men and animals are brought into his charmed circle. Qualities delicate, indescribable, sympathies between nature and human nature are revealed.

A description in Nathaniel Hawthorne's *Transformation* of Donatello and the animals recalls Edwin Landseer as one reads it.

There is a world to which some favoured spirits belong by natural right; others, who are more distant from its simple inspiration, want the interpreter who is to tell them the meaning of those sudden brown lights and wistful glances; those pricking ears and tails a-quiver; those black confiding noses, humorous and simple, snuffing and sniffing the heathery breezes. It is he who has summoned those little feet for us, coming, as in Donatello's charm, suddenly scampering down the mountain pass; we seem to hear the gentle flurry; or again, we are on the mountain itself; the figures lie motionless wrapped in their plaids, the stag is unconscious and quietly grazing, in branching dignity; it is the little doe, watchful, with sweet, up-pricked head, who is turning to give the alarm; or again it may be a tranquil mist through which the light forms are passing : or a stag wounded and trailing across the sunset waters to die.

Who does not know the picture called 'Suspense ? the noble hound watching at his master's closed door. The painter has painted a whole heart, tender reproach, silence, steady trust, anxious patience. The theme is utterly pathetic, and tells its story straight to the bystander ; the door is closed fast and will never open ; the frayed feather from the master's plume has fallen to the ground. He must have been carried by, for there is a drop of blood upon the feather and another on the floor beyond, and the helpless tender friend has been shut out. I can hardly imagine any picture more tranquil, more pathetic. Who that has ever been shut out but will understand the pang?

And then, again, what home-like glimpses do we owe to Land-eer? Has he not painted warmth, content, and fidelity for us? Look at that fireside party; the tender contentment of the colley, whose faithful nose is guarding the old shepherd's slippers; or the Highland breakfast scene, with its gentle, almost maternal, humours; the baby, the proud mother, the little fat puppies that are a pleasure to behold. In the well-known painting of the 'Shepherd's Last Mourner,' the pathos consists as much in that which is not as in that which is there. The dog with silent care rests his head upon the lonely coffin. He does not understand very much about it all: life he can understand, not death. His feeling is more touching in its incompleteness than if he could grasp anything beyond the present strange wistful moment. Is there aspiration in such a picture? There is natural religion most certainly, as there must be in all true nature. No saint depicted in agony, no painted miracle, could give a more vivid realisation of simple natural feeling, of the mysterious love and fidelity which is in life, and which the very dog can understand, as he silently watches by his old master's coffin.

As I write a friend is saying that some people complain, and not without justice, that Landseer in some instances makes his animals almost too human. The picture of Uncle Tom and his wife in chains has been instanced. In the 'Triumph of Comus' the blending of animal and human nature is most painful to look at, and it is a relief to turn from its nightmare-like vividness to those peaceful cliffs hanging on the wall beyond, where the fresh daylight comes over the crisping waters, where the children are at play and the sheep grazing at the cannon month.

One can recognise in some of the earlier paintings of Sir Edwin the impression of the mental companionship of those who influenced the school of art at the beginning of this century. Regarding this, the school of Wilkie, of Mulready, I can only turn once more to Leslie's temperate criticisms. 'Every great painter,' he says, 'carries us into a world of his own, where, if we give ourselves up to his guidance, we shall find much enjoyment; but if we cavil at every step, we may be sure there is a greater fault in ourselves than any we can discover in him.'

We do not lower our individuality because we submit for a time and learn to see life from different points of view.

The school which preceded Edwin Landseer was a placid and practical school, looking for harmonies rather than for contrasts, somewhat wanting in emotion and vividness of feeling. The meteor-like Turner blazed across the path of these quiet students without inspiring them with his own dazzling and breathless grasp of time and light. Leslie, writing of art, looks back wistfully to the times of Stothart, Fuseli, of Wilkie, Lawrence, Etty, and Constable; but, with all their harmony of colour and merits of natural expression, they do not strike the chords that Sir Edwin has struck in his highest moments of inspiration. This much one cannot deny that his pictures are unequal, sometimes over-crowded, sometimes wanting in tone and colour; there are subjects too which seem scarce worthy of his consummate pencil. His very popularity is a hard test, and the constant reproduction of his pictures on every wall must needs blunt their fresh interest. But this is hypercriticism. How many blank front parlours, how many long dull passages and tiresome half hours of life has he changed and illuminated. Remembering some of these half hours, one could almost wish that none but pleasant associations might belong to those familiar apparitions of playful paws and trustful noses. A pretty little page returning from the chase was the playfellow of our own early life; the sun fell on his innocent head as he hung on the wall of our high-perched Paris home. Here, by a foggier fireside, the children grow up companionably with the dear big dog that is saving the little child from the sea. It was the beneficent painter himself who sent this big dog to live with us with a friendly cypher in a corner of the frame.

A friend has told us the story of another dog bestowed by the same kind hand : ' About ten years ago Sir Edwin wished me to keep a dog, thinking that when I came home I should not be so lonely; he also said that he would look for one for me himself. I told him that my business occupations would not allow me to give a dog proper attention, and although Sir Edwin mentioned the subject more than once I still refused. About a month afterwards he came to dine with me one day, and when he arrived he brought a beautifully finished picture of a dog, saying, " Here H., I have brought you a parlour boarder ; I hope you won't turn him out of doors." '

A writer in the ' Daily News,' in a charmingly written notice, describes Sir Edwin's manner of working :—

' His method of composition was remarkably like Scott's, except in the point of the early rising of the latter. Landseer went late to bed and rose very late— coming down to breakfast at noon ; but he had been composing perhaps for hours. Scott declared that the most fertile moments for resources, in invention especially, were those between sleeping and waking, or rather before opening the eyes from sleep, while the brain was wide awake. This, much prolonged, was Landseer's time for composing his pictures. His conception once complete, nothing could exceed the rapidity of his execution. In his best days, before his sense of failing eyesight and the rivalship of rising pre-Raphaelite art aggravated his painful fastidiousness, his rapidity was quite as marvellous as Scott's. The speed was owing to decision, and the decision was owing to the thorough elaboration of the subject in his mind before he committed it to the management of his masterly hand.' The stories are numberless of the rapidity with which he executed his work. There are two little King Charles' in the South Kensington Museum, wonders of completeness and consummate painting, whose skins are silk, whose eyes gleam with light. They are said to have been painted in two days. I have read somewhere also the melancholy fact in addition that both the poor little creatures died by violent deaths.

The ' Daily News ' quotes a rabbit picture exhibited in the British Gallery under which Sir Edwin wrote, ' painted in three-quarters of an hour.'

The first time I was ever in Sir Edwin's studio was about twelve years ago, when we drove there one summer's day with my father to see a picture of the ' Highland Flood ' just then completed. We came away talking of the picture, touched by the charm and the kindness of the master of the house, laden with the violets from the garden, which he had given us. Another time the master was no longer there, but his house still opened hospitably with a greeting for old days' sake from those who had belonged to him and who had known my father. We were let in at the side gate. There stood the great white house that we remembered; we crossed the garden, where the dead leaves were still heaped, and some mist was hanging among the bare branches of the trees, and so by an entrance lined with pictures we came into the great studio once more, where all the memories and pictures were crowded, hanging to the walls, piled against the easels. We seemed to be walking into the shrine of a long life, and one almost felt ashamed, and as if one were surprising its secrets. All about the walls and on the ceiling were time stains spreading in a dim veil; he used to say that he hated whitewash, and that he would never allow any workman but himself about the place. It seemed to me at first as if the cloud of his later days still hung about the room, where he had suffered so many cruel hours.; but, looking again, tnere were his many bright and sweet fancies meeting us on every side, and the gloom suddenly dispelled. Everywhere are beautiful and charming things, that strike one as one looks. Perhaps it is a tender little calf's head tied by its nose, perhaps a flock of sheep against a soft grey sky. There are old companions over the chimney, Sir Roderick and David Roberts looking out of a gloom of paint; there is a lion roaring among the rocks that seems to fill the room with its din.

As we look round we see more pictures and sketches of every description. There is a little princess, in green velvet, feeding a great Newfoundland dog; there is the picture of the young man dying in some calm distant place, with a little quivering living dog upon his knee looking up into his face; near to this stands a lovely little sketch about which Miss Landseer told us a little story. One day the painter was at work when they came hurriedly to tell him that the Queen was riding up to his garden-gate, and wished him to come out to her. He was to see her mounted upon her horse for a picture he was to paint. It seemed to me like some fanciful little story out of a fairy tale, or some old-world legend. The young painter at his art; the young queen cantering up, followed by her court, and passing on, and the sketch remaining to tell the story. He has painted in the old archway at Windsor Castle; the light and queenly figure is drifting from beneath it, other people are following, the sun is shining. Many of these sketches are hasty, but there is not one that does not bear traces of the master's hand

We all know Sir Joshua's often-quoted answer to Lord Holland, when he asked him how long he had been painting his picture.

'All my life,' is written in many a picture, as it is written indeed in many a face. Take the likeness of Gibson, with his keen downcast head, simple, manly, and refined. Is not his whole life written there? With the *thrill* of this noble portrait rises a vision within a vision of another studio miles and years away. The click of the workman's hammer comes echoing through Roman sunshine—the marble dust is lying in a heap at our feet --there stands the sculptor in his working dress, pointing to the band of colour in the Venus waving hair.

There is another portrait in the room, to which the painter has given all his best and noblest work. He has opened his magic box—Pandora's was nothing to it—and there stands a lady with a child in her arms, endowed with a gentle might of grace, of womanly instinct and beauty. The baby's little foot is caught in the lacework of the shawl; the mother's face is turned aside. It is a charming group, refined, full of sentiment. But for all women Edwin Landseer had this courteous feeling of manly deference. There is a Highland mother sitting with a little Highland baby in her arms among limpid grays and browns; there is a lovely marchioness with a dear little chubby innocent-eyed baby upon her knee. It is all the same feeling, the same grace and tenderness of expression.

Ruskin describes somewhere the attitude of mind in which a true artist should set to work. Sham art concocts its effect bit by bit; it puts in a light here, a shade there; piles on beauties, rubs in sentiment. The true painter will receive the impression straight from the subject, and then, keeping to that precious impression, works upon it with all his skill and power of attention. Anybody can understand the difference. Even great artists like Landseer sometimes paint pictures out of tune with their own natures, where the painter's skill is evident, and his industry, but his heart is not.

But here is his heart in many a delightful sketch and completed work : in the 'loveable dogs' heads,' that my companion liked so much, with eyes flashing and melting from the canvas; in the pointer's creeping along the ground; in the sportsmanlike eagerness and stir of the 'otter-hunt;' in the tender uplifted paw of the little dog talking to Godiva's horse; in many a sketch and completed picture.

When Landseer first became intimate with Mr. Jacob Bell, he was not a rich man, nor had he ever been able to save any money, but under his excellent and experienced good advice and management, the painter's affairs became more flourishing. When Mr. Bell died, his partner devoted himself, as he had done, to Sir Edwin's interests. The little old cottage had been added to and enlarged meanwhile, the great studio was built, the park was enclosed, the pictures and prints multiplied and spread, the painter's popularity grew.

One wonderful—never to be forgotten—night my father took us to see some great ladies in their dresses going to the Queen's fancy ball. We drove to —— House (it is all very vague and dazzlingly indistinct in my mind). We were shown into a great empty room, and almost immediately some doors were flung open, there came a blaze of light, a burst of laughing voices, and from many a twinkling dinner-table rose a company that seemed, to our unaccustomed eyes, as if all the pictures in Hampton Court had come to life. The chairs scraped back, the ladies and gentlemen advanced together over the shining floors. I can remember their high heels clicking on the floor: they were in the dress of the court of King Charles II.; the ladies, beautiful, dignified, and excited. There was one, lovely and animated, in yellow; I remember her pearls shining. Another seemed to us even more beautiful, as she crossed the room all dressed in black—but she, I think, was not going to the ball; and then somebody began to say, ' Sir Edwin has promised to rouge them,' and then everybody began to call out for him, and there was also an outcry about his moustaches that ' *really* must be shaved off,' for they were not in keeping with his dress. Then, as in a dream, we went off to some other great house, Bath House perhaps, where one lady, more magnificently dressed than all the others, was sitting in a wax-lighted dressing-room, in a sumptuous sort of conscious splendour, and just behind her chair stood a smiling gentleman, also in court dress, and he held up something in one hand and laughed, and said he must go back to the house from whence we came, and the lady thanked him and called him Sir Edwin. We could not understand who this Sir Edwin was, who seemed to be wherever we went. Nor why he should put on the rouge. Then the majestic lady showed us her beautiful jewelled shoe. Then a fairy thundering chariot carried off this splendid lady, and the nosegays of the hanging footmen seemed to scent the air as the equipage drove off under the covered way. Perhaps all this is only a dream, but I think it is true: for there was again a third house where we found more pictures alive, two beautiful young pictures and their mother, for whom a parcel was brought in post-haste, containing a jewel all dropping with pearls. Events seem so vivid when people are nameless, are only

faces not lives, when all life is an impression. That evening was always the nearest approach to a live fairy tale
that we ever lived, and that ball more brilliant than any
we ever beheld.

No wonder Edwin Landseer liked the society of these
good-natured and splendid people, and no wonder they
liked his. To be a delightful companion is in itself no
small gift. Edwin Landseer's company was a wonder of
charming gaiety. I have heard my father speak of it
with the pride he used to take in the gifts of others.

I see a note about nothing at all lying on the table,
which a friend has sent among some others of sadder import; but it seems to give a picture of a day's work,
written as it is with 'the palette in the other hand,' at
the time of Sir Edwin's health of labour and popularity.

'I shall like to be scolded by you,' he writes. 'This
eve I dine with Lord Hardinge, and have to go to Lord
Londesborough's after the banquet, and then to come
back here to R. A. Leslie, who has a family hop—which I
am afraid will entirely fill up my time, otherwise I should
have been delighted to say yes. Pray give me another
opportunity.

'Written, with my palette in the other hand, in honest
hurry.'

Perhaps Edwin Landseer was the first among modern

painters who restored the old traditions of a certain sumptuous habit of living and association with great persons. The charm of manner of which kind Leslie spoke, put him at ease in a world where charm of manner is not without its influence, and where his brilliant gifts and high-minded scrupulous spirit made him deservedly loved, trusted, and popular. To artistic natures especially, there is something almost irresistible in the attraction of beauty and calm leisure and refinement. These things seem to say more perhaps than they are really worth in themselves.

Lords and ladies have to thank the intelligent classes for many of the things that make their homes delightful and complete; for the noble pictures on their walls, the books that speak to them, the arts that move them; and, perhaps, the intelligent classes might in their turn learn to adorn their own homes with something of the living art which belongs to many of these well-bred people, who sometimes win the best-loved of the workers away from their companions and make them welcome. No wonder that men not otherwise absorbed by home ties are delighted and charmed by a sense of artistic fitness and tranquillity, which after all might be more widely spread, and which is no mysterious secret only taught by prosperity, it is the gentleness of goodwill and the self-respecting deference of generous interest in others.

A friend has sent me the following pages, which describe Sir Edwin at this time, and I cannot do better than give them here as they have come to me.

' " The world knows nothing of its greatest men," was not applicable to Landseer. Though not one of its greatest men, he was a man of acknowledged genius, and was courted, admired, made much of, by all who knew him. " Landseer will be with us," was held out as an inducement to join many a social board, where his wit, gaiety, and peculiar powers of mimicry rendered him a delightful guest. But I am speaking of him as he appeared before the fine spirit was darkened by one of the heaviest of calamities !

' Landseer's perceptions of character were remarkably acute. Not only did he know what was passing in the hearts of dogs, but he could read pretty closely into those of men and women also. The love of truth was an instinct with him ; his common phrase about those he estimated highly was that ' they had the true ring.' This was most applicable to himself; there was no alloy in *his* metal; he was true to himself and to others. This was proved in many passages of his life, when nearly submerged by those disappointments and troubles which are more especially felt by sensitive organisations such as that which it was his fortune—or misfortune to possess.

It was a pity that Landseer, who might have done so much for the good of animal-kind, never wrote on the subject of their treatment. He had a strong feeling against the way some dogs are tied up, only allowed their freedom now and then. He used to say a man would fare better tied up than a dog, because the former can take his coat off, but a dog lives in his for ever. He declared a tied-up dog, without daily exercise, goes mad, or dies, in three years. His wonderful power over dogs is well known. An illustrious lady asked him how it was that he gained this knowledge ? " By peeping into their hearts, ma'am," was his answer. I remember once being wonderfully struck with the mesmeric attraction he possessed with them. A large party of his friends were with him at his house in St. John's Wood ; his servant opened the door ; three or four dogs rushed in, one a very fierce-looking mastiff. We ladies recoiled, but there was no fear ; the creature bounded up to Landseer, treated him like an old friend, with most expansive demonstrations of delight. Someone remarking, " how fond the dog seemed of him," he said, " I never saw it before in my life."

' Would that horse-trainers could have learnt from him how horses could be broken in or trained more easily by kindness than by cruelty. Once when visiting him he came in from his meadow looking somewhat dishevelled and tired. "What have you been doing?" we asked him. "Only teaching some horses tricks for Astley's, and here is *my* whip," he said, showing us a piece of sugar in his hand. He said that breaking-in horses meant more often breaking their hearts, and robbing them of all their spirit.

'Innumerable are the instances, if I had the space, I could give you of his kind and wise laws respecting the treatment of the animal world, and it is a pity they are not preserved for the large portion of the world who love, and wish to ameliorate, the condition of their "poor relations."

'There were few studios formerly more charming to visit than Landseer's. Besides the genial artist and his beautiful pictures, the *habitués* of his workshop (as he called it) belonged to the *élite* of London society, especially the men of wit and distinguished talents—none more often there than D'Orsay, with his good-humoured face, his ready wit, and delicate flattery. "Landseer," he would call out at his entrance, "keep the dogs off me" (the painted ones), "I want to come in, and some of them will bite me—and that fellow in de corner is growling furiously." Another day he seriously asked me for a pin, and when I presented it to him and wished to know why he wanted it, he replied, "to take de thorn out of dat dog's foot; do you not see what pain he is in?" I never look at the picture now without this other picture rising before me. Then there was Mulready, still looking upon Landseer as the young student, and fearing that all this incense would spoil him for future work; and Fonblanque, who maintained from first to last that he was on the top rung of the ladder, and when at the exhibition of some of Landseer's later works, he heard it said, "They were not equal to his former ones," he exclaimed in his own happy manner, "It is hard upon Landseer to flog him with his own laurels."

'But, dear A——, I am exceeding the limits of a letter. You asked me to write some of my impressions about Landseer, and I am sure you and all his friends will forgive me for being verbose when recalling, not only the great gifts, but delightful qualities of our lost friend.'

' My worn-out old pencil will work with friendly gladness in an old friend's service,' he writes to my father, who had asked him to draw a sketch for the *Cornhill Magazine.* Elsewhere will be read the facsimile of a second letter he sent him on the same subject.

' I quite forgot that I dined with a group of doctors (a committee) at two o'clock. R.A. business after dinner. This necessity prevents me kissing hands before your departure. Don't become too Italian ; don't speak broken

English to your old friends on your return to our village, where you will find no end of us charmed to have you back again ; and amongst them, let me say, you will find old E. L. sincerely glad to see his unvarying K. P. once more by that old fire-side.'

So he writes in '63 to the friend to whom I owe the notes already given here. There is the 'true ring,' as he himself says, in these faithful greetings continued through a lifetime. And now that the life is over, the friend still seems there, and his hand stretches faithfully from the little blue page.

He writes again September 2, 1864 :—

'Do you think you could bring Mrs. Brookfield to my lion studio to-morrow between five and six o'clock? I have forgotten her address, or would not trouble you. Have you still got that cruel dagger in your sleeve? If you can also lasso my friend Brookfield I shall be grateful, and beg you to believe me your used up old friend,

'E. L.'

A little later I find a note written in better spirits. His work is done, and those great over-weighing sphinxes are no longer upon his mind. 'The colossal clay,' he says, 'is now in Baron Marochetti's hands, casting in metal. When No. 2 is in a respectable condition remind me of

Colonel Hamley's kind and highly flattering desire to see my efforts. We can, on the 3rd, discuss pictures, lions, and friends.

'Your's always,   E. L.'

What efforts his work had cost him, and what a price he paid for that which he achieved, may be gathered from a letter to another correspondent, which was written about this time :—

'Dear H.,' he says, ' I am much surprised by your note. The plates, large vignettes, are all *the same* size. The sketches from which they were engraved for the deer-stalking work being done in a sketch-book of a particular shape and size. Those of the O form all the same, as also the others. I have got quite trouble enough ; ten or twelve pictures about which I am tortured, and a large national monument to complete. . . . If I am bothered about everything and anything, no matter what, I know my head will not stand it much longer.'

' I cannot even leave off to read Gosling's letter,' he says, writing to this same T. H. ' If you will call at three you will find me.' Then comes, ' the matter which you are kind enough to express willingness to look into ; ' it is one long record of good advice rendered and gratitude freely given. Elsewhere Landseer writes to this same correspondent. 'I have just parted from your friend P. He strongly urged me going to 45, where I have been so kindly received of late. I told him you were an object for plunder in this world, and that I was ashamed of living on you as others do.' This letter is written in a state of nervous irritation which is very painful; he wishes to make changes in his house; to build, to alter the arrangements; he does not know what to decide or where to go; the struggle of an over-wrought mind is beginning to tell. It is the penalty some men must pay for their gifts; but some generous souls may not think the price of a few weary years too great for a life of useful and en-nobling work.

The letters grow sadder and more sad as time goes on. Miss Landseer has kindly sent me some, written to her between 1866 and 1869. The first is written from abroad :—

'I have made up my mind to return, to face the ocean! The weather is unfriendly—sharp wind and spiteful rain. There is no denying the fact, since my arrival and during my sojourn here I have been less well. The doctors keep on saying it is on the nerves; hereafter they may be found to be in error. Kind Lady E. Peel keeps on writing for me to go to Villa Lammermoor, and says she will undertake my recovery. I desire to get home.

With this feeling, I am to leave this to-morrow, pass some hours in Paris (with W. B., in a helpless state of ignorance of the French language); take the rail to Calais at night, if it does not blow cats and dogs; take the vessel to Dover; hope to be home on the 6th before two o'clock. If C. L. had started to come here he might have enjoyed *unlimmitted* amusement and novelty.   B. M. and I wrote to that effect; he leaving on Sunday night . . . . would have found me and B. M. waiting his arrival to bring him to dinner.'

The next is a letter from Balmoral, dated June 1867 :—

'The Queen kindly commands me to get well here. She has to-day been twice to my room to show additions recently added to her already rich collection of photographs.   Why, I know not, but since I have been in the Highlands I have for the first time felt wretchedly weak, without appetite.   The easterly winds, and now again the unceasing cold rain, may possibly account for my condition, as I can't get out.   Drawing tires me; however, I have done a little better to-day.   The doctor residing in the castle has taken me in hand, and gives me leave to dine to-day with the Queen and the "rest of the royal family." . . . . Flogging would be mild compared to my sufferings. No sleep, fearful cramp at night, accompanied by a feeling of faintness and distressful feebleness . . . . All this means that I shall not be home on the 7th.'

He seems to have returned to Scotland a second time this year, and writes from Lochlinhart, Dingwall :—

' I made out my journey without pausing, starting on the eve of Thursday the 3rd, arriving here the evening of Friday (700 miles) the 4th. I confess to feeling jaded and tired. The whole of hills here present to the eye one endless mass of snow. It is really cold and winterly. Unless the weather recovers a more *generous* tone I shall not stay long, but at once return south to Chillingham. I was tempted yesterday to go out with Mr. Coleman to the low ground part of the forest, and killed my first shot at deer. I am paying for my boldness to-day, Sunday. All my joints ache ; the lumbago has reasserted its unkindness ; a warm bath is in requisition, and I am a poor devil. Unless we have the comfort of genial sunshine, I shall not venture on getting out. . . . I am naturally desirous to hear from you, and to receive a report of the progress of goings on at my home. We have here Mr. C. M. and a third gentleman, just arrived. Mr. Coleman has returned to London on account of his mother's ill-health. I have written to H., but in case he has not received my note, let him know my condition ; say I shall be very glad to hear from him when he goes to Paris, and how long he remains in foreign parts. I hope you have found Mr. B. and the maids respectfully attentive.

'My dear Jessy, affectionately yours,

'E. LANDSEER.'

The years seem to pass slowly as one reads these letters written in snow and rain and depression. Here is another dated Stoke Park, July, 1868 :—

'Dear Jessy,—Strange enough, but I have only just found at the bottom of the bag your little package of letters. Many thanks for your pale green note, so far satisfactory. I believe it is best to yield to Mr. C.'s advice, and remain here another day or two. It is on the cards that I try my boldness by a run up to my home and back here the same day. It is quite a trial for me to be away from the meditation in the old studio—my works starving for my hand.'

The next letter is written in 1869 from Chillingham Castle, where he seems to have been at home and in sympathy, although he writes so sadly :—

'Very mortifying are the disappointments I have to face; one day seeming to give hope of a decided turn in favour of natural feeling, the next knocked down again.

If my present scheme comes off, I shall not be at home again for ten days. If on my return I find myself a victim to the old impulsive misery, I shall go on to East-well Park, as the Duchess of Abercorn writes she will take every care of me. Since I last wrote I have been on a visit to the Dowager Marchioness of Waterford, Ford Castle, a splendid old edifice, which C. L. would enjoy. Love to all.'

I go on selecting at hazard from the letters before me :—

'Again accept my gratitude for your constant kind-ness,' he writes to his faithful T. H. H. 'The spell is broken in a mild form, but the work is too much for me. The long long walk in the dark, after the shot is fired, over rocks, bog, black moss, and through torrents, is more than enough *for twenty-five!*

'Poor C. has been very ill rewarded for his Highland enterprise. Fifteen hundred miles of peril on the rail; endless bad weather whilst he was here, without killing one deer; finally obliged to hurry off. . . . I have begged him not to think of undertaking another long journey on my account, even in the event of his being able to leave home. . . . It is like you to think of my request touching medicines for the poor here. . . . We have a dead calm after the wicked weather; not a dimple in the lake. I am not bold yet. Possibly reaction may take place in the quiet of the studio. I shall not start on great difficulties, but on child's play.'

Here is another note, written in the following spring:—

'March 11, 1869.

'I know you like water better than oil; but in spite of your love of paper-staining, I venture to beg your acceptance of these oil studies, which you will receive as old friends from the Zoo.

'In some respects they will recall the interest you took in my labours for the Nelson lions, and I hope will always remind you of my admiration for your kindly nature, to say nothing of my endless obligations to your unceasing desire to aid a poor old man, nearly used up.

'Dear T. H. H., ever sincerely yours,

'E. LANDSEER.'

Here is a note which is very characteristic:—

'Saturday Eve, 5th June.

'Dear H,—I am not quite content with myself touching the proposed suggestion of our taking advantage of an offer made by —— for the two pictures. He has not put his desire to have the pictures in writing, has he? We must talk it over to-morrow if you come up at four o'clock, or sooner. . . . The enclosed letters are most friendly, as you will see. Read them, and bring them up to-morrow. I am anything but well ; botherations unfit me for healthy work. You must pat me on the back to-morrow ; at the same time, if anything has turned up more attractive don't bind yourself to me.

'I should not dislike a drive or a walk to-morrow before dinner.'

He writes once again :—

'I have a great horror of the *smell* of a trick, or a money motive.'

'My dear Hills,—My health (or rather condition) is a mystery quite beyond human intelligence. I sleep well seven hours, and awake tired and jaded, and do not rally till after luncheon. J. L. came down yesterday and did her very best to cheer me. She left at nine. . . . . I return to my own home, in spite of a kind invitation from Mr. and Mrs. Gladstone to meet Princess Louise at breakfast.

'I wonder if you are free to-morrow. I shall try and catch you for a little dinner with me, tho' I am sure to find you better engaged.   'Dear H., ever thine,

'E L.'

Then comes the sad concluding scene—the long illness and the anxious watch.   Was ever anyone more tenderly nursed and cared for?   Those who had loved him in his bright wealth of life now watched the long days one by one, telling away its treasure.   He was very weak in body latterly, but sometimes he used to go into the garden and walk round the paths, leaning on his sister's arm.   One beautiful spring morning he looked up and said, 'I shall never see the green leaves again;' but he did see them, Mrs. Mackenzie said.   He lived through another spring. He used to lie in his studio, where he would have liked to die.   To the very end he did not give up his work; but he used to go on, painting a little at a time, faithful. to his task.

When he was almost at his worst—so someone told me—they gave him his easel and his canvas, and left him alone in his studio, in the hope that he might take up his work and forget his suffering.   When they came back they found that he had painted the picture of a little lamb lying beside a lion.   The Queen is the owner of one of the last pictures he ever painted.   She wrote to her old friend and expressed her admiration for it, and asked to become the possessor.   Her sympathy brightened the sadness of those last days for him.   It is well known that he appealed to her once, when haunted by some painful apprehensions, and that her wise and judicious kindness came to the help of his nurses. She sent him back a message: bade him not be afraid, and to trust to those who were doing their best for him, and in whom she herself had every confidence.

Sir Edwin once told Mr. Browning that he had thought upon the subject, and come to the conclusion that the stag was the bravest of all animals. Other animals are born warriors, they fight in a dogged and determined sort of way; the stag is naturally timid, trembling, vibrating with every sound, flying from danger, from the approach of other creatures, halting to fight. When pursued its first impulse is to escape; but when turned to bay and flight is impossible it fronts its enemies nobly, closes its eyes not to see the horrible bloodshed, and with its branching horns steadily tosses dog after dog, one upon the other, until overpowered at last by numbers it sinks to its death . . .

It seems to me, as I think of it, not unlike a picture of his own sad end. Nervous, sensitive, high-minded, working on to the last, he was brought to bay and over-powered by that terrible mental rout and misery.

He wished to die in his studio—his dear studio for which he used to long when he was away, and where he lay so many months expecting the end, but it was in his own room that he slept away. His brother was with him.

His old friend came into the room.   He knew him, and pressed his hand . . .

As time goes on the men are born, one by one, who seem to bring to us the answers to the secrets of life, each coming in his place, and revealing in his turn according to his gift.   Such men belong to nature's true priesthood, and among their names not forgotten, will be that of Edwin Landseer.

A BOOK OF PHOTOGRAPHS

THERE are all sorts of books, and those of which we have so many, and of which we shall have so many more before the end of the year, are not the only ones which are published. Type, and printers' ink, and paper, after all, are but the record of things as they are; of facts, laws, states of being and feeling, which might perhaps be more quickly and more fully described in many other ways, if we could only find them out; and certainly of late years one great new method of communication has been discovered. A photograph of your friend will, to a certain point, tell you more about him in one minute than whole pages of elaborate description. You see him himself—the identity is there, the dull, worn look or the familiar cross-grained expression, or the humorous twinkle of the eye, or the little vanities or negligences of dress which always belonged to him. They are all before you, summed up upon a little bit of card which tumbles out of his letter, and which you are pretty certain to examine even if you have not time to go on trying to decipher the words with which he accompanies his offering. There he is, more or less like, but always with a certain essence of personality, so to speak, which is produced in no other way. And if one little piece of prepared pasteboard is able to express so much about B., J., and R., the most uninteresting of men, it would seem strange, indeed, if it were not able to say still more, and to describe the interest and sentiment belonging to some people, as well as the utter absence of either in others. This latter quality, especially feeling or sentiment, which is so hard to put into words, seems to have a language of its own, which utters in many different ways, and is often quite beside and beyond the words which try to speak of it. It comes out in music as the notes thrill and suddenly master the listeners; it speaks from the pictures hanging on the walls of great galleries, where the people coming and going, stop, called they know not why or how. When some poets sing, suddenly you know that their song is alive with this mysterious soul of inanimate things; or, again, you find it in the fields and the woods, and along the hill ranges, or in a look which comes into a familiar face, and which, perhaps, you had never seen before. What-

ever it may be, it is certain that some people are blind
to it all their lives, and we all remember how to
Peter Bell—

> A primrose on a river's brim
> A yellow primrose was to him,
> And it was nothing more.

A great many people are blind, a great many others go
about peering through spectacles more or less green, blue,
concave, convex ; while a few great masters there are,
certain Shakspeares and Raphaels of ancient and of latter
times, who seem to see things with their clear natural
eyes, and to point out to those who follow after them
truths which are almost beyond the apprehension of some
of their disciples, though they know that they exist, and
have faith to believe in them.

A book, or rather a portfolio, although it may be here
reviewed as a book, has been lately published,[1] in which
as one turns over the pages one cannot but be struck by
the indescribable presence of this natural feeling and real
sentiment of which we have been speaking.   Mrs.
Cameron, the author of the work in question, is a
photographer who has tried to photograph something more than a mere inanimate copy of this or that
object before her, and yet the commonest stories and

---

[1] It is to be seen at Messrs. Colnaghis' by anybody who likes to go
there.

events of everyday life are the subjects of her art. 'Trust,' 'Resignation,' 'Meekness,' 'Thy Will be done,' are the names she has given to some of her pictures. Children's solemn eyes and fair waving locks, mothers tending them, Madonnas, here and there an old friend greeting us out of a sea of marginal pasteboard, these are all her materials; but it is difficult to believe that these quiet and noble-looking people are of the same race as those men and women whom we are accustomed to meet with in all our own and our friends' photograph books.

A vision rises before one of the throng of gentlemen and ladies, dining-room chairs, small tables, and plaster pedestals to which photography has accustomed us, and of the devices by which popular artists have imagined how to give both dignity and repose to their sitters. You may choose both or either, at your will. If dignity is desired, the plaster column is brought into requisition; if repose is considered more characteristic, the dining-room chair and the small and rickety table are produced. You are requested to place one elbow on the table, to turn your head back over one shoulder, to point out your little finger if you are a lady, to put one hand into your pocket if you are a man. Art can go no farther. With the tasteful addition of a vase, or a small bronze statuette of a horse, and a volume negligently placed upon the small table, the composition is complete.

It is, perhaps, no disparagement to Mrs. Cameron to say that she is *not* a popular artist, and does not deal in these original effects. People like clear, hard out-lines, and have a fancy to see themselves and their friends as if through opera-glasses, all complete, with the buttons, &c., nicely defined. These things Mrs. Cameron's public may not always find, but in their stead are very wonderful and charming sights and sug-gestions in this unbound book of hers. A well known photographer said the other day that hers was the real and artistic manner of working the camera; that he, too, had tried to photograph ' out of focus,' as it is called, but the public would not accept it, and he had therefore been obliged to give it up.

As we are writing, at this moment, we look through a window into a garden, and across a sloping country, where the bare trees have not yet put on their leaves, and stand out in soft and delicate lines against a gentle spring mist, through which the birds are singing. A thatched cottage roof, the hedges, the distant clump of trees, are all painted with the soft mysterious grey. An effect very much like this seems to be occasionally the result of Mrs. Cameron's method of working. And yet the very mystery seems in many cases to add to the wonderful charm of the pictures, although as photographs some of the clearer specimens are the finest. There is one portrait of George Watts which is Holbein-like in its perfection of detail, while another, much fainter and less distinct, for repose and solemn flow of outline puts one in mind of some stately figure of Michael Angelo's. Among the portraits, those of Sir Henry Taylor, Mr. Holman Hunt, and Mr. Spedding, are remarkably fine. A sweet intent woman's head, a child safely cradled in her arms, the old tender maternal story retold once more is called 'Resting in Hope.' 'The Salutation' will recall to many a picture now in our National Gallery. In 'Aurora,' less perfect as a photograph than many of the others, the child's eyes shine out with a depth and intensity that put one in mind of those wonderful children's eyes in Millais' 'Autumn Leaves.' 'Annie Lee' might be a Leonardo, from a certain stately grace. 'Trust,' a quiet woman with a noble head, with children clinging about her; 'Paul and Virginia,' an exquisite little pair, and 'Good Night,' are only a few among the many one would like to mention. A painter, writing of these very photographs, says:—'There is a quality about many of them as pictures which I do not remember in any other photographs. They suggest colour so completely that it does not seem that painting could add anything to their beauty.' Photographers will appreciate the difficulties overcome in the larger picture called 'The Wise and the Foolish Virgins;' but it does not require any knowledge of the art to do justice to the noble and honest and beautiful effects which are here brought before us. Now-a-days Wordsworth would be thinking of other pictures than Sir George Beaumont's were he to write of the—

> Soul-soothing Art, whom morning, noontide, even
> Do serve with all their changeful pageantry,
> Thou, with Ambition, modest, yet sublime,
> Here for the sight of mortal man hast given
> To one brief moment caught from fleeting time
> The appropriate calm of blest eternity.

A COUNTRY SUNDAY.

I am always well pleased with a country Sunday, and think if keeping holy the seventh day were only a human institution it would have been the best method that could be thought of for the polishing and civilising of mankind. . . . Sunday clears away the rust of the whole week, not only as it refreshes in their minds the notion of religion, but as it puts both the sexes upon appearing in their most agreeable forms, and exerting all such qualities as are apt to give them a figure in the eyes of the village.—*Spectator.*

THIS does not seem less applicable now than it did in Addison's time, when perhaps men and women did not work so hard as they do now-a-days, or need the day of rest so greatly; when the village where Addison wrote was smaller than it is now; when Piccadilly was a single line of houses, looking out on fields at the back; when all the painful information, and the army of recollections and allusions which are expected from well-informed persons at every turn, were still in the future, and did not exist to trouble the lazy and haunt the ignorant; when the weeks did not come laden with letters to read and to answer, with 'Times,' with 'Telegraphs,' with 'Saturday Reviews;'

when there were a hundred thousand less books to cut, a hundred thousand less people coming and going, each in turn to be seen, visited, attended to, conciliated, solicited, as the case might be ; when whole streets and districts round which we now laboriously ply in the dusty east wind were unbuilt and unthought of; when one single little welcome sheet, brought in with the tea-equipage by Betsy (who knew her mistress's tastes so well that when breakfast delayed it was because the ' Spectator' had not yet come, but the water boiled, and she expected it every minute), was all that anybody was required to master before the teapot was drained.

That small sheet, short, well considered, written by the wisest penmen of the day, who took so great an interest in its little moralities, and quirks, and kindly conceits, suggested, perhaps, another publication which is at this moment in the reader's hands: but anyhow it is to be feared that a few pleasant reflections on Sir Roger de Coverley's household, or the story of Theodosius and Constantia, or a paper on the abuse of metaphors, would scarcely suffice to us jaded beings who are in pursuit of the latest intelligence from India, Asia, China, and Abyssinia, besides particulars of the American war, the speeches in the two Houses, the accidents on the railways, and the latest abuses' of the day.   A law should be passed to compel such people to spend at least one Sunday out of every seven in the country, where Sundays in England seem to dawn with a sweet peace and tranquillity that are inexpressibly quieting and comforting to the weary. In France people try hard to follow this advice, but we may all of us possibly remember, as a vision, the long straight roads leading from the gates of Paris, with the sun beating fierce upon the dust and the stone-heaps and the stunted trees (acacias, and such like) along the arid wayside, the grey flat horizon, the city with its white stone houses and glittering placards in the distance, the contented people pouring out of its many barriers, and straggling along the road, or resting on the stone-heaps under their sunshades and umbrellas, while the children fill their little blouses and white pinafores with pebbles and with dust instead of flowers and grass. At the time one could not help being touched by the cheerful content of the sun-baked little groups. Father in Sunday blouse; mother in smart ribbons; grandmother in her country cap, producing the basket with the provender and sour bread ; and, perhaps, a friendly gendarme with his lass coming up to join the party. Then there are Roman Sundays, steaming with incense; Scotch Sundays, when the gardener refuses to pluck fresh vegetables, and the children go to church three times ; there are Sundays at sea. . . . But it seems to me that there can be no Sundays in the world like an English country Sunday, such as that which most of us, let us hope, can look back to at some time in our lives.

Lord Bacon in his essays used to like to describe castles in the air with commodious galleries, and servants' offices, and gardens laid out to his fancy, all of which good things were far removed from many of his readers, who yet liked to read of the great man's conceits. In a humble way I too would like to describe an ideal of which most of the component parts are within anybody's reach.

The ideal Sunday should be spent at a country house not many miles from London. We will call it Pleasance. You should come to it through fresh country lanes and commons, and across broad fields where the cows are browsing. Pleasance should have a great hall through which the garden might show, and from which the doors should lead into a library, a dining-room, a drawing-room, all with windows looking across the lawns and fields and green distant slopes and acres far away gently rising and falling. There should be scattered here and there flocks and herds, to give life and animation to the green pastures and the still waters, and close at hand a few great trees under which one or two people are strolling and enjoying the early spring. All the mists and shadows of London life are left behind, and lie in wait for them when they

cross the river; here is only a bright winter's morning,
the song of birds piping, among the bare branches and
bushes, with sudden notes and cadences of exceeding
sweetness. In the ideal country house there should be a
farm-yard, with live toys for grown-up children : cocks
that crow, hens sitting with their little bead-eyed yellow
brood nestling round them. There should be cows that
moo and shake their heads, and crop the grass with a
pleasant crunch as you watch them in the meadow, or
stand meekly in their stalls when milking-time has come,
with their names, such as Cowslip, Daisy, Bluebell, painted
over each pair of horns.

In the morning, instead of hurrying through the
streets and past the closed shops and gin-palaces to a
crowded church with high square pews and dingy windows
and dust, and a fierce-looking pew-opener in a front, you
wend your way quietly across the fields, where the air is
sweet with coming spring, and you pass by narrow
swinging gates and under elm-trees to the church door.
As you enter, though it seems dim at first, and the
stained glass windows temper the light, yet you have a
sense of the pleasant sights and sounds beyond the walls,
of the great arch of the sky over head, of the birds joining
in the chaunt, of the preacher without, telling in silent
language of new hope, new life ; of courage and endurance,

of peace, and beneficence, and wisdom. There are still Sir Roger de Coverleys, thanks be to Heaven! now-a-days, though perhaps they do not stand up and publicly rebuke the sleepy and inattentive, and as soon as Lady de Coverley sees you (for our Sir Roger is a married man), she finds room for you in her big pew with a welcoming look, and makes you quite comfortable, with hassocks, and hymn-books, and psalters. Coming out of church, Lady de Coverley greets her acquaintance, and nods to the village children. There is a certain Amelia I know of, in little hob-nailed shoes, who turns her back upon the congregation, and stands stock-still, tied up in a little flannel cape. There is also a delightful little fat plough-boy in a smock, who smiles so pleasantly that we all begin to laugh in return.

You cross the fields again on your way back to Pleasance. The cows have scarcely moved. A huge pig that was grazing under a tree has shifted a little, and instead of a side view now presents its tail. The farmyard, as you pass on your way to the house, is all alive in the midday sunshine. The Cochin-China cocks and hens, looking like enchanted princes and princesses, come ambling up to meet you, shaking out their soft golden plumage. The Spanish population, and the crève-cœurs, black-robed, with crimson crests, are all in their respective countries, with beautiful sunset tints, purple, violet, green, and golden, showing among their feathers in the sunshine. There is a great discussion going on among the Poles. Gallant generals, with spurs and cocked-hat and feathers, impatiently pace their confines; fiery young captains and aides-de-camp seem to be laying down the law; while the ladies, who also look very important, and are dressed in a semi-military costume, evidently join in the proceedings with the keenest interest. As for the white ducks, what do they care for anything that is going on? their Sunday is spent squatting on the grass in the field with the young Alderney calves. They see both sides of the world at once with their bright eyes, and do not trouble themselves for anybody.

Some people like to go to church a second time; some go for a long walk in the afternoon: they have only to choose. Park, and lawn, and common, hills and dales lie before them; and though the distance begins to fade into the soft grey mist of an English March, yet even the mist is gentle and beautiful, and the air is moist and refreshing, and the brown turf yields under foot with a delightful spring. I seem to forget myself, and to fancy that these are the days of the *Spectator* come back to us, when I venture to write thus at length of ducks and of brown turf, and it is time I should cease.

AN EASTER HOLIDAY.

Is that enchanted moan only the swell
  Of the long waves that roll in yonder bay?
And hark ! the clock within, the silver knell
Of twelve sweet hours, that past in bridal white
  And died to live. . . .—MAUD.

IT is late to begin to write of Easter holidays and holiday makers when Easter is past and the holidays are rapidly coming to an end—when all the people who only yesterday, in a glamour of sunshine and laziness, were to one another distant figures dotting the cliffs, groups upon the beach, couples strolling on the smooth lawn of the hotel, or voices calling from unseen places through the clear spring air, are common-place, uninteresting men and women again, packing up their portmanteaus and bags, disputing over their bills, and driving away in flys and breaks to the platform, where the same railway carriages and steamers which conveyed so many to ease and pleasant hours, now wait, remorseless and unrelenting, to carry unwilling victims back to desks, pulpits, pupil-rooms, consultations, household duties, social cares, clerks, dust, office paper, and red tape.

For the last week or so it has seemed to some of us as if a sort of millennium had set in in many places. Lawyers have been disporting themselves, suddenly freed, as if by magic, from the blue bags and tin boxes to which they are usually chained, Prometheus-like, by strings of red tape. Clergymen, without their pulpits, have been climbing the cliffs with surprising agility, their white neckcloths gleaming in the sun and marking them distinct from other men. Pupils have ceased to be altogether in this happy hour, and are transformed into the well-loved Toms and Harrys of home and domestic life. Illnesses and patients have also vanished out of sight; although the doctors do not quite put aside their professional manner with their practice, and walk in a brisk and business-like way along the seashore, or alertly read the 'Times,' cross-legged, upon the benches in front of their hotels. Here at F——, if one may be allowed to instance one place among the rest, there have been students from Oxbridge and Camford. Two mighty dons have come down from their high places, and may be seen looking at the primroses in the lane; while in the adjoining field a painter, whose name is reckoned high among his compeers, is with some boys, leaping over a cat-gallows; and a councillor who has forgotten the cares of empire for a while, is strolling in the shade of a hedgerow, and repeating odes of Horace to a young companion.

Horace would have most certainly written an ode or two if he had come to F——. He would have liked the pinewood on the hillside, where the river bubbles from its source, and where you climb among trees, across mosses starred with primroses and tiny dog-violets, and as you climb you see the horizon between the flaked stems of the pines, until at last you come out upon a wide down which reaches to the summit of the hill.

But, in truth, we have no need of Horace here to tell us of 'groves of pine on either hand,' to teach us how to look for 'the shining steps.' For the Lord of the Manor of Faringford has written of these full-toned seas and breaking waves, 'these happy blossoming shores,' and 'thymy promontories,' 'where the rainbow lives in the curve of the land,' 'and the golden chords run up the ridged sea.'

Only yesterday, I think, two countrymen who were driving stakes, ceased their work for a while to tell us, 'They were a-putten up of a fence to keep Misterr Tennyson's sheep from strayen — for he wer Lord of the Manor, he wer, and the sheep wer always goen astray.'

It seems almost as if the song of poets came to life upon some spring days and took visible form and voice and being. Rhythm, music, the great flow of their melodies, the secrets of their philosophy, are vibrating all round and about. One seems to learn the meaning of many a poem by heart as one lies on the hill-side in the sunshine. A bumble-bee buzzes by and floats away down the slope over sweet gorse, thrift, wild thyme, rock-roses, violets, and soft green grass. A chorus of piping, whistling, thrilling, chirruping, twittering mounts from all the hedges and copses at our feet, a soft wind from the sea comes blowing into our faces, while the distant sound of the waves washing against the shore down below seems to flow like an accompaniment to the concert of the birds. Townbred folks cannot tell the different notes and instruments of the concerts, but there is a very sweet piping to the measure of 'Come hither! come hither!' and then among the many, one clear note (a nightingale's most likely) struck over and over again with wonderful vivacity and sweetness. Meanwhile the sun streams over the country ; far away, water and landscape, towers and villages, are tender with sudden lights, and everything thrills in answer to the first touch of spring; the leaves are budding, and blackthorn blossoms flowering on the bare branches, and rivers of tender green go flooding over the land, and reaching even into dark city courts where the grass sprouts greenly between the stones, and the poor little flower in the garret window begins to put out its feeble shoots.

And as this season comes on beneficent, silent, and bountiful for us, another also begins in London far away. Cabs, flys, and carriages go quicker and quicker and in more bewildering circles; linkmen suddenly emerge like gnomes out of the earth, with lanterns in their hands; the doors of the houses fly open; the ladies and gentlemen get excited, spring out from the carriages, tear off their cloaks, and begin in their turn to go whirling round and round, and as they go they drag invisible circles in their train of servants, milliners, children, governesses, tradespeople and what not, and the talk will hum on and the music jangle until the night is nearly over, and the stars begin to wane over the waking city, as they do here when the last light has been extinguished in the lattice window, and country folks lie peacefully dreaming, with their dogs whining in their sleep.

But London is four hours off, the sun is not yet set, nor the holidays quite over, and we are still safe on the hill. One tries to climb the steep flanks, slipping over the smooth turf. It is so smooth that the furze bushes seem gliding over the precipitous sides of the down, and one wonders that the very shadows do not slide away. As we climb on, the browsing sheep first appear against the clear sky, then comes more yellow gorse, and then at last the sea from the summit of the cliff.

It lies quite calm, a pale-blue ocean, streaked with straight and solemn lines where the currents flow. The ships seem sailing in the air, for you cannot tell where the horizon finishes or where the sky begins. We stand on the edge of the cliff, listening to the strange stillness of far-away sound, to the song of the waves and the birds. All the air is swept with sunlight and the sweet smell of gorse bushes. There are no words to tell of such silence and sweetness and greatness. A gull swoops over the cliff at our feet with a sudden cry; the sheep straggle away, tinkling their bells, stopping now and then to browse the grass and the wild thyme. Faint tender scents, faint cries, wide colours flowing. A sudden awe and wonder overcome one—a thrill of exquisite calm and gratitude and comfort, like an unspoken psalm of wonder and of praise. A week ago the churches were done out for Easter with flowers and graceful garlands : now it is the whole world which seems decked and garlanded in season. Along the lanes, scattered across our path, under our feet, hanging from the branches in the woods below, flowers, and green and white blossoms are scattered. An Easter hymn is in the air.

P.S.—The councillor to whom I happened to read the beginning of the essay had not patience to hear the end, but interrupted me by quoting two verses from his favourite poet. Mr. Martin has translated them into English.

> Whether thy days go down
>   In gloom and regrets,
> Or, shunning life's vain struggle for renown,
>   Its fevers and its frets,
> Stretched on the grass, with old Falernian wine,
> Thou givest the thoughtless hours, a rapture all divine . .
>
> Where the tall spreading pine
>   And white-leaved poplar grow,
> And, mingling their broad boughs in leafy twine,
>   A grateful shadow throw,
> Where runs the wimpling brook in its slumberous tune,
> Still murmuring, as it seems, to the hushed ear of noon.

IN FRIENDSHIP.

Il faut dans ce bas monde aimer beaucoup de choses,
  Pour savoir après tout ce qu'on aime le mieux. . . .
Il faut fouler aux pieds des fleurs à peine écloses ;
  Il faut beaucoup pleurer, dire beaucoup d'adieux. . .
De ces biens passagers que l'on goûte à demi
  Le meilleur qui nous reste est un ancien ami.—

So says Alfred de Musset, in his sonnet to Victor Hugo :
and as we live on we find out who are in truth the
people that we have really loved, which of our companions belongs to us, linked in friendship as well as by
the chances of life or relationship. Sometimes it is not
until they are gone that we discover who and what they
were to us—those 'good friends and true' with whom
we were at ease, tranquil in the security of their kind
presence.

Some of us, the longer we live, only feel more and
more that it is not in utter loneliness that the greatest
peace is to be found. A little child starts up in the
dark, and finding itself alone, begins to cry and toss in

its bed, as it holds out its arms in search of a protecting hand ; and men and women seem for the most part true to this first childish instinct as they awaken suddenly : (how strange these awakenings are, in what incongruous places and seasons do they come to us !) People turn helplessly, looking here and there for protection, for sympathy,[1] for affection, for charity of human fellowship ; give it what name you like, it is the same cry for companionship, and terror of the death of silence and absence. Human Sympathy, represented by inadequate words, or by clumsy exaggeration, by feeble signs or pangs innumerable, by sudden glories and unreasonable ecstasies, is, when we come to think of it, among the most reasonable of emotions. It is life indeed ; it binds us to the spirit of our race as our senses bind us to the material world, and makes us feel at times as if we were indeed a part of Nature herself, and chords responding to her touch.

People say that as a rule men are truer friends than women—more capable of friendship. Is this the result of a classical education ? Do the foot-notes in which celebrated friendships are mentioned in brackets stimulate our youth to imitate those stately togas, whose names

[1] 'I felt nobody to have existence at all until existing in the minds of other people, and positivism without sympathy between people to be like a religion without its devotion.'—A CORRESPONDENT.

and discourses come travelling down to us through two thousand years, from one country to another, from one generation to another, from one language to another, until they flash perhaps into the pages of Bohn's Classical Library, of which a volume has been lent to me from the study-table on the hill? It is lying open at the chapter on friendship. 'To me, indeed, though he was snatched away, Scipio still lives, and will always live; for I love the virtue of a man, and assuredly of all things that either fortune or nature has bestowed upon me, I have none which I can compare with the friendship of Scipio.' So says Cicero, speaking by the mouth of Lælius and of Bohn, and the generous thought still lives after many a transmigration, though it exists now in a world where perhaps friendship is less thought of than in the days when Scipio was mourned.[1] Some people have a special

---

[1] Grimoald, 'chaplain to Bishop Ridley,' quoted by Robert Bell in his edition of English poets, has left some quaint hobbling verses which seem to have pre-written my little article—

Friendship, flower of flowers, oh! lively sprite of life!
Oh! sacred bond of blissful peace, the stalworth staunch of strife!
Scipio with Lælius, didst thou conform in care
At home, in wars, for weal and woe with equal faith to fare
Gisippus eke with Tyte, Damon with Pythias,
And with Menethus' son Achill, by thee combined was.
Eurialus and Nisus gave Virgil cause to sing;
Of Pylades do many rhyme and of Orestes ring.
Down Theseus went to hell, Pereth his friend to find.
Oh! that the wives in these our days were to their mates so kind.
Cicero the friendly man to Atticus his friend
Of friendship wrote . . .

gift of their own for friendship; they transform a vague and abstract feeling for us into an actual voice and touch and response. As our life flows on—'a torrent of impressions and emotions bounded in by custom,' a writer calls it—the mere names of our friends might for many of us almost tell the history of our own lives. As one thinks over the roll, each name seems a fresh sense and explanation to the past. Some, which seem to have outwardly but little influence on our fate, tell for us the whole hidden story of long years. One means perhaps passionate emotion, unreasonable reproach, tender reconciliation; another may mean injustice, forgiveness, remorse; while another speaks to us of all that we have ever suffered, all that we hold most sacred in life, and gratitude and trust unfailing. There is one name that seems to me like the music of Bach as I think of it, and another that seems to open at the Gospel of St. Matthew. 'My dearest friend,' a young man wrote to his mother only yesterday, and the simple words seemed to me to tell the whole history of their lives.

'After these two noble fruits of friendship, peace in the affections, and support of the judgment, followeth the last fruit, which is like the pomegranate, full of many kernels. I mean aid and bearing a part in all actions and occasions,' says Lord Bacon, writing in the spirit of Cicero three hundred years ago.

To be in love is a recognised state; relationship without friendship is perhaps too much recognised in civilised communities; but friendship, that best blessing of life, seems to have less space in its scheme than almost any other feeling of equal importance. Of course it has its own influence; but the outward life appears, on the whole, more given to business, to acquaintance, to ambition, to eating and drinking, than to the friends we really love: and time passes, and convenience takes us here and there, and work and worry (that we might have shared) absorb us, and one day time is no more for our friendship.

One or two of my readers will understand why it is that I have been thinking of friendship of late, and have chosen this theme for my little essay, thinking that not the least lesson in life is surely that of human sympathy, and that to be a good friend is one of the secrets that comprise most others. And yet the sacrifices that we usually make for a friend's comfort or assistance are ludicrous when one comes to think of them. 'One mina, two minæ; are there settled values for friends, Antisthenes, as there are for slaves? For of slaves one is perhaps worth two minæ, another not even half a mina, another five minæ, another ten.' Antisthenes agrees, and says that some friends are not even worth half a mina; 'and another,' he says, 'I would buy for my friend at the sacrifice of all the money and revenues in the world.'

I am afraid that a modern Antisthenes would think a month's income a serious sacrifice. If a friend is in trouble we leave a card at his door, or go the length of a note, perhaps. And when all is well, we go our way silent and preoccupied. We absent ourselves for months at a time without a reason, and yet all of this is more want of habit than of feeling; for, notwithstanding all that is said of the world and its pompous vanities, there are still human beings among us, and, even after two thousand years, true things seem to come to life again and again for each one of us, in this sorrow and that happiness, in one sympathy and another; and one day a vague essay upon friendship becomes the true story of a friend.

In this peaceful island from whence I write we hear Cicero's voice, or listen to *In Memoriam,* as the Friend sings to us of friendship to the tune of the lark's shrill voice, or of the wave that beats away our holiday and dashes itself upon the rocks in the little bay. The sweet scents and dazzles of sunshine seem to harmonise with emotions that are wise and natural, and it is not until we go back to our common life that we realise the difference between the teaching of noble souls and the noisy bewildered translation into life of that solemn printed silence.

> Is it, then, regret for buried time,
> That keenlier in sweet April wakes,
> And meets the year, and gives and takes
> The colours of the crescent prime ?
>
> Not all : the songs, the stirring air,
> The life re-orient out of dust,
> Cry through the scene to hearten trust
> In that which made the world so fair.

Here, then, and at peace, and out of doors in the spring-time, we have leisure to ask ourselves whether there is indeed some failure in the scheme of friendship and in the plan of that busy to-day in which our lives are passed; over-crowded with people, with repetition, with passing care and worry, and unsorted material. It is perhaps possible that by feeling, and feeling alone, some check may be given to the trivial rush of meaningless repetition by which our time is frittered away, our precious power of love and passionate affection given to the winds.

Sometimes we suddenly realise for the first time the sense of kindness, the treasure of faithful protection that we have unconsciously owed for years, for our creditor has never claimed payment or reward, and we remember with natural emotion and gratitude that the time for payment is past; we shall be debtors all our lives long—debtors made richer by one man's generosity and liberal friendship, as we may be any day made poorer in heart by unkindness or want of truth.

Only a few weeks ago a friend passed from among us whose name for many, for the writer among the rest, spoke of a whole chapter in life, one of those good chapters to which we go back again and again. This friend was one of those who make a home of life for others, a home to which we all felt that we might come sure of a wise and unfailing welcome. The door opens, the friend comes in slowly with a welcoming smile on his pale and noble face. Where find more delightful companionship than his? We all know the grace of that charming improvised gift by which he seemed able to combine disjointed hints and shades into a whole, to weave our crude talk and ragged suggestions into a complete scheme of humorous or more serious philosophy. In some papers published a few years ago in the ' Cornhill Magazine,' called ' Chapters on Talk,' a great deal of his delightful and pleasant humour appears.

But it was even more in his society than in his writing that our friend showed himself as he was. His talking was unlike that of anybody else ; it sometimes put me in mind of another voice out of the past. There was an earnest wit, a gentle audacity and simplicity of expression, that made it come home to us all. Of late, E. R. was saying he spoke with a quiet and impressive authority that we all unconsciously acknowledged, although we did not know that the end of pain was near.

Of his long sufferings he never complained. But if he spoke of himself, it was with some kind little joke or humorous conceit and allusion to the philosophy of endurance, nor was it until after his death that we knew what his martyrdom had been, nor with what courage he had borne it.

He thought of serious things very constantly, although not in the conventional manner. One of the last times that we met, he said to me, ' I feel more and more convinced that the love of the Father is not unlike that of an earthly father; and that, as an earthly father, so He rejoices in the prosperity and material well-doing of his children.' Another time, quoting from the ' Roundabout Papers,' he said suddenly, ' " Be good, my dear." Depend upon it, that is the whole philosophy of life; it is very simple.'

Speaking of a friend, he said, with some emotion, ' I think I love M. as well as if he were dead.'

He had a fancy, that we all used to laugh over with him, of a great central building, something like the

Albert Hall, for friends to live in together, with galleries for the sleepless to walk in at night.

Perhaps some people may think that allusions so personal as these are scarcely fitted for these pages; but what is there in truth more unpersonal than the thought of a wise and gentle spirit, of a generous and truthful life? Here is a life that belongs to us all; we have all been the better for the existence of the one man. He could not be good without doing good in his generation, nor speak the truth as he did without adding to the sum of true things. And the lesson that he taught us was— ' Let us be true to ourselves; do not let us be afraid to be ourselves, to love each other, and to speak and to trust in each other.'

Last night the moon rose very pale at first, then blushing flame-like through the drifting vapours as they rose far beyond the downs; a great blackbird sat watching the shifting shadowy worlds from the bare branch of a tree, and the colts in the field set off scampering. Later, about eleven o'clock, the mists had dissolved into a silent silver and nightingale-broken dream—in which were vaporous downs, moonlight, sweet sudden stars, and clouds drifting, like some slow flight of silver birds. L—— took us to a little terrace at the end of his father's garden. All the kingdoms of the night lay spread before us, bounded by dreams. For a minute we stood listening to the sound of the monotonous wave, and then it ceased—and in the utter silence a cuckoo called, and then the nightingale began, and then the wave answered once more.

It will all be a dream to-morrow, as we stumble into the noise, and light, and work of life again. Monday comes commonplace, garish, and one can scarce believe in the mystical Sunday night. And yet this tranquil Sunday night is more true than the flashiest gas-lamp in Piccadilly. Natural things seem inspired at times, and beyond themselves, and to carry us upwards and beyond our gas-lamps; so do people seem revealed to us at times, and in the night, when all is peace.

PRINTED BY
SPOTTISWOODE AND CO., NEW-STREET SQUARE
LONDON